A SWORD IN TIME

Also By Cidney Swanson

The Ripple Series

Rippler
Chameleon
Unfurl
Visible
Immutable
Knavery
Perilous

The Saving Mars Series

Saving Mars
Defying Mars
Losing Mars
Mars Burning
Striking Mars
Mars Rising

The Thief in Time Series

A Thief in Time
A Flight in Time
A Sword in Time

Books Not in a Series

Siren Spell

Cidney Swanson

Copyright © 2017 by Cidney Swanson
Cover art © by Nathalia Suellen. All rights reserved.

All rights reserved, including the right to reproduce this book or portions thereof in any form whatsoever.

This is a work of fiction. Names, characters, places, and incidents are products of the author's imagination or are used fictitiously. Any resemblance to actual events or locales or persons, living or dead, is entirely coincidental.

ISBN 978-1-939543-49-3

For Kimberley,
who makes painting look effortless,
even when it's watercolor.

A little Neglect may breed great Mischief; for want of a Nail the Shoe was lost; for want of a Shoe the Horse was lost; and for want of a Horse the Rider was lost, being overtaken and slain by the Enemy, all for want of Care about a Horse-shoe Nail.

—Benjamin Franklin, Poor Richard's Almanac, 1758

The Present
July

1
· DAVINCI ·
California, July

The moment the Caterpillar's jawlike bucket bit into the roof, DaVinci knew it had been a mistake to come watch the demolition of her childhood home. The flat roof, which had been a star-watching platform, *plein air* studio, and refuge for six siblings needing alone time, crackled and gave way, exposing the abandoned bedrooms below: bare, skeletal. DaVinci swallowed. Shuddered, as if it were her bones giving way, her skeleton snapping, exposed, a carcass for scavengers.

This was her *home*. More and more in the past two years, home had become all she had. Well, home and art. Her best friends were far-flung—Jillian to Florida and Halley to the set of whatever movie she happened to be working on at the time. And besides having left her behind in Montecito, her best friends had each found true love.

Like that was fair.

Not only that, Halley had *married* Edmund, and DaVinci suspected Everett was dying for Jillian to say she was ready. They behaved like an old married couple already. DaVinci's mouth twitched into a sad smile. She was happy for her friends. Of course she was happy. But with all the *together* happening around her, a girl couldn't help feeling . . . well, lonely at times.

Of course, as Halley and Jillian frequently reminded her, she had siblings. A plethora of them. But Chagall and Toulouse had moved out last year, and her brother Yoshida was probably going to move in with Ana soon. As for Klee and Kahlo, well, the twins already lived in their own private world even though they still shared her bedroom.

Or rather, *had* shared it before the family had moved out of their home three days ago.

DaVinci shuddered as the Caterpillar removed another wall. Her home had been the only thing she'd had left, the one thing that kept her feeling like she belonged, even if the belonging was to a place and not a someone. She *fit* here, even more than in her studio space at UCSB.

"*Home,*" she whispered into the clenched fists pressed to her mouth.

The ramshackle hippie dwelling had perched on Montecito's East Mountain Drive for half a century—two and a half times longer than DaVinci had been alive. It had not been constructed to code and shook like Jell-O during tremors, rendering it completely uninsurable, which hadn't seemed like a problem—until it was.

Neighbors had called it an aqua-blue eyesore, and DaVinci herself had called it ugly, but everything about this shabby, crooked building grounded her, reminded her who she was, kept her anchored. She'd always known that so long as her house stood, there would be a place where she belonged.

The bucket lifted again and swung left, gently biting into the corner nearest the road. Into her older brother Yoshida's bedroom. Yoshi, like DaVinci's parents, hadn't wanted to watch the demolition.

It was somebody else's house now, somebody else's problem, her parents had said, shrugging.

Klee and Kahlo were away at art camp, but they wouldn't have come to watch, DaVinci was sure of it.

Don't go, Yoshi had said.

She should have listened. She shouldn't have come. She should have stayed "home," in the sterile three-bedroom condo her parents had bought in Goleta with money from the sale of their land, still valuable without a house.

She shouldn't be here. She was going to cry in front of everyone. Blinking rapidly, she took a slow breath. Reminded herself why she was here. Not to freak out, but to psych herself up to make things right again—to rewind the clock and rescue her home.

For a girl with access to a time machine, this was more than merely wishful thinking.

The bucket descended. Took another bite. Flayed and exposed another bedroom.

DaVinci swiped at her eyes, hands bunched into fists inside the sleeves of her UCSB sweatshirt from freshman year. She needed to gather courage for the next step. Until now, she'd been too afraid to use the time machine by herself. She was still afraid. Terrified! But there were no other options—not if she wanted her home back.

She had to be brave. Braver than she'd been that

day in fifth grade when she'd punched sturdy Charlie Esposito for making fun of Halley's clothes. Braver than she'd been last year when she'd exhibited paintings one of her professors had called "infantile."

She *would* be brave.

Brave like Princess Leia facing the loss of her son, her husband, her brother. DaVinci wasn't going to find that kind of brave by running away from the demolition. She needed to watch this: *No looking away*.

She fixed her gaze on the metal monster. The excavator's movement was disturbingly graceful as the bucket nudged the walls. No. *Graceful* wasn't the word she wanted. The Caterpillar was . . . *feline*. It was a cat toying with a mouse; it could have destroyed everything with one mighty swing of its jointed arm. As far as DaVinci could tell, the Caterpillar operator only refrained to keep flying debris to a minimum.

She had to stop this. Reverse what had happened. Her house was coming down because of nothing more than a slow drip, drip, drip under the floors. Because of hidden rot eating away at the underpinnings of their aqua-blue eyesore—their castle, their *home*. Well, that and the fact that they'd had no insurance.

> For the want of a nail the shoe was lost,
> For the want of a shoe the horse was lost,
> For the want of a horse the rider was lost,
> For the want of a rider the battle was lost,
> For the want of a battle the kingdom was lost,
> And all for the want of a horse-shoe nail.

The nursery rhyme lines had seared themselves into DaVinci's brain these past weeks since their home had been condemned and then sold.

She glanced around at the neighbors who'd gathered to watch. Some she'd known from the time she could walk. Others she barely knew—the newer, wealthier neighbors who'd bought up properties like her family's, tearing down all but a few walls for a "Montecito remodel," doubtless costing millions.

One of these approached her now.

"It's exciting, huh? And a little scary!" The woman laughed and held out her hand. "I'm Barb. I guess we're neighbors?"

When DaVinci didn't answer—she couldn't—the woman added, "I was told you're part of the owner's family?"

"Previous owner," DaVinci managed to choke out, her throat swelling. "We sold."

"Oh," replied Barb.

Just *Oh* because, really, what else was there to say?

It didn't matter. DaVinci couldn't speak anyway. Her throat was closing. She turned away from Barb, away from the scene of destruction. She didn't want to be here. This was no place to find courage.

Cru-unch!

There went the kitchen. Gone. DaVinci choked on a sob. Swiped at brimming eyes. She slunk past her neighbors in silence, like some wounded animal in retreat. Because her own driveway was full of demolition equipment, she'd parked her borrowed car in front of the Van Sants' house. She fished for her keys and slid into the car. From inside, she felt the ground shudder. Was that the final collapse? Her chest tightened. It was so unfair. So wrong. She started the car.

A SWORD IN TIME

> This was no place to find courage, but it was a heck of a place to harden your resolve.

2

· DAVINCI ·

California, July

Done with from her attempt to "find courage," DaVinci was now bent over a credit card wrapped in Princess Leia duct tape. She was trying, unsuccessfully, to remove the tape. Already, she'd torn a nail, and her fingers were gummy with residue. Her parents had given her the card two and a half years ago for emergencies, and she'd promptly wrapped it in tape to make it hard to use. That part was working well.

As for why she'd chosen Princess Leia duct tape and not basic gray duct tape, that was simple. Potential credit card charges had to make it through a filter: *What Would Leia Do?* Until today, the card had never been used. The Leia filter was awesome like that.

As DaVinci continued to pick at the tape, she stared at Princess Leia. Blaster gripped and ready, iconic white hood raised, it was a classic image. Today as always, DaVinci tried to match that gaze, but what chance did she have, really? She was *always* the first to break eye contact.

Truth was, she was making zero headway trying to peel the tape off. So what would Leia do in this situation? Well, for starters, Leia wouldn't keep trying the same useless tactic, expecting a new result.

Maybe she could soften the adhesive somehow. If she'd been home, she would have grabbed the bottle of Goo Gone. But she wasn't at home. She hated calling the new condo *home*. It wasn't. For this reason, as well as for her need of a time machine, DaVinci was staying at Jillian's. To be precise, she was staying in the Martian Chronicles suite in the west wing of her best friend's estate. Jillian was off finishing her degree in Florida, having moved there to be close to her swoony boyfriend from 1903, Everett Randolph IV, who was studying engineering physics (and, secretly, time travel) under Dr. Littlewood.

Luckily, DaVinci had a standing invitation to stay at the Applegates' even when Jillian wasn't around. Whenever DaVinci stayed, Jillian's mom insisted on putting her in the Martian Chronicles suite: *"Right in here, dear, with your lovely performance art sculpture."*

The "sculpture" was not, in fact, a sculpture. Nor had it been made by DaVinci. Rather, it was an advanced piece of scientific equipment made by Jules Khan, deceased, using designs he'd stolen from Dr. Littlewood. It was a singularity device capable of focusing space–time, although DaVinci simply called it "the scary time machine." Today, however, it was the piece of equipment that was going to help DaVinci fix everything. Help her get her ugly blue house back, assuming she could get the duct tape off her credit card. She needed the card to get a cash advance in the amount of $600 to pay a plumber when she traveled back in time.

Taking a short break from duct tape peeling, DaVinci gave the time machine the side-eye. She never slept great in this room, worried the machine would zap her into some other time and place against her will and then proceed to either duplicate her or mummify her. She'd seen these things happen before. Both Jillian's boyfriend and Halley's had been duplicated by space–time as part of some weird effect whereby space–time kept history rolling. If you yanked something forward in time, an original version remained behind. It was space–time's way of preserving temporal continuity. *The temporal law of mass-energy conservation*, Jillian called it. What it meant was that there were two Edmunds and two Everetts, although only the ones who'd been dragged into the twenty-first century were aware of the existence of duplicate selves. And of course, the originals were long dead by now.

If the duplicating was creepy, the mummifying was even worse. The way Halley and Jillian had explained it, whether the time machine was turned on or not, space–time yanked time travelers who didn't belong in the past back home again after a short delay. But if the machine was turned off by accident before a traveler returned, the machine couldn't provide temporal focus for the return journey, which would no longer be swift for the traveler. A traveler returning from, say, the sixteenth century, would journey through space–time for five hundred years from their perspective, even though it would appear to take only a minute from the perspective of those in the present. Unfortunately, during the longer trip, travelers would first asphyxiate and then eventually . . . *mummify*.

Of course, Jillian and Halley both insisted none of those things would happen to DaVinci just by sleeping in the same room with the machine.

But still. She was keeping her eye on that thing.

She turned the credit card over in her hands, frowning at it. She had to get the tape off to get her cash, but peeling the tape still wasn't working, and she had no Goo Gone. What would Leia do? Drive to the store. Or, duh, Leia would ask the internet for some help. Feeling vaguely embarrassed she hadn't already tried this, DaVinci Googled *removing duct tape* and read that hot water—really hot water—should soften the glue. She crossed to the bathroom.

DaVinci let the water run until it was scalding and then started soaking the card. Ten minutes later, the Princess Leia duct tape was soft enough to peel off. With this success, it was time to bring the proverbial horse-shoe nail to the proverbial horse. It was time to save her kingdom, and DaVinci was ready for battle. Or at any rate, ready for a trip to the bank.

3
·DAVINCI·
California, July

Twenty minutes later, DaVinci strode away from the Coast Village Road Union Bank with $600 in her bag. It had been ridiculously easy to get the cash advance. Scary easy. First chance she got, she was wrapping the card in duct tape again. Double layers.

The teller had asked how she wanted the cash, to which DaVinci had replied she needed bills marked 2016 or earlier. When the clerk gave her an odd look, DaVinci floundered for an explanation that didn't involve time travel and ended up murmuring something about a film project set in 2016, but by then her stomach had tied itself into a macramé project. Her knotted gut was insisting the teller knew what DaVinci was planning and had already pushed a hidden button that would bring the National Guard in to arrest her for operating a time machine without a license.

Her stomach still twisting, DaVinci drove back up the hill to Jillian's to use the time machine. But by the time she walked back into the Martian Chronicles suite, she was more doubt-ridden than her Grandmother Shaughnessy's favorite apostle.

She made a mental note to ask the doubting Saint Thomas to put in a good word for her impending journey.

The doubt was rational—a sort of instinct to avoid the untried and potentially deadly—because, while her BFFs Halley and Jillian were expert time machine operators, DaVinci had never operated it before. Fortunately, one year ago, Jillian had created an operations checklist to make sure every journey was accomplished in total safety, according to set rules. Which was *so* Jillian.

It went without saying that DaVinci came from a long line of rule-breakers and instruction-ignorers, but she would *not* be following in the family's footsteps today. This was no time for artistic license. DaVinci read through the instructions for safe operation three times. At the bottom, Jillian's rocketry-obsessed boyfriend, Everett, had written "Launch Readiness Checklist" in orange Sharpie.

DaVinci shivered. If you thought about it, this sort of travel had to be at least as dangerous as a rocket launch. *Why* had she thought this was a great plan, exactly? She wiped clammy palms against her jeans and tried to find her courage, which had apparently snuck off for a nap.

This called for more Princess Leia.

Opening her wallet, DaVinci pulled out a trading card she'd had since she was fourteen. Worn around the edges, cracked in the middle from the time Yoshi had folded it in half and threatened to eat it, this was

DaVinci's favorite image of Leia, dressed as General Organa in her vest and boots, older and wiser and probably a little heartbroken, but still ready to kick some First Order butt.

So. What would Leia do if her courage was catnapping?

DaVinci frowned. Leia would think about the worlds that would be destroyed if someone didn't blow up the First Order's death-dealing planet. Leia would zip up her vest and start giving orders.

DaVinci forced herself to remember the Caterpillar, to think about her home reduced to shredded lumber and cracked cinder blocks.

And there it was: her courage. She was ready. The Leia protocol was awesome like that.

She mounted the platform of the time machine, a cool smile forming on her thin, tight lips. What would Leia do?

"She'd punch the freaking controls," muttered DaVinci.

And then, asking Thomas the Doubting Apostle to put in that good word, DaVinci launched herself and her $600 back to spring break 2016.

Six Months Earlier
January

4

· *KHAN* ·

Nebraska, January

Jules Khan was driving across Nebraska in a vehicle he'd stolen from, well, *himself*, and looking for signs indicating Omaha was getting close. Fortunately, the freeway was clear of snow and ice. There had been snow in Reno and ice outside of Salt Lake City. How he'd pined for Santa Barbara's mild climate driving through Utah. But even if Nebraska's stretch of I-80 was free of ice, it wasn't free of the occasional law enforcement vehicle, so Khan was keeping his speed at only seven miles over the posted limit. He couldn't afford to get pulled over. If a state trooper ran the plates on his BMW, he'd be thrown in jail for burglary and grand theft auto.

The problem was, he was a *duplicated* Jules Khan—an identical version of himself, created by the vagaries of space–time during a little inadvertent time travel. He had tried passing himself off as the same Jules Khan who owned the BMW and the rest of the vast estate in Montecito, California, but it had not gone well. His lawyer, or rather, the lawyer of the *dead* Jules Khan, had seen right through him, remarking that the so-called "real" Jules Khan was much older. And missing a section of his pinkie finger. The lawyer had then called him an imposter and threatened to charge him with the murder of the actual Jules Khan. *Murder!* Well, it put grand theft auto into perspective.

But Khan didn't intend to be charged with either. His plan was to sell the BMW, thereby obtaining cash for what he really needed: parts to build his own singularity device. Because once he built a singularity device and could time-travel at will, he would have the means of getting all the money he needed for, well, *anything*. He wouldn't need the dead Jules Khan's stupid estate or his stupid lawyer or his stupid anything.

There was, of course, the issue of locating a car buyer with . . . *flexible* morality—someone who wouldn't ask questions about the vehicle's provenance—but in Khan's experience, people with flexible morals weren't impossible to find. He'd found one in Omaha, hadn't he?

Selling the BMW in Omaha was a better option than crawling back to his former postdoctoral employer, Dr. Arthur Littlewood. His former employer—whom he'd held at gunpoint, mind— seemed willing to forgive and forget. In fact, Littlewood had called twice a day for a week and even dangled the tantalizing prospect of scientific glory in front of Khan, promising to introduce him to all the right people at all the right conferences.

But Khan had decided he could wait for scientific glory. Something had shifted inside him when he'd seen the sprawling estate in Montecito that had belonged to his duplicate self. Why settle for acclaim in the scientific community when you could have limitless wealth *and* acclaim? He would put off recognition until the time was ripe. Until after he'd rebuilt the singularity device. Until he was financially secure and no longer on the run. He wanted fame, not infamy. A little patience and he had no doubt his name would make it into the history books alongside those of Copernicus, Newton, and Einstein.

No, he did *not* wish to rejoin Littlewood in that backwater Florida university of his. Jules Khan had his sights set a little higher than that, thank you very much. Not to mention, he had no intention of sharing the glory. Especially not with someone whose ambitions were so small-minded.

All of which meant Khan had to sell the stolen BMW.

He had assumed this sort of transaction would involve a dingy warehouse located in a part of town locals knew to avoid after sunset. Probably to someone named Mick with mob connections. In actuality, however, after posting a purposefully vague "For Sale" ad on Craigslist in Omaha, Nebraska, Khan found himself exiting I-80 and driving into a very ordinary suburban neighborhood to meet his potential buyer.

Khan scowled as he drove past edged brown lawns and painted mailboxes. How was one to tell the good guys from the bad guys if the bad guys lived in neighborhoods with *edged lawns*?

Even more insulting to Khan's sense of decorum, his shady buyer turned out to be a clean-shaven guy named Mark, whose closest connection to the mob was probably watching *The Godfather* on Netflix. It was all very irritating.

But also, Khan reminded himself, very necessary.

Khan shared the story he had at the ready: the car was part of an estate left to him by his grandmother, who was terrible with paperwork, and he'd spent his last cent traveling to her funeral only to find her estate was being confiscated to cover her back taxes, and now how was he going to get home to Michigan? And yes, he might have driven off in Nana's car without exactly asking permission.

Whatever impression Mark's neighborhood might have given, the man himself showed signs of having suitably flexible morals. Mark nodded at Khan's story, kicked the tires, looked under the hood for an unconscionable length of time, and finally offered Khan $2,000 in cash. For a car worth easily four times that amount (Khan had consulted *Kelley Blue Book*).

"It's vintage," said Khan, glaring at Mark's tidy winter-brown front lawn. "It's worth five times that."

Mark shrugged. "Not if it don't have a clean title." Then he grinned, revealing a single gold canine. "From what you've told me, your title's as far from clean as a dog that likes chasing skunks."

Khan scowled.

"Lemme see the pink slip."

Before Khan could stop him, the gold-toothed mongrel opened the glove compartment, at which point several things happened in rapid succession. A heavy *something*, wrapped in cotton wadding, fell to the floor with a thud, revealing what looked very much like a thick gold chain. Khan lurched to grab it, but

18

Mark got there first, lifting the item, examining it, and then—unthinkably—*biting* it!

"Hey!" shouted Khan.

Mark, his eyebrows raised, muttered, "*Huh*," and began picking bits of cotton fluff off a large, rather ugly necklace.

"That's not for sale," snapped Khan.

A knowing grin spread across Mark's face. "Had a peek inside Granny's jewelry box, did we?" Then, with aggravating slowness, he returned the item to Khan.

"It's *mine*," Khan said, stuffing the necklace in a pocket. True, he had been unaware of its existence until a moment ago, but that didn't mean it wasn't his.

"That's pure gold," said Mark. "Soft enough it might be twenty-four karat—"

"It's not for sale," Khan said coldly. At least, not to a plebian like Mark.

The financial return on his BMW had turned out to be disappointing, but the necklace would net a pretty penny. The thing weighed over a pound and was set with precious stones. He would sell it—oh yes, he would sell it—but he would do some research as to its value first. Khan was no expert on antique jewelry, but he'd flipped through his duplicate self's sales ledger. The other Khan had been in the habit of snatching valuable items from the past, and none of the jewelry—mostly small rings and pins—had been sold for less than five thousand.

Mark might have just uncovered a small fortune for him. His luck was beginning to improve.

"Okay, then," said Mark. "So do we have a deal on the vehicle?"

Khan frowned as if contemplating his options.

A SWORD IN TIME

With the necklace in his hands, getting a good price on the BMW mattered less. Although he still needed to put as much distance as possible between himself and the stolen vehicle.

"You might do better finding someone willing to strip it for parts on your own," said Mark. "You'd have to nose around a little."

Mark had taken Khan's hesitation for reluctance to sell at such a low price.

In actual fact, Khan did not wish to "nose around a little," seeking out chop shops, or whatever they were called.

"I'll take your offer," snapped Khan. Better to accept cash here than to risk his neck in some dark alley. He still had the necklace to cover the balance for the parts he needed to rebuild the time machine. He'd heard Littlewood say parts for the device in Florida had run close to fourteen thousand. Khan, however, was clever and thrifty and convinced that anything Littlewood built for fourteen thousand, *he* could build for twelve. He had two thousand and a necklace that had to be worth *at least* a pair of those $5,000 rings he'd seen in the ledger.

After completing the transaction, Khan took a bus to Kansas City (the farthest destination he could reach by bus for under fifty bucks), where he checked into a hostel, occupying the top bunk in an out-of-the-way corner. Legs crossed on the mattress, he opened his computer to make a parts list from the plans he'd copied onto a thumb drive. It was then that he realized he hadn't seen his thumb drive for a while. In fact, he hadn't seen it for a *long* while.

He patted his pockets—front, back, interior, exterior—checked his wallet, searched the small messenger bag containing the sum of his earthly possessions and nearly two thousand in cash, but the drive was nowhere to be found. A bead of sweat ran down the back of his neck. He needed that thumb drive. It contained his only copy of the schematics for building a new time machine. He'd left Florida in haste, without taking the time to transfer the information from the thumb drive to his computer. After all, when was he going to need it? He'd only transferred the information to a thumb drive in the first place because it amused him to steal information from Littlewood while the man was standing right next to him in the lab, droning on about his favorite, missing, fountain pen. It had been one of many petty acts, that transfer. And while he'd made a point to grab the thumb drive before leaving Florida, he hadn't expected to need it, or not so soon.

Methodically, he searched a second time, and then a third time, rather less methodically, and a fourth time, quite frantically. It was only then that the truth sank in. The thumb drive was gone. He'd lost it. He'd lost the instructions to rebuild the device upon which his future rested.

Which meant he had two options: crawl back and ask Littlewood's forgiveness, or break into the Florida lab and take what he needed. Only one of these options was remotely appealing.

The Present
July

5
· DAVINCI ·
California, July

DaVinci had timed her arrival into 2016 with care. It had to be *after* the leak in the pipes under the kitchen had been discovered and diagnosed, or she wouldn't be able to tell the plumbing contractor that, yes, they'd like to go forward with getting it fixed. It had to be while her family was away, or Mom and Dad would notice the plumber hammering (or whatever plumbers did) and chase the plumber off, insisting there was no money for the repair.

She'd chosen to send herself back to spring break of her senior year in high school, a few days before her family returned from their annual drive to Baja California for lobster and plein air coastal painting.

DaVinci strolled inside her quiet 2016 house. Or *almost* quiet house. Was it her imagination, or could she hear water dripping? She shuddered, horribly aware of the leak that was literally destroying her house while she stood there in the kitchen. Picking up her avocado-green landline phone (long since gone), she called the plumber.

The call went straight to voice mail. Which really sucked, because if Jillian's time chart was any good, space–time was going to haul DaVinci's butt back where it belonged in less than three hours. What if the plumber didn't call back before DaVinci's time in 2016 was up? She was *not* loving the idea of using the machine over and over until she finally got the plumber on the phone. There had to be a better solution. One that involved less messing around with space–time. The plumber's "leave a message" was followed by a beep.

"Hi, yeah, this is DaVinci Shaughnessy-Pavlov. So yeah, we want to have you, *um*, fix the leak under the house after all. Today. The one you said would be six hundred dollars? It's an emergency. So like, now. *Um* . . . I'm going to leave the money on the kitchen counter in case, you know, no one's home when you swing by. I hope that's okay?"

DaVinci grimaced. She sounded so unprofessional.

"I might have to, *uh*, step out before you arrive. I'm leaving the back door unlocked, so you know, come by whenever. I mean, the sooner the better, obviously. Because it's an emergency."

She grimaced again.

"Okay. That's everything. Bye. Oh, and thanks! And remember your money is on the counter waiting for you. No receipt needed. In fact, yeah, definitely don't leave a receipt. Okay. That's everything. Bye for reals this time."

She hung up before she said anything else even more stupid than all the stupid stuff she'd already said.

Definitely don't leave a receipt?
Bye for reals this time?
"Ugh!"
She was no good at voice messages. She should have texted the plumber. She shook her head and strolled outside to sit on an exceptionally large boulder from which her family had painted, drawn, sketched, and etched views of the ocean since at least the dawn of time. It had butt-size divots that made it perfect for observing the ocean, two miles downhill.

Home. She was home. Everything was going to be okay. She was home and she wasn't going to lose it again. She would fix everything, and then she would always have a place to return to, a place where she belonged. A place where she never felt alone.

She could sense her shoulders unclenching, her breath softening. Even her tightly coiled hair seemed to relax. Settling, she gazed at the ocean. There were maybe a dozen sailboats out this afternoon, tiny white sails bobbing in vivid contrast to the dark water. The ocean was showing off a little today, its surface rendered in shifting lazuli blues that reminded DaVinci of her mother's blue sodalite wedding ring.

DaVinci sighed with pleasure. She had a solid two hours until space–time yanked her back to the present. Two glorious hours to herself with nothing to do: no deadlines, no workshops to teach, no family home to save from destruction. Given her crazy summer, two hours without any responsibilities sounded like heaven.

About thirty minutes later, the plumber, a muscled woman in her forties, showed up. DaVinci greeted her and let her in, going with the strategy of "say as little as possible."

As DaVinci headed back outside, though, a book on the kitchen table caught her eye. *Janson's History of Art*, sixth edition. Her missing book! It had been "misappropriated" by someone, and she hadn't managed to replace it yet because the sixth edition was out of print, hard to find, and expensive.

Grinning, DaVinci grabbed the book. *Some* of space–time's duplicating behaviors weren't so bad.

Falling asleep on her favorite boulder with a copy of *Janson's History of Art*, sixth edition, in her arms was lovely. Waking to the grip and grind of space–time as it pulled her forward through time, less so.

Several uncomfortable seconds passed before DaVinci, now back in the Martian Chronicles suite, was able to pry her eyes open. The discomfort was just one of the things she hated about time travel. Not that she was complaining. She was grateful for time travel. She loved time travel. She wanted to pepper its face with kisses.

As soon as her muscles were freed from the machine's grip, DaVinci smiled.

"Thank you for saving my life," she said to the time machine.

If her voyage to the past hadn't exactly *saved* her life, it had certainly *fixed* her life.

She hoped. She really needed to see it for herself. The not-rotted foundation. The not-demolished home.

As quickly as possible, DaVinci finished shutting down the machine. She waited for its drone to die back to the decibel level of a garbage disposal before deciding it was safe to leave and drive home. Her *real* home. The home that no rich lawyer or plastic surgeon or app developer was going to buy and demolish.

Had she done it? She would find out soon. Back when she'd first hatched the idea, she'd thought about consulting Jillian and Halley. But she knew they would just hem and haw and nothing would get done. Who was it who had gotten them all into VADA? Into art shows? Who had made a million decisions when the two of them couldn't? DaVinci, that's who. She'd always been the make-it-happen girl, deciding what things needed doing and doing them, and she didn't need to hear a bunch of tired arguments against doing the right thing. In the end, she'd decided she wouldn't tell Jillian and Halley about her plan until she'd succeeded.

But now, if all had gone well, she realized that when she tried to tell them about saving her house, they would have no idea what she was talking about. For them, the house would never have been condemned or sold.

Which was strange to contemplate.

Closing the door of the Martian Chronicles suite, DaVinci strode down the silent hall. Same old hallway. Same old scent of beeswax polish on the same old dark wood wainscoting. But then she saw something that wasn't same-old, same-old.

What was *that* old thing doing in the hallway of the west wing?

She paused to stare at one of her precollege paintings. Actually, as she looked farther along the hall, she realized there were *three* of her old paintings. The ones she'd painted for her UCSB application portfolio. Later, she'd discarded these from her portfolio in favor of a series of plein air oils that had gained her a prestigious scholarship. A slight shiver passed along her shoulders as she gazed at the discarded paintings. Someone walking over her grave, Grandmother Shaughnessy would have said.

Well, it wasn't like she cared about these paintings. She just didn't remember giving them to Jillian. Of course, there was no way she could keep track of every single canvas she'd given away or discarded in the past few years. Maybe she'd given them to Jillian's mom, who'd had them framed and hung. Weird that she missed noticing them earlier . . . Well, she *had* been pretty focused on time travel. That, and not losing her nerve or becoming a mummy.

She gave the three canvases one last appraising look. They weren't very good. She'd done much better work since. Obviously. Even her plein air oils, done only a month after these, when she'd started using the roof as a studio, were far superior.

An image flashed in her mind: the Caterpillar taking a bite out of that same flat-topped roof. She shuddered. No need to think about *that*. It was the nonexistent past, assuming everything had worked. It better have; she'd brought the freaking nail to the freaking horse, hadn't she?

Giving herself a good shake, she raced down the hall and out of the house.

6

· DAVINCI ·

California, July

Her car wasn't outside. Well, not *her* car, but the car for which she had permanent borrowing privileges. The car she'd driven to the bank and back. Only now, it was missing. She placed her hands on her hips. Had Branson seen it and put it away in the garage? That couldn't be right. Branson wasn't supposed to be here—he had time off when the family were away. Which they were. All of them. Away.

Something was wrong.

The garage was the only place DaVinci could imagine the car might be, so she marched over to the building—a massive six-car structure that could have eaten her family's garage for breakfast and still been hungry.

There it was in the second bay: the blue Smart car. Shrugging, DaVinci climbed in. It took her most of the two-mile drive from the Applegates' estate to her house to figure out what must have happened—why the car hadn't been where she'd left it. In this time

A Sword in Time

line, this just-tweaked-by-DaVinci time line, the car had never been borrowed and left outside in the driveway.

It hadn't been borrowed because DaVinci hadn't needed it to go watch the demolition of her home. She hadn't driven it to the bank or back to Jillian's, either. In some sense, she hadn't even used the time machine. Or had she? Obviously she *had*, but . . .

Trying to make sense of it made her head hurt. But the bottom line was this: in this tweaked—*fixed*—time line, the car had never left the garage in the first place.

It made sense; you just had to think about it a little. In a way, it was reassuring. If she *hadn't* spent the night at the Applegates', that meant she must have spent it in her own bed. Laughter burbled up inside her. *Her own bed!* Her very own ancient, squeaky, sagging-in-the-middle twin bed! In her very own shared-with-Klee-and-Kahlo bedroom!

How was she *ever* going to keep this secret from her family? At least she could tell Jillian and Halley. And Edmund and Everett. Well, technically she could tell Dr. Arthur Littlewood, too, although she didn't see that happening. Outside this tight group of time travelers, DaVinci was sworn to secrecy. Which was fine by her. If people found out time travel was possible, it would be complete chaos. Countries-at-war, destroy-the-fabric-of-society type chaos. And even if it were next to impossible to make large-scale changes to the time line—and according to Dr. Littlewood, it was—history would get super weird, super fast if hundreds of people were constantly altering the past.

Turning onto East Mountain Drive, she slowed for the stretch of road that crossed right through the flow of Cold Springs Creek. The road was a little flooded thanks to a rainy week. Not a lot of water, but she slowed anyway, just to be safe.

As she crept through the three or four inches of creek flowing over the road, she glanced uphill at the large boulders dividing the creek into tiny spillways. Jillian had explained that history was a lot like a creek. If you dropped a big old boulder in the creek, the water would part around it temporarily, but the division would disappear on the downhill side of the boulder where the creek would continue, whole again. In the same way, if someone went back in time, say, to prevent James W. Marshall from finding gold at Sutter's Mill, the California Gold Rush would still have happened, but someone *else* would have been the first to discover gold.

DaVinci had never been entirely comfortable with the way Jillian dismissed the imagined alteration to the California Gold Rush. It might not have mattered to history in a generalized sense, but it sure as heck would have mattered to James W. Marshall.

The car cleared the creek and began the climb back out of the gully. DaVinci was almost home. Just one more horseshoe bend in the road and she would get her first glimpse of her beloved aqua-blue eyesore. A few curves after that and she'd be pulling into the driveway. Her heart began to beat faster. What if she hadn't done enough? What if the plumber hadn't been competent? DaVinci banished the thought. The plumber had been Applegate-vetted. The Applegates hired only the best. The plumber would have known her stuff. But what if something else had gone wrong? What if DaVinci came around the corner and saw the Caterpillar still at work?

She swallowed hard.

"Then you figure out what happened, and you go back and fix *that* problem, too, until everything is normal."

She rounded a curve and the ocean came into view. The sight eased something inside her, slowing her heart to a more normal pace. One more curve. She took it slowly—the Van Sant kids liked to play in the road no matter how many times they were told not to.

And then, as her house came into view, DaVinci gasped. It was there, but it was the wrong color! Someone had painted her aqua-blue house a rosy terra-cotta. Her heart raced, skipping beats. This was all wrong. Her family would *never* have painted over the aqua blue. It was iconic, according to her father. Too ridiculous to change, according to her mother. So who had done it? More to the point, who was living in the house now?

Five Months Earlier
February–March

7
·FATHER JOE·
Florida, February

Father Joe, properly Father Josef Novotny, was worried about his latest stray, a young man with seemingly no past. Through the years, Father Joe had nursed kittens, cats, dogs, and one time a crow back to health, finding homes for those that seemed likely to enjoy a home. But he had never, perhaps oddly for one whose life was dedicated to human souls, taken in a stray *human*. Or never for more than a night or two. Quintus, however, had been with him for more than four weeks.

Long enough for Father Joe to have ascertained Quintus wasn't a missing person, wasn't a fugitive, wasn't a felon. Wasn't exactly crazy, but was not, perhaps, entirely in his right mind, either.

Their friendship had not begun in a promising manner, but then, many people approached Catholic priests with suspicion. Father Joe could agree this wasn't entirely unwarranted. However, Father Joe had never been approached before by someone tickling his ribs with the business end of a sword and asking if he could speak Latin. (He could, a little.) Not a promising beginning at all, even if the sword had long since been dispensed with.

The Latin, however, had not been dispensed with. In the weeks since that memorable night, Father Joe's stray had continued to communicate only in Latin. Very *good* Latin. Father Joe continued to address the young man (who called himself Quintus Valerius, a very good Latin name) in English, but Quintus gave no indication he spoke English, much less understood it. Father Joe had tried Spanish, but Spanish had been met with only marginally more success than English. The young man sometimes seemed to catch a phrase or two but never attempted to reply in Spanish, sticking as resolutely as ever to Latin.

Quintus's attire that memorable night before Christmas had suggested he might be in the employ of a local amusement concession. The Holy Land Experience, maybe, or Medieval Times. Father Joe couldn't recall Roman legionnaire costumes being used in the Disney or Universal parks.

For reasons best known to himself, Quintus had disposed of most of his costume that first night of his stay. On seeing Quintus in the predawn darkness the following morning, Father Joe had thought the young man must have grabbed a white cassock from the vestry, belted it, and torn a good eighteen inches off the bottom. Upon closer examination, however, Father Joe realized Quintus hadn't stolen a cassock. The young man was merely wearing his own tunic, which had previously been hidden by the layers of protective outer gear. It had taken over a week for the priest to persuade Quintus to wear something besides the tunic.

Father Joe had sent an email to his friend Arthur Littlewood asking if the University of South Central Florida had a Latin program hidden somewhere in the classics or history departments (it did not), so that had been one more possibility crossed off.

Father Joe's sister Ivca, a Prague psychiatrist visiting America with her new husband, had stopped by for a brief visit. After observing Quintus, she was perplexed. In most ways he presented normally. She guessed it was a stress disorder, likely the result of trauma the young man wasn't yet ready to revisit.

"But he won't get better until he does," Ivca cautioned.

Ivca further surmised the young man, twenty by his own account, was raised a Catholic or he wouldn't have sought shelter with Father Joe, now would he? Ivca advised Father Joe to continue conversing in Latin until the young man indicated a preference for English or Spanish. (Ivca was sure it would be Spanish—the young man radiated machismo, and his bronze complexion, dark eyes, and dark hair hinted at a childhood in the islands nearby: Cuba perhaps?) Having Googled "Cuban goodbyes," Ivca kissed Quintus on the cheek when she departed, but if Quintus was familiar with this style of embrace, he gave no indication.

In spite of Ivca's conviction concerning Quintus's Catholicism, Father Joe believed the young man was not a Christian of any stripe. Case in point: Quintus had at first indicated a willingness to cross himself like Father Joe did when entering the sanctuary. However, after Father Joe explained the ritual was performed as a reminder of Christ's crucifixion, the young man refused to cross himself—or even to enter the sanctuary at all.

"Why?" Father Joe asked out of curiosity, in English, which Quintus was gradually acquiring.

"It is an incautious and unlucky god," Quintus replied in Latin, "who would allow himself to be executed in such a manner."

As to how the young man had come by his excellent Latin, well, Father Joe knew of the example of his parishioner, Mrs. O'Shea, who had taught herself Klingon using online resources. Why shouldn't Quintus have done the same? When Father Joe inquired as to how Quintus had learned Latin, Quintus had shrugged and asked, "How does a bird learn birdsong?"

How indeed?

Quintus was not forthcoming about his presumably troubled past, and Father Joe did not try to force conversation. In spite of his sister's belief it would help, Father Joe did not believe in forcing confessions of any sort. The young man would speak when he was ready.

But then things took a slight turn for the worse. Quintus stopped getting up for breakfast. Two days later, he stopped getting up for lunch. With a few gentle questions, Father Joe established that Quintus wasn't sleeping well. Or at all, some nights.

"Perhaps you might read yourself to sleep?" asked Father Joe, in his halting Latin.

Quintus grunted his assent.

Father Joe procured books in Latin, English, and

A SWORD IN TIME

Spanish for Quintus, setting them in the vestry, where Quintus slept. He noticed the Spanish and English ones remained untouched while the Latin Vulgate Bible showed signs of having been read.

"Do you like the book?" asked Father Joe one evening, first in English and then, haltingly, in Latin.

The young man, speaking in his customary, lyrical Latin, replied, "With these . . . *sewn pages*, you do surely entrust me with treasure."

"Treasure, indeed," replied Father Joe, his smiling gaze resting on the Vulgate. Did his young stray require spiritual counsel at last?

"Such gathered pages does Gaius Julius Caesar prefer," said Quintus. "For scrolls, no patience has he."

Ah. Merely another of Quintus's cryptic comments and not an invitation for spiritual counsel. Father Joe said good night, musing as he departed on Quintus's penchant for odd pronouncements. This one tickled at the priest's mind. Was it true about Caesar? An internet search revealed that, yes, Caesar had had his correspondence cut into pages and sewn together—a precursor to books in an age of scrolls.

The following morning, curious, Father Joe asked Quintus where he had learned about Caesar's preference for books over scrolls.

Quintus seemed on the point of responding, but then checked himself as if uncertain. Or perhaps as if . . . afraid to reveal a secret?

Who was this young man? And what was his story?

8

·*QUINTUS* ·

Florida, March

Quintus had fallen into deeper and deeper despair. How would he ever return home? How would he ever deliver Gaius Julius Caesar's message? About his location, Quintus was less certain than ever, even though three months had passed.

He could not sleep for trying to work out what was to be done. But if he did not sleep, he would be unfit to do whatever *might* be done, should an opportunity present itself. Yet the fear no opportunities would arise kept sleep far off, inviting despair and insomnia. It was a vicious circle.

When Pater Joe brought books to Quintus as a means of inviting sleep, he read the one in Latin, both to pass the nights and to gain what knowledge he could of the tribe of the *Floridae*, among whom he now dwelt. Florida was not mentioned in Pater Joe's book, although there was mention of other lands Quintus knew—Egypt and Judea—but where were the references to the great empire of *Roma*? He had progressed little through his text, but still, to mention Egypt and leave out *Roma*?

Where was he? And from here, where was Roma?

He asked Pater Joe about the phrase "Roman Catholic" written on the sign before the priest's temple, but Pater Joe's response was confusing. His Latin was not of the best sort. Quintus, a natural linguist, was beginning to prefer when the priest spoke in English, the tongue of the Floridae.

In any case, rather than telling Quintus about a city or land designated "Roman Catholic," the priest had spoken of gods, whom he called the gods of *Catholica Romana*, the "holy three." The greatest god was referred to as *Pater* to all, so Quintus thought of him as Jupiter Optimus Maximus. Pater Joe, however, chiefly revered the youngest god of the holy three, who seemed to have been murdered by priests and then resurrected, which sounded like an Egyptian tale Quintus had heard in Alexandria. Although in this matter, too, there was confusion. Pater Joe's god had been crucified, which, so far as Quintus knew, was a uniquely Roman form of execution. It was all very odd. In addition to the holy three, there was a fourth, a divine mother, and to this divine mother was Pater Joe's temple dedicated. Her image stood out of doors, ringed with blooming flowers and seats. Quintus thought she might have been Vesta or the Bona Dea, although at times she sounded more like Diana, the ever-virgin.

Pater Joe invited Quintus to ask these gods for aid, but the gods of the Floridae were not Quintus's gods, so how could they be expected to act for Quintus's good? Quintus gave up trying to puzzle out the relationship of Roma to Catholica Romana and asked Pater Joe more directly where Roma was to be found. If he understood the priest correctly, Roma lay across a vast *oceanus*, which the tribe of the Floridae called *Atlantic*.

If, as Quintus feared, this Atlantic was one and the same with the sea Gaius Julius Caesar called *mare Oceanum*, then he was lost indeed. How was a man to cross such a sea without aid? Without a great ship and slaves to row when the winds were contrary? Pater Joe suggested Quintus should "fly" if he wished to reach Roma, pointing to great winged creatures of the sky that belched fog in their wake. But Quintus could no more compel such a creature to swoop down and carry him than he could grow wings and fly himself.

Returning to Roma seemed impossible, and when he was not raging against Julius Canis for having stolen him from thence, Quintus's despair threatened to swallow him, as surely as the Atlantic would swallow him if he sought to cross it.

9
· KHAN ·
Missouri, February–March

In the weeks following his discovery that the thumb drive had disappeared, Khan neither crawled back to Littlewood to ask forgiveness nor broke into Littlewood's lab to steal the information he needed. He worked on plans for the singularity device, occasionally obsessing over the location of his missing thumb drive. Annoyingly, the missing object made him think of Arthur Littlewood and his penchant for leaving important items lying around. These recollections were infuriating; Khan was not Littlewood. Khan was not forgetful. He was organized and alert and careful with his things.

So where was this most important of things?

He had no idea.

Once, he had enjoyed plaguing Littlewood with the question "Where did you last see it?"

Such a seemingly innocent question but so infuriating when directed at oneself. Where had he last seen his thumb drive? He didn't know. He simply couldn't remember.

Since his initial search he had made many similarly fruitless searches of his pockets, his bag, his wallet. He spent one evening combing the youth hostel kitchen, bathroom, and grounds. He lay awake many nights, trying to reconstruct his movements, only to rise to stuffy sinuses and thunderous headaches. Finally, after three weeks of searching, he admitted the truth: he'd lost it for good. He'd lost the key to wealth immeasurable and all that wealth could buy: comfort, amusement, better health, better toys.

"Better *weather*," he muttered to himself. And then he put his head down and set to reconstructing the design he needed, from scratch.

Kansas City in February was a hell of ice and dirty snow. He shivered miserably in a studio apartment over a bakery that he moved into because the owner accepted cash and asked no questions. The bakery listed "free day-old baked goods" as a perk of renting the space. The problem with "free" food was that it was made up of the items that didn't sell out. If Khan never saw another pineapple cream cheese Danish, it would be too soon.

However, he ate his way through those, and the *TastiKrab*-stuffed profiteroles, carob chip brownies, and other out-of-favor items, reminding himself every dollar he saved was a dollar that could be spent on rebuilding a time machine. He'd sold the necklace—Elizabethan era, he was told—for a tidy $14,000, but small expenses were constantly gnawing at his spoken-for stash of money. He reduced his rent by half when he offered to keep the sidewalk in front of the bakery free of ice and snow seven days a week, and he brought his heating bill to zero by cutting into some floorboards to access the bakery's heating ducts—something about which he had no intention of informing his landlord.

But two months of carbohydrates and shoveling snow had yet to provide him with a workable schematic for rebuilding his portal to warmth, wine, and Wagyu beef. He spent all his waking hours working through the systems he remembered, but he was running into gaping holes in his knowledge. It wasn't, he insisted, that Littlewood had been more intelligent; rather, Khan simply hadn't paid attention to certain aspects of the singularity device.

February gave way to March and a handful of days above freezing, but then the snow returned with a vengeance. He spent a memorable Saturday shoveling the bakery sidewalk *four* times. This could not go on. Late that night, after dining on whole wheat brioche and a carton of cheap red wine, Khan came to a painful (if rather drunken) conclusion. He had neither the financial resources nor the will necessary to continue this way indefinitely. He needed the lost designs. And the only place he could get them was in Florida. Florida was nice in March. Khan wanted "nice" for a change. The baker could damn well shovel his *own* sidewalk.

On the four-day bus ride to Wellesley, Florida, Khan went back and forth trying to decide whether or not it would be best to simply present himself to Littlewood along with an apology for the regrettable events of last December. Littlewood's messages three months earlier had indicated he was willing to forgive and forget. Khan had nearly persuaded himself that such an apology was within his power, but when he stepped off the bus in downtown Wellesley, he realized the truth: he didn't have it in him. He didn't trust Arthur Littlewood. He didn't *like* Arthur Littlewood. He'd pulled a gun on Arthur Littlewood. And honestly, he would rather kiss Arthur Littlewood than apologize to him.

So theft it was. After casing the laboratory facility for three days, Khan concluded the attempt had to be made between the hours of midnight and four in the morning when the lab was always unoccupied. He then spent a day snatching up an entire wardrobe in black (it wasn't his fault if people didn't police their Laundromat items) and commenced his attempt to break in to the lab at 2:37 a.m. on a Thursday, coincidentally the Ides of March.

10
· SPECIAL AGENT NEVIS ·
Washington, DC, March

It had been a lateral move, not a promotion. Electrical grid terrorism? Who were they kidding? Not Special Agent Benjamin Nevis, that was for damn sure. Why didn't they just take away his FBI badge and be done with it? Sure, it was still National Security Branch. It was still counterterrorism. But sending him out to places like backwoods Georgia and rural Florida? Calling it a promotion was an insult—as if Nevis didn't get enough of those already. Of furtive looks, of eyes resting on him just a millisecond too long as he strode to the elevator, to the copy machine, to the john.

What an idiot.
You heard about him, right?
Can you imagine?

Nevis was used to the whispers when colleagues thought he couldn't hear. And the ones who didn't care if he *could* hear. Nevis was used to all of it. The staring, the whispering, the wide berth in the gym. All because he'd been stupid enough to trust his brother-in-law, then Special Agent-in-Charge Lewiston. It always came back to Lewiston and the events six years ago.

I've got your back, man.

Only it turned out Lewiston had never had anyone's back. Not Nevis's and certainly not Nevis's sister's—Lewiston's ex-wife. After, Lewiston had sent Karen a very large check drafted on a bank somewhere in the Caribbean. Nevis couldn't remember which island. One that had strict banking secrecy laws, that was for sure. The check was supposed to be . . . what? An apology? A severance package? It didn't matter. She'd cut it into pieces and burned the pieces in a coffee can. Folgers, if he remembered right.

It was getting harder and harder to remember things about his sister, Karen. She'd lost her battle with lung cancer five years ago. Maybe things would've been different if she were still alive. Orphaned at sixteen and eighteen, respectively, they'd been each other's only family for years. Until Lewiston came along with his big grin and big plans and big lies. Nevis had introduced them, a sin for which he would feel guilt the rest of his life. But Lewiston was hard to say *no* to. Still, Nevis *had* refused to introduce him to Karen for over a year.

Anyway, what was done was done. Nevis had considered quitting the FBI after Lewiston's betrayal. It would have been easier, maybe. But it would have meant losing access to certain channels of information, and Nevis still harbored the hope he'd find Lewiston someday. Find him and pay him back.

Stay here and watch that door. I'll come around from the

other side. We'll trap them.

And then that magnetic smile.

Don't worry man, I've got your back.

But what Lewiston had gotten was . . . *away with it*. Followed by *out of the country*. He'd made off with $7 million in unmarked bills. Nevis had remained behind—a top suspect in the theft and Lewiston's subsequent disappearance. They were friends, after all. They were related by marriage. It was a natural assumption. Heck, the details revealed during the investigation had practically convinced *him* that he'd been party to the heist.

I've got your back.

Nevis hadn't been kicked out or demoted or even reprimanded, in the end. But he'd become a pariah by association, and all his moves within the bureau since that time had been lateral. As though maybe, if they kept shuffling him sideways long enough, he'd get the hint and leave.

But he wasn't going anywhere until he figured out where Lewiston was.

He turned his gaze back to his file. His next assignments monitoring the electrical grid for terrorist threats were scattered throughout the South. Which, no doubt, would be as stimulating as his previous assignments in the Midwest. He ran his eyes down the list. Savannah, he'd heard of at least. But Eclectic, Alabama? Who named their town *Eclectic*? And where the heck was Wellesley, Florida? He hadn't known there *was* a University of South Central Florida. It was insulting. He'd done good work for the bureau. He was better than this.

But he wasn't ready for a career change. Not yet.

Nevis shook his head and opened a new browser window. Lands' End. Where he was heading, he was going to need a lighter blazer, not to mention shorts and sandals.

11
· *FATHER JOE* ·
Florida, March

It pained Father Joe to see Quintus sinking into depression, as he plainly was. The reading material might have helped Quintus's insomnia (although Father Joe wasn't sure of that, either), but it had not cheered him.

Over a breakfast of toast and coffee, Father Joe broached the subject in hesitant Latin.

"Friend, are you troubled?"

Quintus didn't answer right away.

Father Joe wondered, ought he to have used *terreo* or *tribulo* instead of *conturbo*? Reading the Latin Vulgate was easy; speaking in Latin was a constant challenge.

But Quintus didn't look confused by the question, nor did he ask Father Joe to repeat himself.

"I am troubled," said Quintus after his lengthy pause. "I lack occupation," he added, as if this explained everything.

Privately, Father Joe thought unemployment was the least of Quintus's troubles.

And yet . . . if that was what he believed was wrong . . .

"May I employ you in labor?" asked Father Joe.

He must have phrased his Latin oddly, because Quintus seemed intent on covering a smile. These fleeting attempts to stifle laughter over Father Joe's Latin were the only smiles the priest saw. At least the young man remembered *how* to smile. That was something.

"To you will I . . . give . . . labor," Quintus said, in halting English.

Father Joe smiled and reached for a legal pad on which he kept a running list of chores that never seemed to get any shorter. There were always areas of the church and grounds that needed cleaning or clearing or planting or weeding.

He chose the most urgent concern: clearing space for additional parking to accommodate the surprising number of lapsed parishioners who'd kept New Year's resolutions to attend Mass more regularly.

In the area Father Joe hoped to clear, there were rocks, some large and some half-buried, in addition to plentiful saw palmettos and weeds. Father Joe expected they'd be at it all week.

Father Joe had underestimated Quintus.

By two in the afternoon, Quintus had removed nine boulders and seventeen saw palmettos from the far end of the new parking space. All while Father Joe had done nothing more than weed the rose bushes edging the lot. In addition to the removals, Quintus had backfilled the holes left by the plants and rocks. The young man reminded Father Joe of the oxen he had observed during his youth in Poland; Quintus had the same strength and determination, not to mention his ability to work in the heat.

"Time for a rest," said Father Joe, handing Quintus another water bottle, his third or possibly fourth.

"I am not weary," replied Quintus. Then, shading his eyes from the sun and looking at Father Joe, he smiled. "But I observe that you are."

Over their midday meal, Father Joe told Quintus of a plan he'd concocted to replant the garden surrounding the Madonna with fruits and vegetables that they might be available for those in need.

Quintus nodded and replied in his lyrical Latin, "Those like myself you would aid, lest they are constrained to steal from farmers their oranges."

"Yes."

"It is a noble endeavor," replied Quintus. "I shall aid you."

What was more, Quintus needed next to no instruction, either for preparing the soil or planting the seeds, although once Father Joe stopped him from applying water to the garden using his water bottle, Quintus had seemed inexplicably fascinated with the garden hose.

Father Joe asked how Quintus had learned about planting.

"My mother managed a great garden," Quintus explained.

"Have you considered working as a gardener?" asked the priest.

"I am no man of agriculture. I have stood guard over—" Quintus fell silent.

"You were a security guard?" asked Father Joe

after a moment of silence.

Quintus's expression had grown remote, unreadable. "It matters not."

"I did not mean to pry," Father Joe said, his voice gentle.

"Forgive me," replied Quintus. "I am glad to aid you in this work, but I am no gardener."

Perhaps not. But it begged the question: What *was* he, this puzzle of a young man?

12
·LITTLEWOOD·
Florida, March

Arthur Littlewood had been drinking more than usual. A lot more than usual. And usually alone.

Neither was a habit he wanted to cultivate, but he was worried and not sleeping well, and this led to drinking. A lot. Alone.

Littlewood was worried about Jules Khan.

In those first days after his (now former) postdoc had held them all at gunpoint, Littlewood had repeatedly attempted to contact Khan. He'd left messages urging Khan to turn himself in. (It appeared Khan had stolen a valuable vehicle to make his getaway.) Littlewood had promised to speak on Khan's behalf, to get any potential sentencing reduced by any means possible. He knew Jules Khan. He *knew* what a great scientist he could be. Would be. Should be. But day after day, Khan refused to pick up, the calls going straight to voice mail, until New Year's, when the phone *didn't* go straight to voice mail because the number was no longer in service.

At this point, Littlewood had had the locks at his lab changed.

He also began to have recurrent nightmares in which Khan appeared, gun drawn. Several times when Littlewood drove home late at night, he would see the Honda Accord he'd loaned to Khan, parked in the darkness, and he would panic for a moment, believing Khan had returned and was waiting to ambush him. On one of these occasions, Littlewood found the need to march over to the car and make sure it really was empty, which it was, except for trash.

Inside the Honda, Littlewood discovered a half-eaten and completely moldy hamburger, along with several empty bottles of VOSS water, and, between the driver's seat cushion and back cushion, a thumb drive, which for all Littlewood knew had been left by himself long before Khan had been given use of the car.

He tossed the burger, recycled the bottles, and stuck the thumb drive in his linen sport coat pocket, to be investigated later. After, he decided it was high time to move the Honda *behind* the mother-in-law unit at the back of his property so that he wouldn't experience any more moments of panic.

In addition to moving the Honda, Littlewood took some very practical steps to ensure his safety. Over President's Day weekend, he changed his house locks and installed *another* new lock at the lab—electronic this time. Then on the first of March, Littlewood added a security camera to monitor the laboratory stairwell.

Halfway through the month, Littlewood's new security camera caught something. It recorded the approach of an intruder just after two o'clock in the morning. The figure was dressed head to toe in black, face hidden underneath a balaclava that looked homemade, but there was something unnervingly familiar about the intruder's gait. Littlewood felt certain it was Khan.

Which made it nearly impossible for Littlewood to sleep, well into the month of April. Was he in mortal peril? Should he hire a bodyguard? Most of the time—in daylight at least—Littlewood was able to calm himself, to listen to the voice of reason. After all, Khan hadn't succeeded in breaking in, had he? No. So just report the incident to the police. It was their job to handle men like Khan. It was his job to do *his* work. Focus on his research. On his students.

Littlewood tried to do this, but he was finding it harder than ever to sleep. Khan knew where he lived. Khan carried a gun. Had *fired* said gun. After an especially bad weekend, Littlewood decided to pay a visit to his friend Father Joe, hoping to find him free. Littlewood wasn't entirely sure what Catholic priests did, other than celebrate Mass. Littlewood wasn't religious. At least, he wasn't Catholic, in spite of his mother's prayers offered to that end. He supposed he believed in a Being or Force that had struck the match to light the big bang and that possibly kept things running, but he didn't really like church.

He did, however, like Father Joe.

The two had met in a liquor store, of all places, years ago. Littlewood had gone to the liquor store to buy *krupnik*: a spiced, honeyed spirit of Polish invention that he'd acquired a taste for when his mother had served it on special occasions in his youth.

On his way out of the liquor store, Littlewood overheard the priest who'd been behind him asking for *krupnik* as well. Littlewood paused at the door. How unexpected. Littlewood had never met anyone else who knew what *krupnik* was, much less wanted to purchase it.

He stood with one hand on the door, debating whether to say anything. The man was a priest. Would a priest be embarrassed to be addressed about liquor? And by a complete stranger?

But when Littlewood heard the liquor store employee tell the priest that there was no more *krupnik* and to try back in two weeks, Littlewood decided to speak. Turning from the door, he offered his bottle to the priest.

Who refused it.

But who agreed to sip a glass with Littlewood that evening.

A single raised glass that night became two glasses, and then three, and possibly more, and Littlewood ended up sleeping in the vestry. After that, the two men, one a Czech of Polish descent and the other the son of an American-Polish mother, met every couple of months to enjoy *krupnik* together, sharing their memories of savory *pierogi* and steaming *babka* and *oplatek* the night before Christmas.

This had gone on for two years before Jules Khan had first intruded into Littlewood's life. Lately, though—since the trip to Santa Barbara, in fact—Littlewood hadn't visited Father Joe. That had been what, Christmas? It was almost Easter now. It was high time to raise a glass of *krupnik* with his friend. At least, it was better than drinking alone.

Krupnik bottle in hand, Littlewood made his way to the Church of Our Lady of Mercy. where he found Father Joe looking dead tired.

"My good friend," said the priest, embracing Littlewood and inviting him inside.

"You look beat," said Littlewood, a bit discouraged. The priest didn't look up to a late night of sipping spirits.

The priest laughed. "You should see the other guy!"

Littlewood didn't know if he should laugh or not.

"I'm joking," said Father Joe. "But there is actually someone I want you to meet. Give me a moment. I'll be right back."

Littlewood made himself comfortable in the priest's shabby little sitting area. He'd grown fond of the room, right down to the framed portrait of Pope Whoever-He-Was. Littlewood poured two glasses and raised one of them to the head of the Catholic faith. And then, thinking ahead, he found and poured a third glass for the mysterious guest.

But when Father Joe returned, he was alone.

"Poor kid fell asleep," he murmured. Sitting, he exhaled heavily. After clinking glasses with Littlewood, the priest took a sip of *krupnik*.

"You have a . . . *kid?*" asked Littlewood, after no explanation had been offered.

Father Joe laughed. "I ought to have spoken more carefully. I've taken in a stray. A most singular young man."

Saying no more about the young man, Father Joe listened to Littlewood's woes, his fears, his apprehensions regarding his safety, and his wish that he were wealthy enough to hire someone to stand guard at the lab.

Father Joe promised to pray for his friend, and after that, the conversation returned to the priest's young stray, who had learned a little English but spoke primarily in Latin. Father Joe praised Quintus, relating how helpful he had been today, despite his marked aversion to becoming a gardener.

And then Father Joe paused. He *hmm'ed* to himself. His brows rose.

"Goodness," he said. "You just told me you were thinking of hiring a security guard, didn't you?"

Littlewood nodded gloomily. "I can't afford one. It's only wishful thinking."

Father Joe smiled. And then he poured himself another small allowance of *krupnik*. "What is that American saying? Ah yes, to kill two birds using a single rock. Allow me, if you will, to offer a solution to your concerns regarding the affordability of a security guard."

13
·KHAN·
Florida, March

Later, Khan would tell himself that it was the combination of four days on a bus with little sleep and sheer bad timing that kept him from successfully breaking in to Littlewood's lab in Florida on the Ides of March. But none of those was the real reason. The real reason had to do with sirens.

Sirens had been troubling Khan ever since his narrow escape from the sheriff back in Montecito, California, right after he'd shot that kid and driven off in the stolen BMW. He had recurrent nightmares in which he heard the wail of police sirens and knew he should flee but couldn't. Sometimes his feet weighed too much to move. Sometimes he was in a car, but he couldn't locate the right key to start the engine. Sometimes he was trapped in a basement by a large couch wedged against the door and preventing his escape.

He always woke before the sheriff or police or National Guard caught him, but waking up to find himself safe and sound did nothing to cure him of a steadily worsening panic response to the sound of sirens. Unfortunately, his apartment over the bakery in Kansas City was located just down the street from a fire station—a constant source of fresh alarm. Khan told himself these frequent exposures would lessen his fear over time. In fact, irrational as it sounded, the opposite seemed to be happening.

Just after Khan boarded the bus to travel to Florida and break into Littlewood's lab, a pair of police vehicles had roared into the bus loading zone, and Khan had experienced his first-ever panic attack. He was sure they'd finally caught up with him. Had it been mild-mannered Mark from Omaha who'd provided the missing clue leading to Khan's capture after so many months? Should he run? The bus's exit doors opened in the direction of the red and blue flashing lights. Khan's heart hammered in his chest, and he suddenly felt as though someone was squeezing all the air out of his lungs. Was this a heart attack?

When the police vehicles pulled away ten minutes later without having arrested him, Khan's shirt was drenched in sweat, and he was convinced he'd suffered a cardiac episode of some sort. Eight hours of Googling "heart conditions" later, he was reluctantly persuaded he'd suffered nothing more than a panic attack.

"Nothing more," he muttered.

His second panic attack came four days later at 2:37 a.m. in Wellesley, Florida. He was hunkered down beside the door to Littlewood's lab, hidden from casual view in the below-ground stairwell. A YouTube video on his phone was showing him three possible

A Sword in Time

ways to disarm an electronic door lock.

The moment he heard the wail of the siren in the distance, he knew it was coming for him. He knew Littlewood had been waiting for this moment. Of course, Littlewood had known Khan would return. Khan had been set up.

He stood too fast, and all the blood seemed to drain to his lower extremities, leaving him light-headed and slightly nauseous. A moment later, his heart began to thunder in his chest. Another panic attack. He gripped the metal banister and pulled himself up the stairs, hand over hand, back up to ground level. It was then that he noticed the security camera. It was too late to do anything more than lower his head and feel thankful he'd turned his stolen stretch cap into a makeshift balaclava. Littlewood couldn't prove it was him, as long as he got away.

Damn that siren! Had the security camera alerted the police? Had he fallen right into a trap?

The siren was much louder now. The vehicle was definitely turning into the warehouse complex. Stumbling, Jules Khan backed away, rounding a corner to take himself out of plain sight.

The sheriff was chasing someone. Someone driving a truck. The driver lost control of his vehicle and slammed sideways into a pair of bollards blocking access to an alley between buildings.

Khan watched all this without moving, hidden by night and his black apparel, but even when he could plainly see the county sheriff arresting this *other* offender, Khan didn't make the mistake of returning to have another go at the door. Littlewood had taken all those precautions. The new lock. The camera. Even if the cops hadn't been here for him, the door was monitored, as if Littlewood had known Khan would be back, as if Littlewood had been planning to catch him. Littlewood wanted him behind bars. Khan had been a fool to believe Littlewood's earlier overtures had been genuine. Well, Littlewood wouldn't catch him with his guard down a second time. He wouldn't catch him at all. If there was one thing Jules Khan would *not* risk, it was incarceration.

Khan began a slow, painful jog back to the bus station. He would figure out the schematics another way. He was twice the scientist Littlewood was. He could recreate all of it from scratch, despite his earlier failure. To hell with Littlewood and his machinations to put Jules Khan behind bars. To hell with them all.

Three Months Earlier
April–May

14

·*QUINTUS* ·

Florida, April

Quintus accepted employment as a security guard for Dr. Arthur Littlewood for two reasons. Firstly, it had become evident to him that his host, Pater Joe, was impoverished, and thus in no position to share his meager meals with a man of large appetite such as Quintus knew himself to be. Secondly, if he were to someday purchase a sailing vessel and slaves to sail it, he would require an income. Littlewood had offered both a dwelling place *and* a salary, solving two of Quintus's most pressing needs.

So Quintus had taken his few belongings—all but his soldier's gear were gifts from Pater Joe—to his new dwelling, located in a set of rooms separated from and just behind Littlewood's main villa. Quintus unpacked, placing the gifted tunics and breeches in "drawers" after the custom of the Floridae, and then he awaited the call to dinner.

Quite late that night, Quintus determined it must not be customary for hosts to provide dinner for their

A Sword in Time

guests, even though Father Joe had done so. Littlewood, at any rate, offered neither food nor watered wine. This was less troublesome in a land where the household water was at all times of year fresh and wholesome to drink.

Pulling out a sack, Quintus examined Pater Joe's final gift: sliced bread and something labeled *peanut butter*. The gift made sense now. The priest must have suspected Littlewood would not feed Quintus. So Quintus ate the strange paste spread over the soft bread. In a "week," the seven-day equivalent of Rome's eight-day *nundinae*, he would receive payment, which would enable him to buy other foods. Meanwhile, he set a few snares out of doors, hoping his new host would not upbraid him for eating the birds on his land.

The following evening, Littlewood took Quintus to his new place of employment, driving him there in one of the marvelous horseless chariots used by the Floridae. Overhead, the sky was shifting from pale purple to a deep charcoal. The road stretched smoothly before them. While Quintus found "cars" a marvel, the smooth road raised much deeper feelings of admiration for the Floridae, creators of "asphalt," who, moreover, had the engineering skill to join this creation to the forging of such roads.

They had just turned onto a road of *lesser* perfection when Quintus's senses came to sudden alertness. The buildings looked familiar. He had been here before. His heart began to beat more swiftly. He *knew* this place! How was it possible he should return to the very place where he had awoken after Julius Canis had stolen him out of Rome?

Some god had surely arranged this. He sent a quick prayer of thanksgiving to Mercury, a god who had favored him many times during his days as Caesar's messenger. Quintus vowed that when his work hours ended, Mercury would have the best bird from his snares.

For if Quintus was returning to where he had escaped Julius Canis, did it not stand to reason the wretched man might be found there? And if Quintus could bring the man to justice . . .

"It's a bit tricky finding your way through the buildings," Littlewood said, interrupting Quintus's thoughts.

Quintus, attempting to steady his heart rate, returned his attention to his employer.

"They all look alike," said Littlewood. "I've been known to walk to the wrong door myself." He gave a small laugh and seemed to await a response.

Quintus gave a brief nod to indicate he understood.

"These buildings have been in use since the Second World War, if you can believe it. Complexes just like this all over Florida, I shouldn't wonder. I suppose there's no money to be made in tearing them down."

Quintus experienced a sinking sensation. If Florida contained many buildings that had the same appearance, perhaps this was *not* the place in which he had roused from his drugged sleep. His jaw tightened. How he *yearned* to visit justice upon Canis. This desire was second only to his desire to deliver Caesar's letter. Another hastily uttered prayer ascended to the god of travelers, and a second to the blind goddess Justitia:

Please. Please.

"Just look for the number painted on the side of the building," Littlewood was saying. "You can park anywhere. Oh, I meant to tell you, you can use the old Honda parked behind your cottage. Father Joe said you didn't have a car, so I thought . . ."

Quintus was too distracted to reply. His heart pounded; how greatly this place resembled the one from which he had fled Canis. Would the evil man still be found within? Surely, *surely* . . .

"You can drive, right?" asked Littlewood, exiting the car.

Quintus, forcing himself to attend to Littlewood, exited and made his reply. "I cannot drive."

He returned his focus to his environs, his eyes darting about, seeking Canis.

"Ah. Well—" Littlewood broke off. "I suppose I could drive you over."

Quintus was silent. The stairwell. The door with its small window. *This was the place.* He knew it with certainty.

Mercury should have *all* the birds in his snares.

"Maybe there's a bus," said Littlewood.

"I walk," said Quintus. The phrasing was incorrect; English was a maddening language. "I *shall* walk," he said, amending his reply. It was hard to form his responses knowing Julius Canis might at any moment appear.

"It's three miles," said Littlewood. "You're not seriously suggesting you'd walk six miles a day, every day? *Er,* night?"

"I shall walk," repeated Quintus. In fact, the exercise, though of small distance, would do him good. He had grown soft in this strange land. Shame washed over him. If Canis was inside the building, Quintus would have ample reason to regret his laxness when he attacked.

Together, they approached the door.

"And another thing," murmured Littlewood. "In your prior, *er*, security work, it may have been normal to call 9-1-1 first. Here, however, I'd prefer if you called me instead."

"I shall call you," said Quintus, itching to wield his *gladius*—his sword.

"Right. Ah . . . Father Joe indicated you had no cell phone, so I took the liberty of getting this for you." Littlewood held out a cell phone—an uncanny device by which means the Floridae communicated with one another when they were too far distant to shout and be heard.

Quintus accepted the device and fixed his eyes on the small window in the door.

"Okay. Well, the lock is state of the art," said Littlewood, indicating the door leading into the subterranean chamber.

Quintus felt the back of his neck prickling. Was Canis here?

Littlewood demonstrated the door's locking mechanism. After Quintus succeeded in unlocking the door following Littlewood's instructions, the two entered the room.

"Nothing fancy, I'm afraid," said Littlewood, flicking on the lights. "Just a basic lab."

As Quintus followed Littlewood inside, his hands clenched into tight fists. A dozen details of the room struck him, choking as a blow to the windpipe. He knew this place. He had awoken here when Canis had stolen him from Rome. Swiftly he drew his sword, seeking the man.

"Good heavens!" said Littlewood. "What on earth are you doing?"

"Where is the man called Julius Canis?"

15
·LITTLEWOOD·
Florida, April

When it came to swords, Arthur Littlewood was out of his depth. When it came to Jules Khan, not only was he on solid ground, but he knew enough to proceed with caution.

"How do you know Khan?" he asked his new security guard.

It was a simple question, calmly asked, but it evoked a passionate response.

"He stole me to this place and later attacked me, here in this room. I will exact payment."

"Ah," said Littlewood.

Things were coming together in his mind, which was now filling with dread. In this sudden revelation, Littlewood comprehended *many* things. It was as though the curtain of day had been suddenly swept aside, revealing starlight. It had been there all along, could one but see it. Quintus's strange insistence on speaking only Latin. The odd habits Father Joe had mentioned. It all made sense. *"Ah,"* he said again. He stuffed his hands into the pockets of his linen sports coat, nervously clutching the keys he found there.

For a moment, the two men regarded one another in silence, and then Quintus's gaze fell once more to examining the laboratory. It was an alert gaze, predatory. Quintus looked very much as if he expected—no, *hoped*—Khan would jump out and yell, *Surprise!*

Littlewood reached for his phone and texted Everett. Then added Jillian in as well: Come at once! A time traveler from ancient Rome has arrived. Permanently arrived. Please hurry.

After this, Littlewood tried to think of what he ought to say to this poor young man. He had an idea that this sort of news ought to be given gently, and the thought of doing it . . . well, *wrong*, made him quite squeamish. What if he bungled the whole thing? Honestly, he had no idea how one broke such news.

There was the matter of the sword, however, and the bloodthirsty—*understandably* bloodthirsty— expression on Quintus's face. *That*, Littlewood might address.

"Father Joe has explained to you, I trust," he said to Quintus, "the amount of trouble that your . . . *er, weapon* could get you in? If you were to, say, attack someone with it?"

Would Quintus have learned this from Father Joe? The priest led a very sheltered life, which meant *Quintus* would have had a sheltered existence since his arrival.

"When I encounter Julius Canis," said Quintus, interrupting Littlewood's thoughts, "I shall do what is necessary to obtain justice."

"Ah, well, there's necessary and there's *necessary*, you see . . ."

Quintus, hearing the air conditioner rattling to life, spun, brandishing his sword.

Littlewood felt his mouth go suddenly dry. Oh dear. Oh *dear*. "Would you mind, just for now, putting that weapon away?"

Quintus lowered his sword, frowning darkly. "Canis has done wrong things and must pay. The goddess *Justitia* cries out for it. I shall have the revenge that is my due."

Oh dear.

Littlewood's keys slipped through the hole in his coat pocket, jangling noisily as they hit the floor. He really needed to take his coat in for a repair before he lost something important.

"Well," murmured Littlewood, bending down to retrieve his keys, "let's set aside the discussion of your revenge for just a moment. You say he attacked you and then brought you here?"

"Somehow he overcame me and brought me by force to this place, though I cannot recall the journey," said Quintus. "The man is too slight to have bested me in a fight. I am no believer in magic. Therefore, I conclude he used some drug to overcome me so that he might bring me here. In doing so, he has made himself an enemy of the state of Roma, upon whose business I was engaged."

"Ah."

"For your kindness to me, I will not harm you at present," said Quintus, "but if Canis is your friend, then I must regard you as an enemy and we must part."

A Sword in Time

"He is not my friend," said Littlewood, gloomily. "He was. Or I thought he was, once. But our friendship ended several months ago. I am not your enemy. And Khan is not here."

Quintus's expression dulled. Exhaling heavily, he placed his sword once again out of sight behind his substantial back.

It was time for Littlewood to make a few inquiries.

"Quintus, I want to ask you something."

"Ask what you will."

"Where are you from?"

Quintus frowned as if considering whether to answer. At last he spoke. *"Roma."*

"Oh dear." Littlewood ran a hand through his hair. "Rome. Good heavens. It's true. Does Father Joe know this?"

"I—" Quintus broke off. His frown deepened. "I have not spoken of it before now." After a moment's silence, Quintus added, "And Father Joe is not a man to ask questions."

"Yes. Yes, indeed." Littlewood's mouth had gone completely dry. "Might I ask, who governs the, ah, Roma from which you come?"

"The *consules* Valerius Messala and Gnaeus Domitius," replied Quintus. "Myself, I am a soldier under the authority of Gaius Julius Caesar, twice governor of *Gallia.*"

"*Good heavens.*" Littlewood began to pace. He felt himself swelling with indignation. How could Khan have done this?

How could he have done it and then *abandoned* Quintus?

It was heartless. It was *spineless*.

Littlewood forced himself to stand still. Later, there would be time to be furious with Khan. Right now, he needed to establish a few things about Father Joe's "stray." How had the poor young man survived, let alone learned a new language, learned to pass in a new culture as a *normal* person—well, he wasn't exactly normal, though, was he?

Clearing his throat, Littlewood said, "I'd like you to tell me everything you remember about the moments leading to your abduction."

Quintus's tale took only a few minutes, but Littlewood found it impossible to resist interjecting a few questions: *How had he learned English so quickly?* The young man explained he was skilled with languages, having learned those of the *Aedui*, the *Arverni*, and the *Belgae*, among others, which had made him an invaluable courier for Caesar. *For Caesar!* It was astonishing. It was unconscionable and a host of other things as well, but . . . the man had served *Caesar*.

"I don't suppose you speak . . . Egyptian? Or any language spoken in Alexandria of, ah, your time?"

"Greek is the language of that barbarian city," replied Quintus. "I can speak and write and read Greek."

"How fortunate," said Littlewood, perking up considerably. "I have a pet project . . . just an idea, mind . . ."

At this point, they were interrupted by the arrival of Everett and Jillian.

"Ah," said Littlewood, beckoning the two over. Then he addressed Quintus. "I texted these friends—that is, I thought it might be good for you, well, *hmm*.

Everett Randolph, Jillian Applegate, this is Quintus—ah, I don't know your family name," he said.

"I am of the Valerii."

"Quintus *Valerius* then," said Everett. "From . . . Rome?" Everett looked back at Littlewood as if seeking confirmation.

"Yes," replied Quintus. "Do you know my family?"

"No, I haven't had that pleasure," replied Everett. He turned to Littlewood. "How much have you told Quintus Valerius about where and when he is now?"

"Oh well, now . . ." Littlewood paused, guilty. "I hadn't quite gotten there yet. Perhaps you might . . . ?" He fidgeted with a mechanical pencil in one of his pockets.

Jillian, at Everett's side, looked severely distressed. She turned to Everett.

"You've been through this," she murmured to him. "It does give you a certain advantage in explaining things."

Everett nodded and then extended his arm, indicating a table with four chairs around it. "Perhaps we might retire to the dining table."

And then, while Jillian smiled encouragement and Littlewood fidgeted with his mechanical pencil, Everett explained things to Quintus, up to and including the harsh reality that Quintus could never return to his own time.

16

·*QUINTUS*·

Florida, April

After hearing the news, Quintus was silent for a long time. At first, he considered the possibility that their story was some elaborate ruse. But to what purpose? Besides, as he thought about all the mechanical marvels he had seen, things even Roma could not have dreamt of, he began to realize the explanation these Floridae offered was the most probable explanation: he had traveled forward in time.

As he accepted this, the implications began to sink in. This was worse—far worse—than facing a horde of barbarians. To learn that he could not return to Roma? To his Roma? It was devastating news. He could not deliver the letter from Caesar to Pompeius because Pompeius was dead. Caesar was dead. Everyone he knew was dead. The hairs on his arms raised, prickling. He had failed his general. Caesar had gone to his grave wondering why his letter had never been delivered. How could Quintus live with the shame? His hand drifted to the hilt of his sword. A noble Roman, upon learning of such dishonor, would surely fall on his own blade.

And yet . . . did he wish to die?

His heart began to gallop within his chest as though to argue against death. It came to him that he did *not* wish to die. He wished to know things—so many things. If he had, indeed, crossed a bridge into the future, how could he turn back from the adventure? That would be a coward's course. Shame, he might bear. The taint of cowardice, however, he would not endure.

He removed his hand from his sword.

"It's a lot to take in," said the girl called Jillian.

Quintus raised his eyes to meet hers. "It is," he agreed. It came to him that Orpheus, journeying to the Underworld, must have felt much this way, surrounded by things so wholly unknown. Odysseus, venturing through the lands of Cyclops and monsters and gods, must also have felt as Quintus did now.

"But I will not shrink from it," he added. He felt the truth of his words. He had faced danger before, faced brave foes before. And he would do so now. Starting with vengeance against Julius Canis. For this, he needed information.

"If he is no friend to you, how is it that Canis brought me to this place?" asked Quintus.

"Ah," said Littlewood. "That would be my fault."

Quintus's brows furrowed. It took nobility of spirit to shoulder blame rather than shirk it. Pater Joe had chosen this friend, Arthur Littlewood, wisely.

"How so?" asked Quintus.

Littlewood waved a hand to a . . . *contrivance* at the room's far end. It looked vaguely familiar. "I built the machine Khan used to, ah, kidnap you."

"That . . . *machine* is the bridge that joined my time to yours?" asked Quintus.

"Well, yes, in a manner of speaking. I'm afraid so."

But this was marvelous news, if he understood it correctly. "You said I could not return to Roma. But if you control the bridge between my land and yours, why may I not return? Once I have revenged myself upon Canis, of course."

This time it was Everett who spoke. Everett who explained that while a return might be made, it would be impossible for Quintus to remain in Roma. That an entity called *space–time*—a god of great power, Quintus concluded—would always call him back to this place.

"Six minutes, or thereabouts," said Everett, "would be the longest you could remain, if you went home."

"The time machine is not a toy," Littlewood said gently. "I can't authorize its use to send you home for visits any more than I would have authorized the sort of use Khan made of it."

Quintus said nothing, only nodding once.

"The important thing," said Jillian, "is that there is still a *you* living your life in Rome. Or there was, I mean." She paused for a moment before adding, "So no one you cared about, or were responsible for, has suffered as a result of your coming here. If that helps."

Did it help? Hope seized him at her words. "If I had intended to deliver a message of grave importance—"

"Then likely you did it," said Everett. "You didn't stop being you, back in your own time. If it was important to you, then most likely you did it."

"I do not understand 'likely'," said Quintus.

"It means probably," said Jillian.

Probably. How was he to live with *probably* in such an important concern?

"I never meant for my invention to cause hardships, such as you've suffered," Littlewood said softly. "I'm very sorry."

"I hold you not to blame," said Quintus. "Canis alone is to blame. And he shall pay the price."

This remark began a series of pleas that he would refrain from seeking to take the life of Canis, and the consequences of doing so, should he be caught. The laws of this land were much like those of Roma. Quintus indicated that he understood. He did not, however, indicate that he would forego his revenge.

17
· *KHAN* ·
Missouri, May

Khan's progress was slow. Maddeningly slow. He'd started writing the software he would need to control the singularity, but after initial good progress, he'd run smack into a wall. He needed formulae stored on the missing thumb drive. He chose to take a break and work on recreating the schematics instead, trusting his mind would work the problem on its own if he switched to something new. Back in Florida during his aborted break-in, he'd had a brief look through the window in the lab door and seen things that had jogged his memory regarding the field shaping equipment and a few other components.

After finishing the schematics, he purchased copper and began shaping the coils. It was progress, but his lengthy break from writing the software did not, unfortunately, serve to unblock his memory.

Meanwhile, the finished copper coils were taking up a large portion of his already crowded living space. It was time, he decided, to rent a small industrial space where he could work without the interruption of nosy landlords wanting to bring by day-old bagels.

Soon after leasing the space, Khan found it necessary to order increased power connections. More money. More outlay against a future that continued to feel frustratingly out of reach. Large gaps remained in his memory and knowledge base. At the rate he was going, it might take him years of experimenting to get the singularity device built, much less functioning properly.

Returning to Florida, though, was a nonstarter. What he needed was his thumb drive. That would solve all his problems. He made a list of possible places the drive could have been lost. After a thorough hounding of the Greyhound Bus company, he admitted he ought to contact Mark in Omaha. He should have done this months ago, but up to this point, he'd been too proud to admit he might not be able to reconstruct the device on his own.

He reached Mark by email, describing the missing drive and including a picture of an identical one. Mark replied that, no, he'd found no thumb drives, but he then revealed he hadn't stripped the car for parts after all. Mark had donated it to the Sisters of Saint Joseph in the apparent expectation that Sisters Margarethe and Jill would pray for his soul whenever they drove it out to the far goat pasture. Bizarre.

Bizarre, but also encouraging. If the car had *not* been stripped, the thumb drive might yet be found. It was a stretch, perhaps, but this news that the car was still in one piece was enough to get Khan back on a bus to Omaha, Nebraska. He would at least have the satisfaction of having left no avenue unexplored.

The Sisters of Saint Joseph were happy to allow Khan to give the car a once over, even offering to help him search for the thumb drive containing pictures of his beloved grandmother from the old country. The lie was out of his mouth before he could wonder if lying to nuns might result in significantly worse karma than lying to anyone else, but Khan didn't believe in karma anyway.

Khan diligently searched every cranny and every crevice in the vehicle. In the process, he jammed several things under the nail bed of his right middle finger, which led to vociferous swearing. One of the sisters tittered. The other appeared to have begun praying for his soul.

Unfortunately, the thumb drive simply wasn't to be found.

By midnight, he was back on a bus to Kansas City—and all the gluten-free blueberry muffins he could stomach—no closer to the information he needed. It was as though the drive had vanished into thin air.

"Impossible," muttered Khan.

The next afternoon, he returned to his work, determined to discover his own solutions. And who knew? Perhaps they would prove more elegant than those Arthur Littlewood had come up with. He was twice the scientist—no, ten times the scientist Littlewood was. It was simply a matter of time before the secrets of the singularity revealed themselves to him. Simply a matter of time. Khan smiled grimly and set to work.

The Present
July

18

· *DAVINCI* ·

California, July

DaVinci jumped out of the car and raced to the front door of her inexplicably terra-cotta-pink house, hoping against hope that she would find her family inside. Her heart pounding, she paused, listening for familiar voices. She didn't hear a thing.

At the threshold, however, she noticed that the screen door was propped open with the rock Kahlo had painted in fourth grade to look like Mission San Juan Bautista. That had to be a good sign. If some other family was living here, they wouldn't have kept Kahlo's painted rock for a doorstop, would they?

She burst into the kitchen, clutching her *Janson's History of Art* to her chest.

From beside the refrigerator, the twins turned to gape at her sudden appearance.

"You found your book," said Klee.

"Told you I didn't take it," said Klee *and* Kahlo, in exactly the same intonation.

Dumping the book on the already-full kitchen

table, DaVinci rushed forward to hug both her twin sisters at the same time.

"*Ew!* You're sweaty," said Kahlo.

"Dude. Seriously. Shower," said Klee.

DaVinci stepped back. Ran a hand over her brow. She'd broken out in a cold sweat sometime in the past three minutes. But it was okay! Everything was okay. She could live with a hideous terra-cotta-pink exterior, so long as she had her home back.

"Sorry," she said. "I, *um* . . ." DaVinci trailed off. She had no idea what she was supposed to have been doing. Where her sisters would think she'd been. It was . . . *weird*, not knowing what she had been up to.

"I washed your uniform," said Klee.

Uniform?

"Mom made her," said Kahlo. "For waking you up in the middle of the night."

"*Um*, thanks," said DaVinci. What uniform? Was this twin-speak for "your ratty, paint-splattered sundress that you totally need to retire from your wardrobe"?

"It's on your bed," said Klee.

"Okay," said DaVinci.

"Better hurry," said Kahlo.

"Okay," DaVinci repeated. Uncertain why she was supposed to hurry, much less what else she could safely say, she took the narrow stairs that led up to the kids' bedrooms. She stopped at the second door. It was closed, as usual. The twins were all about privacy. Humorous, considering they shared a room with her. But when she opened the door, she saw only two beds. Two beds with the twins' things all over them.

Her bed was . . . *gone*.

Cautiously, she turned to stare at the door of Toulouse and Chagall's old bedroom. She'd been bugging her parents for the past year to let her take over their now-unused room. Maybe in this version of history, she *had*.

She opened the door, her eyes sweeping over a dry-erase board on the door with some kind of two-week schedule. And then she slipped inside. Inside her new bedroom. She started giggling. She couldn't *stop* giggling. There, in front of her, were her things! This was her room! With just one bed! There was no sign of either Toulouse's *or* Chagall's things anywhere to be seen. She had her own room!

She rose up on her toes, bouncing several times as she took in the room. It was neat. Tidy. Organized. All the things her shared room with the twins had never been. With an enormous sigh of relief, she allowed herself to fall backward onto her bed. It gave a familiar squawk, welcoming her back. Overhead, the *Starry Night* painting Toulouse had done on the ceiling in tenth grade shimmered down on her, just like it was supposed to. DaVinci smiled at it, glad that *some* things hadn't been painted over.

"You're all mine," she said contentedly to the room. And then, flipping, she propped herself up on her elbows to admire the room some more. From downstairs, the side door by the stairs slammed shut, sending a whoosh of air into DaVinci's new room at the head of the stairs. Her new room! It was probably going to take her weeks to stop walking into the twins' room by mistake.

She smiled again. And then sniffed.

The air from downstairs brought some fishy smell

A Sword in Time

with it. Yoshida was probably cooking fish sticks for lunch. He loved fish sticks. She shook her head and noticed the black clothing folded neatly at the end of her bed, between her and the door. On top was a note in one of the twins' handwriting—their handwriting was impossible to tell apart—and a packet of gummy bears.

"Gummy bears?" muttered DaVinci, who didn't like them. She tossed the packet aside and read the note.

"Sorry for waking you up. I know you need your sleep, and I'll do better. Love, Klee. P.S.: I washed your clothes, but there are some smells you can't get out."

DaVinci frowned and sat up. She lifted a black shirt off a pair of black pants. She sniffed again. The fishy smell was coming from the shirt, not from downstairs. The shirt was plain and black. A buttoned shirt with long sleeves that Klee (or someone) had carefully folded to three-quarters length. Since when did DaVinci Shaughnessy-Pavlov wear black? Well, other than her freshman year in high school.

She shook the shirt out. And that was when she noticed a tiny detail. Embroidered over a pocket were the words *Enterprise Fish Co.* This was a uniform. Not just *a* uniform.

This was *her* uniform. Apparently, she worked at Enterprise Fish Company, a restaurant down on lower State Street.

"The heck?" she murmured, setting the shirt down.

Why would she want to work at a restaurant?

Standing, she shook her head. She was turning in

her notice today, that much was for sure. Although . . . wait a minute. If she was working at a restaurant, how did that affect her summer job teaching art? With a terrible foreboding, DaVinci rose to examine the whiteboard on her door. It held a two-week schedule, but it wasn't a schedule that included end-of-summer art workshops for middle school kids. It was a schedule for Enterprise Fish Company. Only. She counted the hours, adding in her head.

Forty.

Forty hours a week? She worked there forty hours a week? How had she been getting anything done? The art workshop job had been perfect because it was only twelve hours a week, leaving plenty of time for her to work on the huge commission she'd accepted from the Applegates' neighbor, Mrs. LaFleur.

She was definitely quitting waiting tables. Today.

She decided to check her email, certain she'd feel a lot better if she dug up a few end-of-term posts regarding her summer activities.

Hastily, she typed in her ID: DaV_Shaugh@umail.ucsb.edu.

When her password didn't automatically populate, she grabbed her phone and looked it up and then typed it into her computer.

ERROR: Your UCSBnetID or password is incorrect. Please re-enter.

She re-entered it. Got the same message. Tried again. And again. It wasn't working. Which was seriously annoying. She must have a different password—or netID—in this time line. Unfortunately, she was out of time to figure it out, for now. If the schedule on her door was correct, she had less than half an hour to get herself down to the restaurant for an eight-hour shift ending at one o'clock in the morning. As tempting as it was to simply quit, she told herself she should go. People would be counting on her. Leia would totally not skip out if people were counting on her. Besides, she probably had *friends* there.

She exhaled noisily and started changing.

Luckily, she'd waited tables at Red Lobster after graduating high school, so she should be able to fake her way through one shift. At least she still had the Applegates' car for transportation. After a quick change into her fishy-smelling uniform, she jogged downstairs.

The twins were eating peanut butter and brown sugar sandwiches. Mom must not be home. DaVinci smiled softly. Some things hadn't changed, at least.

"Hey, guys?" asked DaVinci. "When did I start at, *um*, the Enterprise Fish Company?"

Kahlo raised one eyebrow. Klee raised hers to match.

"Dude. You've been full-time there forever. They just gave you that two-year raise in June, right?"

Two years? That wasn't very likely. It sounded crazy. How had she managed to fit everything in? She would like to meet this DaVinci, the one who had her life so together she could work full time on top of everything else.

Realizing Kahlo and Klee were staring at her and waiting for an answer, she nodded like she was agreeing with what they'd said about working two years. Like she remembered it.

What was with her life choices in this time line?

As she asked herself the question, DaVinci couldn't shake a certain bad feeling. How could so much have changed when all she'd done was pay a plumber to fix a leak under the house?

19

· DAVINCI ·

California, July

As DaVinci drove to work, she nearly talked herself into turning around and calling in her notice, but an inconvenient sense of duty kept her driving to the restaurant. No matter what time line she was in, DaVinci did *not* let people down. Besides, she wouldn't mind a few hours' mindless distraction from all the strangeness of coming home to a home that wasn't quite right. A schedule she couldn't imagine having chosen. Passwords that didn't work.

There had to be an explanation as to why she wasn't working at the Art for Kids camp. Whatever the explanation, she was going to fix it. It had to be a totally fixable mistake. Right?

Tying on a work apron, she listened to the rapid-fire banter between cooks and waiters. Maybe "mindless work" was a little inaccurate. She took a minute to ask three of the staff what their favorite entrées and desserts were, preparing for customers who would no doubt ask her the same question.

Which they did. Along with a laundry list of other questions she had to fake her way through. Her shift turned out to be less of a distraction and more of a disaster. She mangled the orders for an entire table of businesswomen, serving gluten-free rolls to the ones who'd requested sourdough and forgetting to place their crème brûlée orders. Another table got lobster instead of lobster bisque, and she sold mahi-mahi to a third table when there was no mahi-mahi left.

And those were just her interactions with the customers. Her back-of-the-house interactions were . . . not pleasant. Well, all right, one of them was nice. Sort of. A very handsome waiter winked at her several times before finally asking, "Are we still on for tonight?"

DaVinci wasn't sure if they were on for tonight. She had no clue if . . . she squinted to read his nametag—*Carlos*—was her boyfriend or study-buddy or ride home or *what*. The hours dragged past until a lull just after 11:00 p.m., at which point the manager gave her a dressing-down that would have reduced persons *without* the Leia protocol to tears. DaVinci wasn't about to cry over a job she didn't even want, but she'd had enough.

"You're right," she said to the manager. "I don't deserve this job. I screwed up. And I quit."

The manager stared at her.

"I just have one question." DaVinci leaned in closer. "Are Carlos and I, you know, a, *um* . . . menu item?"

When the manager continued to stare at her like she'd sprouted antlers, she tried a more direct approach. "Is it your understanding that Carlos is my boyfriend?"

At that moment, a server rushed up to the manager with an urgent request, leaving DaVinci by herself.

"Fine. Don't tell me." She untied her apron.

"You *wish* he was your boyfriend," said another server, balancing four bowls of clam chowder as she zipped past.

So. She did not, apparently, have a hot boyfriend named Carlos.

"Same old, same old—*there*, anyway," she muttered.

Dropping her apron into the rag tub, she walked the two blocks to where she'd parked the Applegates' car. Only after she'd driven most of the way home did she realize her tips were still in the apron pocket, back at the restaurant.

She did not turn around. It hadn't been a great night for tips.

She got home just before midnight. Yoshi was up, playing some video game involving oversize weapons that would've toppled an actual person trying to carry them.

DaVinci plopped onto a saggy beanbag next to her brother.

"Hey."

He pulled off his headphones and paused his game playing. "Hey, yourself. What are you doing home so early?"

"My manager told me to go sit in a corner and think about what I'd done."

"Did not," said Yoshi, grunting out a laugh.

"Did not," agreed DaVinci. "But I quit."

Yoshi's pale eyebrows rose. "Serious?"

"Yeah. I don't know why I took that job in the first place."

"*Um* . . . the money?" Yoshi put an arm around her and squeezed. "It's okay. You'll find another job."

DaVinci grunted noncommittally.

"In fact," said Yoshi, "my fiancée's mom is hiring."

DaVinci felt a chill run along her spine. Yoshi wasn't engaged. Or, he shouldn't be.

"Ana's family business is booming," Yoshi said proudly.

"Ana, your *fiancée*, Ana?" asked DaVinci. Last thing she knew, her brother had still been saving for a ring.

"Ha-ha." He shoved her shoulder with his.

Great. Yoshi and Ana were engaged. Just one more couple in her life to remind her that she had no one.

"*Um*, remind me when you got engaged?" she asked, as casually as she could.

An eye roll. "*Duh*. Same day you got your splint off."

"My splint?" DaVinci sure as heck didn't remember any splints.

"Oh, *excuse me*," Yoshi said with exaggerated politeness. "I meant your *cast*." He made tiny air quotes as he said *cast*.

Great. She added "broke my something" to the list of things she didn't know about herself.

"Hey, you should play with us again, now that your finger's all healed."

"Play with you?" DaVinci frowned. "Like . . .

video games?"

"You were getting good. Well, you sucked less."

He leaned away from her, and she realized he was expecting her to punch his arm. Which *normal* DaVinci of either time line would probably have done, if she'd felt insulted. But sucking at video games wasn't insulting, and the idea she might have actually *played* them wasn't insulting enough to merit a punch.

Groaning, she sank deeper into the beanbag.

"Seriously, though, if you want a job, just say the word," said her brother.

"I'm going to bed," she said.

Yoshi gave her another squeeze around the shoulder and then grimaced. "*Ew.* You smell like clam chowder."

DaVinci plucked at one sleeve. Sniffed. She *did* smell like clam chowder.

"Hey, Yoshi, do you know my login for my email?"

"Why would I know that?"

DaVinci shrugged. "I was just hoping." And then, because he seemed to be waiting for an explanation, she added, "My, *um*, computer rebooted or something and lost all my passwords. I guess I could call UCSB tech support."

"Why would you call UCSB?" asked Yoshi, fiddling with his game controller. His on-screen avatar picked up a gun the size of a small sofa. DaVinci could hear his friends shouting in his earphones, telling him to use the weapon, already.

"To recover my login, *duh*," muttered DaVinci. But as she spoke, the hairs on her arms rose.

"They only help students. *UCSB* students," added

Yoshi. "They won't help you."

DaVinci tried to suck in a breath, but her lungs weren't working right. *They only help students?* What the heck was that supposed to mean?

Yoshi continued. "If you want, I could ask Miguel. Ana says her brother is amazing with tech."

Yoshi's offer barely registered. *They only help students.* Was she not a student in this altered time line? How could she not be a student at UCSB? What had happened?

"Hey, the team is screaming at me here," said Yoshi, gesturing to the screen with one elbow. He nudged his headphones forward until they settled squarely over his ears.

DaVinci rose and walked to the stairs. Before she reached the top, she had her phone out and was texting Halley and Jillian.

Anybody awake? I need help.

20
· DAVINCI ·
California, July

Halley was the first to answer DaVinci's text.
I'm awake. What's going on?
Wow. How was she supposed to answer that?
"I sort of messed up the historical time line, and I don't like my life anymore" would cover most of the bases, but she couldn't bring herself to type that.

Halley, awaiting a response, texted a series of question marks.

DaVinci spent another minute trying to think of the best way to explain what had happened, during which time Halley sent a second series of question marks and a sad face.

Where was she even supposed to begin?

DaVinci's phone vibrated in her hands. Halley was calling.

"Hey."

"Hey, DaVinci. What's up? Are you okay? Is everyone okay?"

"*Um*, yeah. Sort of. It's . . . well, it's sort of

complicated."

"Complicated is my specialty."

DaVinci thought she heard Edmund's loud guffaw in the background. He was probably mouthing, *She speaketh the trutheth*, or something similar.

DaVinci exhaled heavily. "I shouldn't have woken you up."

"You didn't. I have two zippers to replace before 3:00 a.m. Tell me what happened."

"I did something really . . . stupid," replied DaVinci. "Involving space–time. And history."

DaVinci heard Halley's intake of breath. Heard her whispering to Edmund.

"Halley, I'm scared." The tears DaVinci had been holding back all day swam in her eyes and then spilled onto her cheeks. Her next words came out between sobs. "I . . . screwed . . . up."

Another hushed exchange with Edmund.

"Okay, listen," said Halley. "I'll find out when work can release me, and then I'll come straight to California."

21
· DAVINCI ·
California, July

It would be four days before Halley could get time off from her work on the movie set to visit DaVinci and discuss matters face-to-face, and Jillian couldn't even do *that* much. On top of the divide created by distance, Jillian was catering her first conference, leaving her too busy to do more than send hurried texts in which she dropped subtle hints she would gladly fly DaVinci out to Florida for a visit and less-subtle hints about meeting a hunky ex–Roman soldier named Quintus. She also sent a care package stuffed with gummy bears. DaVinci stared at them, shook her head, and left them untouched. As for Jillian's other offers, DaVinci didn't think going to Florida would solve her problems, and she was doubtful that abs of steel, Roman or otherwise, would fix things, either. Besides, Jillian would be flying to California in ten days for DaVinci's painting exhibit. Halley, meanwhile, texted and FaceTimed several times a day, with more sympathy than DaVinci felt she deserved, considering she'd, well, *changed history*.

To her family, glancing at her with worried looks, DaVinci only said she didn't feel well. She alternated spending time on the roof and in her new-to-her room, but nothing felt comfortable. Nothing was familiar. Nothing was right. It was like wearing clothes washed with someone else's laundry detergent—all the scents wrong and unfamiliar.

Even the private bedroom she'd *begged* her parents for in her "real" past became a reminder of how truly alone she was. Through the wall, she could hear Klee and Kahlo laughing and whispering, and she had to stop herself from barging in, demanding they let her move back. She'd saved her home from destruction, but it no longer felt like a place where she belonged; it was a place that belonged to some alternate version of herself that she didn't know and didn't *want* to know.

She couldn't paint. Even if she'd had the energy, she wasn't sure where her paint box was. Nothing was where it should be. She dragged through her days only to crash into horrible dreams at night, nightmares where she'd lost her scholarship at UCSB or been kicked out of the honors program. The dreams were bad, but even worse were the seconds before she came fully awake. Heart pounding, she would murmur to herself, "Just a bad dream. Just a bad dream." But then she would realize all over again that it wasn't a dream. That she was living a nightmare. And that it was all her fault.

Worst of all, she had no idea how to fix things or even which things needed fixing. Again and again, she asked herself where things had gone wrong. Where had she messed up? But she had no idea where or when or how. It was just a stupid fix to a leaky pipe. How had that lost her a coveted scholarship? Her place in the honors program? Her summer job? The commission from Jillian's mother's friend? She asked the same questions over and over, but there were no answers.

Midmorning on the fifth day of DaVinci's "new" life, Halley's car headlights pierced the clingy, summer fog that had settled in a few days earlier. Fog didn't usually make it all the way up to East Mountain Drive, but it was thick today, visibility no better than fifteen feet in any direction. DaVinci clambered down from the lookout boulder, scraping her ankle on a broken edge of stone she could have sworn hadn't been there before she'd changed history. Swearing, she limped to Halley just as her friend exited the car.

Halley held her arms out and DaVinci fell into them, and then the tears she'd been holding back began to flow. She *should* have been crying from relief that she finally had someone to talk to. And she was relieved, but she was crying because she realized she'd been pinning her hopes on Halley having a solution, and now she saw how delusional that hope had been. She'd clung to it, fooling herself into thinking she just had to wait for her friend to show up and then everything would be okay again. But everything was *not* okay again. Halley was here and Halley was real and Halley loved her, but if Halley had figured out a solution, she would have proposed it already.

What if she never figured out how to fix things? What if she was stuck in this failed-artist life smelling like clam chowder to the end of her days? While these thoughts dragged at her like a riptide, Halley held her and gave her tissues and hugged her fiercely until, at last, the swell of tears receded.

DaVinci, apologizing, blew her nose and said, "Thanks for coming."

"I tried to get away sooner," said Halley. "Edmund and I felt awful knowing you were here dealing with this alone."

New tears welled up at the kind words, but DaVinci forced them back, nodding.

"I'm so sorry I couldn't get here earlier."

DaVinci forced herself to smile. "And I'm sorry about this crap weather."

Halley grunted out a laugh. "Because that's totally your fault."

DaVinci shrugged. "Probably."

"It's practically a whiteout, though, huh?" murmured Halley, shivering. "It's like being in the clouds."

"It's been like this for three days," said DaVinci. "Yesterday, Yoshi tried using a leaf blower to see if he could clear it away."

"Of course he did," said Halley, a single gruff laugh escaping her throat. "I swear, someone should do a reality show on your family."

Halley had said this often, and normally DaVinci played along, offering three or four other strange things her family had said or tried or done, but today she didn't have it in her. Besides, how would she even know what her family had said or done lately?

"Do you want to go inside or stay out here?" Halley asked quietly. "It's fine by me if we stay outside. I got a little queasy on the curves, with the fog shrouding everything." Halley placed her hands on her hips and looked over to the house, shaking her head. "I can't believe how long it's been."

DaVinci frowned. How long *had* it been? She didn't know what Halley had been doing in this time line any more than she knew what she'd been doing. She hugged her arms around her torso as if she could keep it together, keep *herself* together, if she just squeezed tightly enough.

"Oh," said Halley. "I got you these. You know, to cheer you up." Halley handed her a packet of gummy bears.

"*Um* . . . thanks," said DaVinci, puzzled by the gift. Why did everyone in her life think she suddenly liked gummy bears?

"You know," said Halley, "someday you have to tell us what it is with you and gummy bears."

DaVinci had to tell Halley? Yeah. She would get right on that. As soon as she figured it out for herself. Just one more thing that was wrong with this time line.

The two of them walked over to the boulder, looming large and dark in the shifting mists.

"So?" Halley asked softly. "How are you doing?"

DaVinci didn't answer at first. She sat and picked gravel out of the treads of her shoe, like the solution to her problems was hiding in there.

"We don't have to talk about it," said Halley. "Not if you don't want to."

But she *did* want to.

She released her shoe.

"It's like my life is this pair of jeans that doesn't fit," she said. "Like, clearance-item jeans, so you can't return them," she added glumly.

"*Huh*," grunted Halley. "Well, there's a picture."

"I shouldn't have done it," DaVinci said, twisting a coil of hair that had slid over her eyes. Eyes that were filling with tears for the four hundredth time today. "You're supposed to say I shouldn't have gone back and messed with time."

Halley gave a sad half smile. "I might have done the same thing in your shoes."

"I couldn't just stand there and do nothing," said DaVinci. She swiped her eyes with her sleeves. She was so darned sick of tears. "I watched a Caterpillar tear the whole thing down," she said, glancing back to the house. "I thought I had to witness it to . . . I don't know . . . gather my courage or something. But it was so awful." She shook her head. What else could she have done?

Halley hooked an arm around DaVinci's shoulder. "You saved your home. It's here. It's okay."

"My *house* is fine, but—" DaVinci groaned in exasperation. "Nothing else is. My life is a joke. I ruined *everything*, and I don't even have a clue how I did it."

"Oh, DaVinci." Halley's eyes were large and sympathetic. "Not everything. You've got me and Jillian and your whole family—" Halley broke off, a sad smile forming.

DaVinci understood. To Halley, her life seemed perfect. Parents who loved her. *Two* of them, no less. And all those siblings—DaVinci knew Halley would commit highway robbery for even *one* sibling. She had an entire freaking family who loved her, and in Halley's view, that ought to have been enough.

How could she begin to explain this . . . this *aloneness*? How lost she felt, and how cut off. A terrible thought struck her. Maybe in this time line, she and Halley had been drifting for years. Maybe they weren't close anymore. How long *had* it been since they'd hung out?

She squeezed her eyes shut. How would she bear it if she wasn't close to Halley anymore? Or Jillian? Did she even know these alternate-time-line versions of her closest friends? DaVinci's lungs compressed, and for a moment it felt as if all the air in the world had vanished.

But then Halley passed her a fresh tissue.

Squeezed her shoulder, tightly.

Murmured that things were going to be okay.

DaVinci realized she was being an idiot. Of course she and Halley were still close. Halley had left work the first chance she got, hadn't she? No matter what DaVinci had done to the time line, Halley was here for her, like always.

Her lungs began to work like lungs again, and then the words began to flow—a flash flood of words, like Cold Springs Creek swelling and exploding after heavy rains.

"I know you're right. I know I should be grateful for all of it—my family, my friends, this house I love so much, but the thing is, I don't even feel like I'm *me* anymore, and that makes everything feel . . . *wrong*, like it's not really my family or my house or my life. I don't recognize myself. I don't recognize this . . . this . . . *anything!* I'm not an art student at UCSB anymore—no, it's worse: I'm not even in college, *any* college, and I somehow became this person who thought that working forty hours a week at a fish restaurant was a good idea. Like it didn't even occur to me to, maybe . .

. I don't know . . . take a watercolor class at the community college? How could I suddenly not care about improving my art?"

"Wait, wait, wait," said Halley, frowning. "So, if I understand correctly, in the version of . . . of history as you know it, you were in college?"

"Of course I was," snapped DaVinci. How could Halley even ask the question?

"Okay, okay. Sorry." Halley held her hands up apologetically.

"I got into UCSB with a big fat scholarship," DaVinci continued. "I was placed in the honors program with a studio and everything. I won the Virginia R. Parrish Scholarship. Seven thousand a year for four years."

"You won the Parrish?" Halley looked confused. Or doubtful.

DaVinci felt a flare of anger at the questioning look in her friend's eyes. "You don't think I could win the Parrish?"

Halley fidgeted with some necklace DaVinci didn't recognize and shrugged apologetically. "You told me you'd never in a million years have won the Parrish . . ."

"I said that? In your world, I said those words?"

Halley nodded.

All at once, DaVinci felt herself deflating, a blow-up beach ball kicked one time too many. How had she become someone who didn't believe in herself? She sank back against the boulder, its surface cold and rough and unforgiving.

Everything was wrong.

Wrong, wrong, wrong.

She took a slow breath and watched the fog swirling overhead in six shades of white: lead-paint white, albuminous white, paste white, ash, argent, ivory. She released her breath. She needed to hear it. She had to know the truth. *This* version of the truth.

"In your world—time line—whatever," DaVinci said softly, "did I . . . did I at least try to get into UCSB to study art? In their . . . regular program?"

Halley spoke in a murmur. "You don't remember any of it? No—that was a stupid thing to say." She frowned.

"I can't trust anything I know," DaVinci said hollowly. "My brother isn't supposed to be engaged, or is he? I'm working forty-hour weeks in a *restaurant*—or I was until I quit. How did I even find time to paint or weave or throw a pot in the last two years?"

Halley's frown deepened. "You don't do any of those things anymore. You quit. You got into UCSB, but not into the art program you wanted. And then you dropped out midterm freshman year and just . . . stopped making art."

DaVinci felt her throat tightening. That couldn't be right. In what possible world could she have stopped making art?

The answer was right in front of her: in *this* world. In *this* time line.

"I don't understand," she whispered. "All I did was pay a plumber to fix a leak."

"Khan's second law of . . . something," murmured Halley. "Unintended consequences." She worried the chain of her necklace again. And then DaVinci noticed she wasn't wearing her wedding ring.

"Oh my God," whispered DaVinci. Edmund hadn't come with Halley. Were they not together anymore? She tried to remember if Halley had said a single thing about Edmund, but she couldn't recall.

She blurted out, "Are you and Edmund still married in this version of time?"

A frown flickered over Halley's face. "Yes, of course we're married. You were there. There was roast peacock and Edmund's younger self and—"

"Then why aren't you wearing your wedding ring?"

Halley stared at her left hand. "I take it off when I do fine hand-sewing, so the prongs don't catch on the fabric and ruin all my work. I must have forgotten to put it back on."

"Oh," sighed DaVinci. "Thank goodness." She fought back the tiny part of her that would have been ready to comfort Halley for her loss, to say encouraging things about independence and freedom—to have someone else in her life who was, well, doing life solo. She swallowed her selfish thoughts, tasting bitterness as they departed.

"And Jillian?" asked DaVinci. "Is she still with Everett?"

Halley rolled her eyes. "Surgically attached."

"At least I didn't ruin anyone else's life," she said.

"Just yours, it sounds like," Halley replied softly. Her eyes were fixed on the drifting mist. DaVinci recognized her friend's problem-solving face. "There must have been something," said Halley. "Something you did that affected more than just the plumbing."

"But how am I going to figure out what it was, when I can't trust anything I remember since 2016?"

A horrible idea presented itself. According to Halley, she no longer painted in this time line. Would that mean her muscles would have "forgotten" how? Did her body contain the changes made within this time line? Skills involved complex muscle memory. Did her muscles have those original memories or not? *Stop it*, she told herself. They had to. She was being stupid.

Halley interrupted her thoughts. "Maybe Jillian will have some ideas."

"Oh, trust me," said DaVinci, pushing aside her fears about her muscles, "I have a long list of questions for her and Everett when they get here."

Halley frowned. "Jillian and Everett are coming here? Why?"

"For my show next Saturday—" DaVinci stopped herself midsentence. She felt her mouth forming the shape of *Oh*, but no sound came out. It was the rug getting yanked out from under her feet again. Just one more fresh betrayal. Another thing that wasn't real anymore. Angry tears burned behind her eyes.

She balled her hands into fists. "Let me guess. I don't have a show on Saturday anymore, do I?"

Halley spoke softly. "Did you . . . used to have a show?"

Swallowing her worthless tears, DaVinci nodded. "In my world, Jillian was coming out for it. And you—well, you took the movie set job in Santa Ynez instead of the New Mexico job because you would be able to come home for my show easier."

"I took the New Mexico job," Halley said apologetically. Then she added, "It paid better."

Of course. *Of course.* If she didn't have a show, of

course Halley would have taken the higher-paying job.

"So, yeah. I guess Jillian's not coming," said DaVinci. "She has no reason to in this version of reality."

"DaVinci . . ." Halley hesitated, twisting her necklace again. "This isn't a 'version' of reality. Not to me. Or to anyone else, either."

DaVinci collapsed her head into her hands, elbows resting on her knees. Nothing made sense. And Halley was just sitting there accepting it, like it was possible for either of them to believe in a world where DaVinci no longer painted or wove tapestries or threw pots.

"I'm sorry," said Halley, "but you're going to have to get used to *this* reality. My reality. Everyone's reality."

"How?" DaVinci asked bitterly. "How am I supposed to get used to a reality where I'm not *me*?"

Halley shook her head. "I don't know."

DaVinci rose. Paced seven steps forward to where she knew the hill dropped away, even though she could barely see it. Heavy fog filled the canyon and the air above it, a sea of shifting mists.

Halley couldn't help her. Halley couldn't even grasp how *wrong* everything was, how impossible it was for DaVinci to just "get used to this reality." She was in this alone, just like always. Every freaking person in her life had someone they could count on, except for her. Even the twins, who didn't have boyfriends, still had each other. And what did she have? She had a freaking *house*, and that was it, because she had somehow managed to trade everything that mattered in her life for this stupid, ugly, sunburn-pink house.

"I'm on my own." She hadn't meant to say the words out loud, but they were out now, no taking them back. She hugged her arms around her chest.

"How can you say that?" asked Halley, rising to join her. "I'm right here."

"But *I'm* the one who has to figure out what went wrong and fix it," she said quietly.

"DaVinci, listen. I mean . . ." Halley faltered. "Are you sure that's wise?"

DaVinci didn't respond at first. The dank cold seemed to be seeping inside her. "Maybe I don't care what's wise," she said curtly.

"DaVinci." Halley uttered her name like a verdict.

After that, they were both quiet until Halley broke the silence. "You said you didn't remember Yoshi getting engaged, right?"

DaVinci nodded. She stared into the fog, squinting, trying to find something she could focus on within the shifting whites.

"What if you go back and fix things and something *else* goes wrong? You've already proven that the actions you take can affect other people."

"There's nothing wrong with Yoshi getting engaged," DaVinci said tersely.

"Fine. But what if it had gone the other way? What if Yoshi had broken up with Ana because of what you did? How would that feel?"

How would it feel? Halley's words pierced her, stoking a cold fire that ignited, and then, just as swiftly, died back to a thin wisp of smoke, to nothing at all. Suddenly freezing, DaVinci sank to the ground and hugged her knees to her chest, her head falling forward onto her knees.

She wanted to say she didn't care. She wanted to say it didn't matter, not compared to what she was going through. She wanted to say these things, but she couldn't. A tear of frustration splashed the dirt between her legs.

After that, neither of them spoke for a long time. DaVinci waited for Halley to rise. Waited for the sound of her friend walking back to her car. Starting the ignition. Driving away. But Halley just kept on sitting beside her. Kept on not leaving her. Eventually DaVinci raised her head. The air had begun to warm, and the fog had thinned to the point that DaVinci could see a ghostly outline of the tallest sycamore in the canyon. The one where Kahlo had broken her arm trying to get close to a bird's nest. At least, in DaVinci's memory, Kahlo had broken her arm. But who knew if it had happened in this time line? The nest was still there, looking abandoned, unkempt, twigs dangling from its near side.

She felt like that, abandoned, with her twigs dangling.

"I don't know how to keep living like this," she said, breaking the long silence.

Halley turned. "You don't know how to live here in this time line? Or here in Montecito?"

"Both, I guess." The feeling was cold and unassailable—the feeling that this wasn't her life. That even if it *was* her life, she didn't belong inside it. DaVinci dropped her chin until it rested on her knees. She noticed paint spots on her shoes, mocking her from another life—a life where she'd been working on a commissioned mural.

"I don't know what to do," she whispered.

Halley scooted closer and DaVinci leaned her head against Halley's shoulder. "I just don't know what I should do," she repeated.

"Wanna hear what I think?" Halley asked gently.

DaVinci nodded.

"I think there are too many things here reminding you of . . . of who you might have been. If things had been different."

If things had been different.

"Come on," said Halley. "We're calling Jillian. Her catering job ended yesterday, and she's got one of those foldout couches in her apartment in Florida. I don't know what the answer is to your problems, but I'm pretty sure you could use a change of scenery."

DaVinci nodded. It was easier than arguing. And really? She didn't know anymore what she needed. She only knew that she hurt.

Halley got on the phone, and in less than an hour, the trip was arranged.

"Jillian got you a ticket in first class," Halley said.

DaVinci managed a half-hearted smile. "Some things never change."

Halley gave her a quick hug. "Come on. Let's get you packed."

DaVinci rose. She had no classes, no job, no life. Her show had been nixed out of existence. She might as well go. It wasn't like she had anything better to do.

One Month Earlier
June

22

· LITTLEWOOD ·

Florida, June

It was a busy afternoon for Arthur Littlewood, who had scheduled another trip to the Ancient Library of Alexandria. Quintus was proving very useful on these trips, speaking Greek like, well, the native son of the first century BC that he was.

Littlewood examined his calculations for the upcoming journey, during which he hoped to recover certain lost writings of Aristotle. These were quick jobs: in and out in less than six minutes. Accurate insertion of his travelers was critical.

Happily, his calculations checked out. Everything was ready ahead of schedule. It would be two hours until Everett and Quintus showed up to travel to ancient Alexandria. Littlewood was not traveling this time. There had been an . . . *incident* on another trip, and everyone had agreed it was better if Littlewood made no further journeys.

Littlewood sighed and ran a hand over his hair, noting that some of it was sticking straight up. He mussed his hair unconsciously when he was working a problem. Khan had enjoyed laughing at his hair. Khan. Where was he now? Best not to dwell on that whole, sorry debacle.

He was attempting to shift his thoughts to lunch when a stranger appeared in the lab. "Appeared" as in . . . *appeared*. Not entered by way of stairs and door, simply *there* as if by magic.

The stranger's back was to him. It was someone who was old. Elderly, in fact.

"Rats!" said the stranger, gnarled hands on his narrow hips. He was observing the desk where Littlewood normally sat and worked.

The stranger's voice sounded oddly familiar, although it had an unexpected wheezing quality. As Littlewood tried to place the voice's owner, he realized with a frisson of shock that it was his own voice. Being used by someone else. A sudden possibility occurred to him.

"Are you looking for me?" asked Littlewood.

"Ah yes," said the elderly man, slowly turning around. "Memory's a funny thing, you know. In my memory, I was sitting at my desk. That is, *I* was sitting there when, ah, *older-I* appeared in the room. Yes, yes, yes. Now I recall. I had been sitting at Khan's former desk. Where you are now." A look of sadness crossed the old man's face but quickly passed. He held out his hand.

"Good to see you," said the old man.

Littlewood shook hands, adding, "I wasn't . . . expecting you."

"No, no, you wouldn't be," said the elderly man, with a smile. "For you this hasn't happened yet."

"Ah . . . *right*. Yes," said the younger Littlewood. "Might I ask why you are—"

The elderly man interrupted him. "Oh, I'm doing very well. Thank you for asking."

He'd misheard the question. Before the younger Littlewood could ask it again, his older "self" uttered a single laugh and spoke.

"No need for me to ask how *you* are doing. I remember, right down to the lens replacement surgery you're considering. Here's a tip: get the surgery. You won't regret it."

Littlewood's eyebrows lifted. "You've come here to recommend *eye surgery*?"

"Oh, no. I'm here for, well, for several reasons. In part, of course, I am here because I remember having been visited by an older version of myself. It's our birthday today. Many happy returns."

"Same to you," Littlewood said automatically. He'd forgotten it was his birthday. Another year older, and all that. The back of his neck prickled slightly. This was by far the oddest thing that had ever happened to him. And that was saying something for someone who'd invented time travel.

"We'd better get right down to it," said the elderly man, dragging a chair to Khan's desk. "I've brought you some calculations."

"Calculations?" asked the younger Littlewood.

The old man unrolled a semitransparent sheet of . . . *something*, and set it flat on the desk, where it held its new flattened shape. He then tapped it twice and it awoke, some kind of futuristic-looking screen covered with calculations.

"Here is what I came for," said the older man,

indicating the futuristic screen. "We've got forty-nine or so minutes remaining to go over these formulae."

His expression seemed to brighten. "My, but it is nice to see you. Such good memories. I was rather dapper in my middle age, wasn't I?"

Littlewood honestly could not imagine saying such a thing, even though it was obvious he would, one day, say it. The experience truly was very, *very* odd.

Brushing the thoughts aside, he examined the futuristic screen on the desk.

"What am I looking at?" he asked.

The elderly Littlewood cleared his throat. "Thus far in our work with the temporal singularity, we've only been using the fundamental frequency." He paused to indicate a formula with which Littlewood was extremely familiar. "But we can double the frequency by using a higher harmonic—"

"Good heavens!" murmured the younger Littlewood. He stood and began fidgeting with the keys in his pocket.

"You see where I'm going?" asked the older man.

Littlewood nodded. "It never occurred to me . . ." He looked up at . . . himself. "This would mean longer journeys are possible."

"Exactly. The length-of-stay formula is highly nonlinear, but increases rapidly with frequency. The formula is here."

The older man scrolled down to a complex formula on his screen.

"Ah," said Littlewood. "That's brilliant. Please, you must show me the derivation."

"No time for that now. You'll figure it out."

"Are you sure?" Littlewood looked up, uncertain.

"Trust me," the older man responded.

The younger Littlewood sat back down at the desk, his keys falling through the hole in his pocket for the third time in a week. "I can't believe I never thought of this."

"Well, you *did* think of it," said the older man. "In a manner of speaking."

"I did?"

"In a manner of speaking."

"Ah. Yes," said the younger man, "I suppose I did."

"You ought to get that hole in your pocket repaired."

"I've been meaning to."

"I know." The elderly Littlewood seemed to lose himself in thought for a moment. "Well, nothing to be done about it," he said cryptically.

The younger Littlewood noticed the time. "Oh dear. Quintus—that is, my security guard—will be here soon along with Everett. I've planned a trip to the Ancient Library."

"Yes. Quite. *Hmm*. The best laid plans and all that . . ."

He paused and held up a hand. "But I say nothing, of course." He smiled and changed the subject. "Dear Quintus. I've missed him. Between you and me, you could stand to be a little kinder to the boy."

"Kinder?"

"Ah. Well. He is not from an age where men were given to express their feelings of loss or loneliness, but trust me, he suffers."

Littlewood blinked. "I'll try to be . . . kinder."

"Now listen carefully, my boy," said the older man. He consulted his watch. "Should there come a time in the future when you need to, ah, *disappear*, you now have the means to do so for a considerable length of time. You do see that, do you not?"

"Are you saying I'm going to need to disappear?"

"Not *this* year—ah! I forget myself. I say nothing. I make no predictions. I reveal nothing."

The middle-aged Littlewood released an exasperated sigh.

"That is," said the old man, extending a bony finger, "I reveal only what I am supposed to reveal."

"How can you be sure you should be telling me *any* of this?"

"That's pretty obvious, I should think. I'm speaking to you now because *it already happened*," said the elderly Littlewood, smiling.

"Right. Right, of course. It's just . . . you must admit this is very strange."

"Yes. Time travel conundrums *are* very strange. Now then, remember what I said about young Quintus." The old man eyed the younger one sternly. "Make a point of being nicer. Take him to see Father Joe now and again."

Littlewood found himself nodding to his older self.

"Ah," said the elderly man, consulting his watch. "Time's up."

And with that, Arthur Littlewood the younger had the disturbing experience of watching the elder version of himself vanish into thin air. There, and then gone. Just like that.

"Good heavens," he said, sinking into a chair

once more.

Ten minutes later, he was still sitting in the chair musing about harmonics and temporal pocket dimensions when Everett and Quintus arrived, already dressed for the journey to ancient Alexandria.

"Oh," said Littlewood, looking up. *Kinder to Quintus*, he'd promised.

"Ah, how are you both? Today? This afternoon?" He released a single nervous laugh.

"I am rested and prepared for the journey," replied Quintus, who was wearing his first-century military garb—handy in a pinch, since Rome ruled Alexandria during the era Littlewood was sending them to.

Everett smiled and murmured, "I am well, thank you. And yourself?"

Littlewood clapped his hands together once and said, "Well, let's send you off then."

The three crossed to the time machine. Littlewood fumbled for another means by which he might be kinder to Quintus.

"And, ah, how are you finding life as a security guard?" he asked as he reached to awaken the podium screen.

Quintus mounted the platform. "You pay more than is just," he said.

Everett barked out a single laugh.

"Ah. Well . . ." stammered Littlewood. He was only able to pay a dollar an hour above minimum wage, for heaven's sake. "I should think the, ah, terrible hours more than justify a rather better level of pay." He busied himself with the singularity device and thought of something else he could say. "I've noticed your English is improving. We must take you to see Father Joe. He will be impressed."

"I've suggested a few idioms," said Everett. "Well, the selfsame ones Jillian has to remind me to use," he added, grinning.

"Everett has directed me to the . . . *podcasts* on . . . YouTube," said Quintus. "I am learning also the Spanish tongue."

Littlewood considered explaining the proper placement of the modifier *also*, but he decided it could wait since the machine was screaming and almost fully charged. A moment later, Everett and Quintus were frozen in place, disappearing amid a burst of blue electric light.

"Well," murmured Littlewood to himself, "kindness is rather mentally exhausting work."

He spent the next several minutes trying to recall what he might have appreciated most as a college-aged fellow, but he found himself quite at a loss, until his stomach growled, at which point he smiled and pulled out his phone.

By the time the two young men returned six minutes later, scrolls in hand, Littlewood was busily entering a credit card number for a delivery pizza he'd ordered online. He had, for the time being, entirely forgotten anything else pertaining to the elderly Littlewood's visit.

23

· QUINTUS ·

Florida, June

Quintus had been working for Dr. Littlewood for nearly three months since first learning his old life had vanished two thousand years in the past. During those months, his English had improved considerably, in large part thanks to Everett. Improving his English was not, however, Quintus's most important task. He had a far more important goal: to learn how the time machine was operated so that he might return and ensure his letter from Caesar reached its intended recipient, Gnaeus Pompeius Magnus.

To this end, Quintus had offered his services to Littlewood beyond those hours when he stood guard. Of course, spending so much of his life at the lab also furthered his second goal: there was always the possibility, however slight, that Jules Khan would steal into the laboratory again, there to meet his fate at Quintus's hand. Quintus had been given to understand the magistrates of this land neither could nor would punish Khan, so the task fell on Quintus's shoulders.

He was not sorry for this.

But he had his other, more urgent task to complete first: return to Rome and deliver the letter. He had never failed Caesar before, and he would not forget his allegiance and duty merely because centuries divided him from his commander.

Everett had argued that the *other* Quintus Valerius had, in all probability, delivered the letter. But Quintus was not a man to deal in *probabilities*. He dealt only in *certainties*, and until he had placed the message with which he was entrusted into Pompeius's hands, he would not count himself free of his obligation. He had not considered anything beyond this purpose. He could not bear to think of the future, of a life bereft of service to Rome, bereft of family, wife, son—of all the things that had made his life *his life*. At times when thoughts of his empty existence crept round, he would grip his *gladius*. He was a true Roman. He did not fear an honorable death upon his sword. But this could come only after he had fulfilled his obligation to Caesar.

Fortunately, there was little left to learn before he could operate the machine himself. Repeatedly, he had accompanied Everett, traveling through time to Alexandria, two thousand years in the past. Littlewood spoke always of this use of the machine as a noble calling. Perhaps it was. All the world had heard of the great library in Alexandria.

But Quintus had a greater calling. And he let not a single day pass where he did not ask a question, look over a shoulder, study the operation of the computer, observe the list of instructions that must be followed for the machine to function correctly. He listened and learned and studied, waiting for the day when he would be ready. He would return to his own time and he would ensure Pompeius received Caesar's letter.

Or he would die trying.

The Present
July

24
· *NEVIS* ·

Florida, July

Special Agent Benjamin Nevis scanned the administrative office of the University of South Central Florida's physics department. The AC was set at *arctic*. There had to be a sixty-degree temperature difference between the sweltering day outside and the frigid indoor climate. Maybe he should be investigating this office for power surges on the electrical grid instead of investigating . . . whoever he was meeting with today.

Nevis glanced at the name flagged for investigation: Dr. Arthur Littlewood.

Littlewood didn't seem the type to engage in electrical grid terrorism. American born of Polish descent, drawing a tidy little salary as a tenured professor with a multiyear grant in the seven-figure range, over two years' worth of accrued paid vacation. The kind of researcher so stuck in his ivory tower, he probably didn't know who was president or who'd won last year's Super Bowl. Of course, come to think of it, Nevis wasn't sure who'd won last year's Super Bowl, either.

He tapped his fingertips on the counter—a haven't-got-all-day gesture intended to attract attention. Even though he did have all day. He had all day *all* the days. His SAC had given him a list nine miles long of individuals and companies to investigate and approve. Enough for months spent on the road sleeping at Hampton Inns and getting fat on complimentary breakfast waffles. He wondered what it would take to get the bureau to spring for an occasional Garden Inn so he could order an omelet instead?

More finger tapping.

An apologetic administrative assistant crossed back to the counter, complaining that Littlewood was impossible.

"He doesn't remember to charge his phone. Or leaves it in his car half the time." The secretary leaned in and whispered, "Genius, of course, and we're lucky to have him, but zero common sense."

Nevis accepted the campus map and another apology for the wait. As he left the office, the heat slammed into him. My God, how did Floridians do it? DC was bad, but this? It was like walking into a sauna set to masochist level. He'd tried jogging this morning at five forty-five, but by six he'd called it. Too hot. Which had meant a dull hour spent in a musty-smelling fitness center instead. Why did hotel fitness centers all look and smell exactly the same?

He turned a corner and found the building he was looking for. The building's interior wasn't as frigid as the administrative office, thankfully. He entered the lab marked "Littlewood Group," and after a quick glance at the photo of Arthur Littlewood on his phone, began a search for the man himself. He saw only students, however, and a custodian relining a trash barrel.

"Can I help you?" asked a man entering behind Nevis.

Nevis's jaw tightened, and he overrode the instinct to treat the man behind him as a threat. Although, who knew?

"Special Agent Nevis, FBI," he said, turning and flashing his badge.

"Oh yes. That was today? Right. How sloppy of me. Terribly sorry. I'm Arthur Littlewood. Come on in. That is, you're already in. So, ah, how can I help you?"

"Let's step outside to talk in private, shall we?" said Nevis, tipping his head at the students hunched over laptop computers.

"Of course, of course. I forgot our meeting was today. Professional hazard. Forgetfulness, I mean. It runs in the profession." A nervous laugh.

The two stepped into a high-ceilinged atrium. Nevis paused beside a noisy fountain that he felt would provide sufficient cover for their conversation.

"So why am I being 'investigated'?" asked Littlewood, making nervous air quotes around the word *investigated*, a thin smile on his face.

Nevis didn't smile back. "I work in the National Security Branch, counterterrorism. We're conducting a national investigation on stressors on the electrical grid, looking for spike loads that might fry transformers. It's possible terrorists could use such stressors to bring down key substations." At this, Littlewood's countenance seemed to relax, which Nevis found odd.

"Oh. Well, if it's key substations you want," said Littlewood, "I shouldn't think central Florida is much of a—"

"We're taking a no-stone-unturned approach." Nevis arranged his features into a smile that didn't reach his gray eyes.

"No, no. Quite. Yes. Good. Nice to know our little university is on someone's radar." Littlewood swallowed, a nervous signal indicating he was anything but pleased at being "on someone's radar."

Nevis continued. "Our analysis puts the central Florida station as a weak point based on high peak usage incidents that point back to *you*." There. Let him squirm a little.

"You think I'm planning a . . . a . . . an *act of terrorism*?" Littlewood's color went slightly gray, matching the streaks at his temples.

"If I had questions on that count, you and I would be having a different conversation in lieu of this pleasant one. In your case, approval should be straightforward. Your profile doesn't reveal anything that would lead us to suspect you are planning an act of terrorism."

Littlewood released a tiny sigh of relief.

Nervous little fellow, wasn't he?

"However," continued Nevis, "I'll need to have a look around your facility as well as getting background checks on anyone who has regular, unimpeded access to your lab. You can provide me with a list of names?"

"Names? Me? A list?" Littlewood pulled out a

A Sword in Time

handkerchief and patted his brow. "I mean, yes. Yes, of course. Only too happy to cooperate."

"In addition, I'll need to know what it is you're doing that creates the large power surges."

"Of course. Of course." Another nervous laugh.

Nevis frowned. Maybe he *should* add Littlewood to his list of individuals who bore further investigation. "We'll also need you to liaise with local power authorities prior to granting your approval to operate. They will need a schedule of times you'll be drawing large amounts of power. This will provide the additional benefit of allowing the substation to analyze your usage and experiment with ways of lessening the threat associated with heavy usage."

"Happy to cooperate. Whatever I can do. I don't suppose . . . would you like to have a look around the lab now?"

Why the hell else was he in this miserable backwater? Aloud, Nevis said, "Now would be good."

"Please. Follow me," said Littlewood.

Littlewood provided a tour of his laboratory facility, using language Nevis wasn't familiar with to describe activities that he couldn't make heads or tails of. At some point, Littlewood apologized for the technical language.

"Research scientists all work in such narrow fields of study. Even physicists can barely talk to other physicists outside their precise area of interest."

Nevis had no trouble believing that. Supposedly, he'd been assigned this job because he'd spent two out of his four college years as a physics major—he'd later changed to business after a disastrous encounter with an upper-division course in electricity and magnetism, which meant he hardly qualified as a physics specialist. The *real* specialists within the bureau were doubtless doing more important things than gathering power grid data across the hinterlands of the nation.

Littlewood was concluding his remarks on a piece of electrical field shaping equipment that, perhaps— *maybe*, he said—drew significant power at times.

"I'll want a schedule of your intended future use," said Nevis, his tones clipped. "And names and contact information for those background checks."

"My students. Yes. Yes, of course." Littlewood mopped his brow again.

There was something going on here. Nevis couldn't put his finger on it, but something was definitely off with the Nutty Professor.

25
· *DAVINCI* ·
Florida, July

The flight from Santa Barbara to LAX on a noisy propeller plane with no first-class seating was short and crowded. DaVinci felt completely at home. The flight from LAX to Miami was in first class, where DaVinci could extend her seat into a lie-flat bed. She felt even more at home—so much so that she slept the entire flight. When she awoke and deplaned, she felt almost refreshed. At least, more than she had in the past six days. But her good mood quivered at curbside when Jillian pulled up in a car DaVinci didn't recognize. And she was blinking back tears by the time Jillian jumped from the car to give her a sad smile and a hug, carrying a cellophane-wrapped basket, like students sometimes gave DaVinci's dad at the end of the school year.

"Sorry, sorry, sorry," mumbled DaVinci, reaching for one of a dozen crumpled tissues that made her carry-on look like it was stuffed with snow.

"Never apologize for tears," said Jillian.

"That doesn't sound like Applegate wisdom."

Jillian's mouth turned up at the corners. "*That* was classic Branson. Oh, and speaking of Branson, he sends you his love, along with these." She passed DaVinci the basket, which was stuffed full of every size, shape, and color imaginable of . . . *gummy bears*. What was with the gummy bears?

DaVinci accepted the basket and then blew her nose. "I don't suppose Branson is single in this historical time line?"

Jillian's laugh came out as a tiny snort.

"A girl can dream," said DaVinci. She blotted her face one last time, exhaled, inhaled, and noticed the oppressive heat for the first time. "Florida in July, huh? Wow."

"Come on, I've got the AC blasting inside," Jillian said, opening the passenger side door. The interior looked expensive and smelled like leather. "In Florida's defense, the state has so much to offer once you get past the heat. You won't *believe* some of the foods I'm going to introduce you to. When we get to Wellesley, I'm getting you a *Cubano*."

It sounded vaguely like her BFF was offering to hook her up with a Latin lover, but DaVinci couldn't work up more than a pair of raised eyebrows.

"It's a *sandwich*," explained Jillian.

DaVinci's stomach growled. She couldn't remember the last time she'd eaten anything other than a handful of strawberries in first class. *Normal* DaVinci would have accepted the airline's offerings of steak, potatoes *dauphinoise*, and crème brûlée, and then asked if seconds were an option.

She glanced over at Jillian. Jillian was biting her

lip, both hands gripping the steering wheel. It was time to make more of an effort.

"Thanks so much for flying me out," said DaVinci. "A sandwich sounds great. I could probably eat a whole warehouse of sandwiches."

A *slight* exaggeration, but it achieved her goal: Jillian smiled and relaxed her grip on the wheel, saying, "You haven't changed at all."

Icy fingers seemed to play across DaVinci's shoulders.

You haven't changed at all.

If only that were true.

26

· DAVINCI ·

Florida, July

By the time Jillian had driven them both an hour south to Wellesley, Florida, it was five in the evening, and the food truck serving Cubanos had a line fifteen customers deep, which meant that it was 5:50 before Jillian and DaVinci made it to Dr. Littlewood's secret, off-campus laboratory, where the two were joining Everett for dinner.

As they strode to the entrance, DaVinci scrutinized Jillian's eager expression.

"Oh my God. You're glowing. Actually . . . *glowing*," she said to Jillian.

Jillian ignored the remark, although a slight flush joined her glow. She murmured something about a tricky new lock code on the door.

By the time the two entered the lab, Jillian's expression had reached beatific levels of glow. And who could blame her? Everett Randolph was swoonworthy. Long dark lashes covered his eyes as he hunched over a computer, but when he heard Jillian's greeting, he looked up, and his Caribbean-blue eyes sparkled with delight.

Those *eyes*. That gaze. That was totally a gaze that said, "I would take a bullet for you."

Which he had done. He'd taken a literal bullet for Jillian. Well, for all of them, to stop Khan from shooting anyone. Oh the irony.

Everett kissed Jillian, and DaVinci stood holding the sandwiches and feeling vaguely like an awkward younger sister while the embrace drew itself out into a total big-ass Hollywood kiss. The kind that made DaVinci feel all melty-warm with a side of be-fruitful-and-multiply.

She gave herself a mental shoulder-squaring and approached the kissing couple, savory Cuban sandwiches presented at arm's length, which had the effect of making her feel like a Girl Scout hoping someone would buy her cookies.

"DaVinci!" Everett released Jillian (he even did *that* with silver screen grace) and gave DaVinci a hug. A chaste and brotherly hug, vaguely disappointing in the face of the be-fruitful imperative she was currently trying to banish.

"Sandwich?" she said.

Everett smiled with appropriate gratitude, but he didn't take the sandwich. Instead, he strode to a desk, producing plates (actual *plate*-plates) and cloth napkins from a drawer.

"Everett insists we do dinner properly," Jillian murmured to DaVinci.

"Like Branson, much?" replied DaVinci.

Once the three were seated and dining, DaVinci took a moment to examine her feelings, which boiled down to (1) Everett was gorgeous, but (2) she did not in fact want him for herself, although, (3) she wouldn't say no to a DSLR camera to photograph him in high-contrast lighting because . . . those *cheekbones*.

Jillian spoke animatedly about the long line at the food truck, and eventually, the conversation drifted to what Everett had been working on that day.

"I've been reading up on the *Margites*," he said.

When Jillian and DaVinci gave him blank stares, he added, "It's a vanished work of Homer's that predates *The Iliad* and *The Odyssey*. Aristotle praises its comedy, and scholars ever since have been regretting its loss."

"Oh," said Jillian, eyes wide. "You're preparing for another trip to the library."

"So," said DaVinci, "if it's lost, how's a library going to help you?"

"Not *a* library," said Jillian solemnly. "*The* library."

"The Royal Library of Alexandria, also referred to as the Ancient or Great Library of Alexandria," said Everett, after dabbing carefully at the corners of his mouth.

"Wait. The one that burned to the ground a couple of millennia ago?" asked DaVinci. Everything clicked. "*Oh*. Oh wow. You're going back and snatching lost works from the Alexandrian library."

Everett nodded, an eager smile spreading across his face.

"Wow," repeated DaVinci. "That's . . . ingenious."

Everett, giving Jillian's hand a quick squeeze, said, "It was Jillian's suggestion. Dr. Littlewood is trying to plan ahead for the day when we can't keep the secret of time travel anymore. He worries something terrible that people will disapprove of the machine because of the potential for its use in questionable ventures."

"We want to be able to show it can be used for *good*," said Jillian.

"*Huh*," DaVinci said. "How . . . noble." It *was* noble. With a side of dangerous. But then again, this was the guy whose duplicate self had made the ultimate sacrifice for his country back in 1918. It put the bullet-taking and time-traveling-for-noble-purposes in perspective. It also made her want to type into her phone: *note to self—no dating noble soldiers.*

"So you go back in time," said DaVinci, "and grab things the, *uh*, world of scholarship is missing?"

Everett nodded.

Jillian added, "Someday, it may help us argue the only proper application of temporal studies is historical research."

"In essence, we're providing a means by which to justify the study of the temporal singularity," added Everett.

"Yeah," said DaVinci, feeling slightly uncomfortable. "Listen, I know I had no right . . . I know there's no justification . . ." She broke off as her slight discomfort became definite discomfort, flushing her pale cheeks.

"No one is criticizing your actions," said Jillian. "Think about it. I would be the first person in line if anyone deserved criticism for how the machines have been used up till now. Remember how I attended culinary school?"

DaVinci took a bite of her sandwich, hoping to avoid further discussion.

Jillian, with Applegate radar for "uncomfortable," changed the subject. "Do you like your sandwich?"

DaVinci nodded and focused on the food. Sour pickle and melted cheese, roast pork and ham, all wrapped up in buttery bread. Unfortunately, if someone had drawn a Venn diagram just then of "people with appetites" and "DaVinci," there would have been zero overlap. Where had her appetite run off to? Same place as the rest of her life, no doubt.

Everett, meanwhile, lacking Applegate radar, was continuing the discussion of time travel.

"In a pinch, we could probably get by speaking Latin in ancient Alexandria," he said. "But we discovered Dr. Littlewood's security guard—the Roman abandoned here by Dr. Khan—speaks first-century Greek. After that discovery, well, it was too wonderful an opportunity to pass up." He brushed a strand of hair from Jillian's face, smiling softly at her.

At the gesture, DaVinci felt a hollow sensation in her belly. She took another bite of her sandwich, even though she was plenty aware that the feeling in her belly had nothing to do with hunger. Who would've guessed that yearning made its home in the stomach?

Everett, still gazing at Jillian, was sporting another of his star-of-the-silver-screen expressions. Yeah, he was beautiful. Totally yearn-worthy, even if she didn't want Mr. Gorgeous for herself. The thing was, though, this yearning had nothing to do with Everett's appearance. Not really.

It wasn't how he looked—it was how he looked at Jillian.

That, whispered DaVinci's heart. I'll have what she's having.

DaVinci rolled her eyes at herself and looked away. She didn't need to start cataloguing new things missing from her life. She already had plenty of old things missing. Refocusing her attention on her friends, she quickly realized the discussion had returned to the topic of ancient documents.

Nodding at DaVinci, Jillian said, "Right?"

"Uh-huh," she replied. The response had to be at least vaguely appropriate.

"I knew you'd like that part," said Jillian. "It will change the way people think about the relationship of Hellenic Greeks to their art forms."

DaVinci was considering making a generic remark about the art of ancient Greece when the laboratory door slammed shut. She startled and turned, expecting to see Dr. Arthur Littlewood.

But this wasn't Littlewood. Oh. My. *So* not Arthur Littlewood. Not unless Littlewood had suddenly gotten twenty-five years younger, grown a foot taller, and gained fifty pounds of solid muscle. With a side of *hunk*.

"Oh *hello*," she whispered. And then covered her mouth. Her expression of approval was not intended for the public arena.

Arena. Yes. That was where this guy belonged. He must be the Roman. DaVinci swallowed. He definitely belonged in an arena fighting off ten gladiators with swords and maces. And maybe a lion. And DaVinci wouldn't have put odds on the lion.

"This is Quintus," Jillian was saying. "Quintus, this is DaVinci Shaughnessy-Pavlov, a friend of mine and of Everett's, and also an acquaintance of Dr. Littlewood's."

DaVinci was examining the musculature of Quintus's forearm. He could probably strangle that lion one-handed.

"*DaVinci,*" whispered Jillian, drawing DaVinci's attention back from the imaginary first-century BC arena.

DaVinci raised her eyes from the Roman's forearm to his eyes. His meltingly, achingly, shockingly beautiful eyes. "Ungk," grunted DaVinci.

Ungk? Really?

"Nice to meet you," she said, quickly covering. She held out a hand.

Quintus, his light brown eyes narrowed and glued on her like he was assessing her for "potential threat in an arena death match," finally took her hand for approximately one-hundredth of one second. No shake. No squeeze.

Awkward. He was gorgeous but *awkward* as heck.

"So you're the one who speaks Greek?" she asked. Her confidence was returning rapidly now that she knew she wasn't the more socially clumsy of the two of them. At least *she* knew how to freaking shake someone's hand.

"Yes," replied Quintus.

After a final penetrating stare, he turned his back to her and asked Everett, "Do we travel to Alexandria tomorrow morning?"

DaVinci blinked. Her own eyes narrowed. Quintus-the-Barbarian wasn't just socially awkward. No, he'd crossed the border into the Land of Rude.

Still. With those bulked-out shoulders and that well-muscled derriere, she was going to have to draw him. Although getting far enough past that gruff exterior to acquire his *permission*—well, that was going to be loads of fun. She would probably have to stealth-sketch him.

His *latissimus dorsi* rippled under his thin cotton shirt. Wow. Yes. Drawing needed to be happening. Stat. Conté crayon, maybe? Or—no—not Conté. Charcoal. Yes. Charcoal on a toothy, ochre-tinted paper. Just as DaVinci was wondering if Jillian knew of any 24-hour art supply stores, the muscled shoulders in question shifted and Quintus turned. His eyes met hers, and his brow wrinkled like he *knew* she'd been checking him out. Her face flushed. Hastily, she looked away.

As soon as Quintus had returned his attention to Everett, Jillian caught DaVinci's eyes. She raised her brows hopefully, pointedly shifting her gaze from DaVinci to Quintus and back again. DaVinci was familiar with this look. It did *not* indicate an interest in having DaVinci capture Quintus's musculature on toothy, ochre-tinted paper.

DaVinci rolled her eyes and mouthed, *Please*. She might not require Everett or Edmund levels of polish in a guy, but her standards were well above the bar set by a certain *rude* ancient Roman. How could Jillian, the politest person on the planet, even suggest Quintus as dating material?

Leaning in, DaVinci murmured to Jillian, "Drawing Gruff and Grumble? Yes. Dating him? Nope."

Jillian responded with a tiny right-shoulder-only shrug, whispering, "Never say never."

DaVinci snorted and then muttered, "Never with a side of never, drenched in never sauce."

No, the only interaction DaVinci required with the hulking Roman was a little small talk leading to a little permission to sketch him.

27

· *QUINTUS* ·

Florida, July

Quintus had seen eyes like DaVinci's once before. Eyes of pale green, like the waters of *Rhodanus*, where it calved from the glacier. Wide-set eyes of a shade rarely seen in Rome, arresting enough to catch unwanted attention, even in the face of a girl of eleven. Quintus still had nightmares haunted by those empty green eyes.

But the eyes of the girl before him today weren't haunting or empty. This girl—young woman, rather—stared at him boldly, almost as if amused by him. Which aided Quintus in shaking off his dark memories. Stiffening under DaVinci's fearless gaze, he turned to speak to Everett about the day's work.

Everett, however, seemed interested in including the green-eyed interloper in their conversation.

"DaVinci, do you suppose your father might be willing to suggest lost art texts for which we could search?"

"Lost texts?" DaVinci combed pale fingers

through her red-gold hair and shrugged. "My dad is the emperor of lost causes. Why not lost texts?"

"He certainly has connections," said Jillian, who evidently took the question more seriously than did DaVinci. Jillian explained to DaVinci, "We've already got a solid list—history's top-ten lost texts, twenty-five top reasons to regret the burning of the Ancient Library of Alexandria, and so on. These are just things we grabbed off the internet without any real effort. But if you could get your dad to maybe ask around in the art community?"

"*Uh*, sure," said DaVinci. "He knows people that might . . . know stuff."

Quintus was still learning nuance of expression in English, but this girl's speech seemed less precise than that of either Dr. Littlewood, Everett, or Jillian. Perhaps she was uneducated.

"So what do you think of all this, anyway?" DaVinci asked, addressing Quintus with an amused look on her face. "Are the trips to Alexandria a good way to use the machine?"

Why would anyone ask him about the uses to which the time machine was put?

"I owe Dr. Littlewood a debt I cannot repay," Quintus said, wary, "and I am therefore glad to offer my assistance as an interpreter."

The green-eyed girl frowned, causing her full lips to thin. How red those lips were. How pale the girl was. And her hair—even in this artificial light, it seemed to glow. What would it look like in the sun's light?

"That's not what I asked," said the girl. "I mean, that's great you're grateful and Littlewood is made of

A Sword in Time

awesome, yada, yada, but what do you think about visiting the past to collect important things? Is it ethical? Unethical?"

Quintus's jaw tightened. What was the girl fishing for? Did Littlewood or Everett or Jillian suspect he might wish to use the machine for his own ends? Had they sent the girl to trick him into speaking of this?

"I perform my duty without regret," he answered cautiously.

The corners of the girl's mouth twitched. Was she laughing at him? She no longer struck him as uneducated so much as . . . what was that new word? *Wily.* Yes. The girl was wily. She had a hidden aim and was attempting to conceal it. Quintus had been trained to detect such things by a master of the art—Gaius Julius Caesar himself. So what aim was this girl attempting to conceal?

Perhaps Littlewood *had* noticed Quintus's increasing questions about the machine after all. Quintus had tried to keep his interest hidden, but perhaps he had failed, and the girl had been sent to *wile* a confession from him. It would not be the first time a pretty girl had been employed in such work, but it made Quintus sorry to imagine Littlewood suspicious of him. Guilt pinched at him. A good man would not repay his employer thus. And yet, who was Quintus's true employer—his true commander? Was it not Caesar? Had he not pledged to deliver Caesar's letter?

His resolve renewed, Quintus attempted to dismiss the girl.

"If you will excuse me," he said, "it is time I began work."

He crossed to the station from which he

monitored the camera mounted beside the laboratory entrance. Ordinarily, once everyone had departed for the day, he would listen to YouTube videos on conversational English, but everyone had *not* departed for the day, so he could only watch the monitor. Sensing the girl was still watching him, he attempted to look engaged by his job.

The girl, her arms folded delicately over her small chest, walked toward him.

"What is it you don't like about picking up stuff from the past?" she asked. "Clearly, you've got some feelings about this. So, is it just the nausea and dizziness? 'Cause I am not a fan of those, either."

Quintus pressed his lips together. "The discomfort is minor."

She raised one red-gold brow.

"And inconsequential," Quintus added, proud of the new-to-him word. "And in any event, it matters not what I think of the importance of Littlewood's work."

"Huh," she said. She stepped closer and peered at the monitor. "Wow. You do this eight hours a day?"

"Night," Quintus replied tersely.

She was craning her neck between him and the monitor. She had a row of freckles across her tiny nose and below her lovely mouth. Everything about her was fashioned to perfection, as if Venus herself had given the commands. Quintus frowned at himself and returned his gaze to the monitor where it belonged.

"So what would you use the machine for?" asked DaVinci. "If it were up to you? What would be more . . . important, by your standards?"

The girl was persistent, a virtue Quintus normally admired. It had won Gallia for Roma under Gaius Julius Caesar, after all.

"It is not my concern what use Dr. Littlewood puts his machine to," said Quintus.

"But you *must* have an opinion. I'm just curious."

The girl's persistence was striking. Perhaps Littlewood was indeed suspicious. Perhaps he should give the girl an answer to throw everyone off the scent. Quintus could not allow anything to prevent him from carrying out his mission.

"You do know that the items from the past aren't actually stolen out of the past, right?" asked DaVinci.

"Indeed," replied Quintus.

The girl crossed behind him and then examined him from the opposite side.

"So what would you bring to this century, if you could bring anything?"

Quintus's throat felt suddenly thick. It was a question he had asked himself, and often. Could he bring his wife and son here? But as much as he missed his old life, he would not bring them here. Mucia would weep for her sisters, for her *mama* and *tata* and the culinary delicacies of Roma. His son, he hardly knew.

"Seriously. What would you bring back?"

Was *this* what Littlewood wished to learn? Was it for this he had employed the girl? Or was Quintus imagining things? Perhaps the girl was merely an acquaintance of Littlewood's, as Jillian had proclaimed. The girl was probably bored. And accustomed, as pretty girls were, to having their whims met and their questions answered.

"Come on," she said, smiling. "Humor me."

"Very well," Quintus said. "Were it up to me, I should bring Gaius Julius, whom you call 'Caesar' to this century. He would bring your nation under good governance. Yours is an undisciplined land."

DaVinci stared at him, her mouth half-open, and blinked very slowly. "O—*kay*," she said. "Yeah. No. So not a good plan. Stick with the doing-your-duty. As you were, soldier."

Having said this, she turned and marched away.

"I'm beat," Quintus heard her saying to Jillian. "Can we go to your apartment?"

Quintus shook his head almost imperceptibly at the odd girl. He did not rise to add his goodbyes to those of Everett when the friends departed a minute later. But as the door opened, he couldn't help turning to see what the setting sun, now streaming through the basement door, would do to DaVinci's hair. There was a flash of red-gold fire, and then the girl was gone.

Several hours after the girl had gone, after everyone had gone, Quintus thought again of her green eyes. Her shining hair. He tried not to. He opened a computer browser to episode thirty-four of his favorite conversational English channel on YouTube and pressed play. He told himself it was only that her eyes reminded him of the green eyes and golden hair of the girl he had tried to save so long ago. The girl whose pale-green eyes had caught the attention of Glavius, a fellow soldier during Quintus's first campaign with Caesar. Glavius had been a great oaf of a man tasked with distributing slaves awarded after victories. He'd procured the green-eyed girl, a child of eleven winters, and while Quintus was no more squeamish about slavery than any of Caesar's men, he had been furious when word reached him of Glavius's plans for this newest slave.

The oafish soldier had crossed a line, proposing to deflower her before a paying audience of drunken legionnaires. Quintus had pushed his way to the front of the forming queue and demanded speech with Glavius.

"Are you paying to watch? Or to watch and have a turn?" asked Glavius's groom, an onerous, toothless leer on his face.

Quintus did not dignify the question with a response. Ignoring the groom, Quintus grabbed Glavius by the tunic. "This must stop," he said, his voice low and even.

Glavius shoved Quintus's hand away and continued addressing his supporters, detailing the acts he planned to perform on the green-eyed girl.

"She is a child," said Quintus, shifting himself so that he stood in front of Glavius.

Glavius made a show of examining Quintus from his feet to his face before emitting a harsh laugh. "You and she have that in common then," said Glavius.

"Gaius Julius will not permit—"

Quintus was cut off by Glavius. "*This* for Gaius Julius," he said, gesturing rudely.

"You forget yourself, soldier!" snapped Quintus.

The men encircling them had gone quiet, all attention on Glavius and the interloper, Quintus.

"No, boy, I do not forget myself," said Glavius. "But perhaps you have forgotten a few important things. Such as bringing *Tata* Julius along with you to back up your demands."

Quintus widened his stance. Below his cloak, he inched his hand toward his sword.

"Call off this . . . this spectacle at once," said Quintus.

The girl, all the while, continued to stare into the distance, unblinking. Quintus had seen children in the aftermath of battle. But this girl with her ghost-green eyes, her gaze as unfocused and unblinking as one of the dead, made him shiver.

"Or what?" demanded Glavius.

"Or face the consequences," said Quintus. With one smooth motion, he threw back his cloak and drew his sword.

Glavius laughed. It was an ugly laugh, full of disdain. He threw back his own cloak and rose. He was large, but he was also nimble, and his swordsmanship was legendary, some calling him *Gladius* instead of Glavius on account of his skill with the Roman short sword. Quintus struck first, hoping to end the fight quickly, but Glavius was ready. He parried Quintus's strike and, with lightning speed, landed a blow using the flat of his sword on the back of Quintus's thighs. It stung—it was meant to humiliate, and the drunkards surrounding Glavius laughed, making comments on Quintus's youth.

The two went round and round for several minutes, neither able to land a serious blow. Quintus, however, was now bleeding in several places. He was beginning to think Glavius had no plans to seriously wound; the man was fighting a war of pinpricks and scratches, bloodying his opponent so that his handiwork might be admired throughout the camp. Quintus grew angrier, and in doing so, struck faster and faster while unintentionally letting his guard down. Glavius, it seemed, had been biding his time for this. He sprang forward, his blade singing toward Quintus's head.

At that moment, Quintus slipped on a gnarled root, sending himself wide of the trajectory of his opponent's blade. His fall saved his life. Glavius's blade continued its unalterable course and drove deep into a log awaiting the fire. Glavius hunched forward, straining to remove the blade, which was solidly lodged. With shock, Quintus realized that Glavius had struck to kill. Hot anger, livid and blinding, overtook Quintus. With a fierce cry, he plunged his sword into Glavius's exposed neck. There was no honor in the blow, but the fight was over.

Glavius pitched face forward. There was a burbling, gurgling noise as he tried to speak, and then the ground grew dark as his heart pumped his life's blood into the cold earth.

The crowd that had gathered around Glavius dispersed rapidly. Quintus withdrew his sword and then plunged it into the earth, swearing. Not for the waste of such a life, but because he must answer for what had happened. And then, in the confusion of the scene, the girl seemed to come awake. Dashing forward, she pulled Quintus's sword from the ground, and, before Quintus could stop her, fell on it, her aim as true as any soldier's.

That night, a parlay with the defeated tribe commenced, and among other concessions granted by Gaius Julius, the tribe was given the body of the girl, who had been a barbarian princess. As the enemy retreated with her body, Quintus had stared after her red-gold hair until it had been swallowed by the dark forest.

A loud musical refrain summoned Quintus back to the present. The conversational English video had ended.

Grunting at himself for allowing the dark memory to resurface, he rose and crossed to the time machine. Enough wasting of time. He had work to do. Caesar's work. And tonight was the night.

28
· DAVINCI ·
Florida, July

"So, about Quintus the Barbarian," DaVinci said to Jillian as soon as they were inside Jillian's apartment. "Who put grumpy sauce in his coffee?"

Jillian's brow wrinkled with worry. "Please don't judge him based on this evening. He's been through so much. Khan just dropped him here with no explanation. No assistance. Nothing. He was completely on his own for days before he found a friend."

"Friend as in *Littlewood*? Well, no offense, but I guess that could account for the appalling lack of social graces."

Ignoring the slur, Jillian said, "Littlewood didn't meet Quintus until months after he'd arrived. A Catholic priest found Quintus first and befriended him. Like a good Samaritan."

"Oh," said DaVinci, nodding. "Well, I guess you don't exactly go to catechism to learn manners, either."

Jillian laughed. "Father Joe can be . . . disarming. He's really sweet. And as for Quintus," she continued, "he's very nice, once you get to know him."

"Which he totally goes out of his way to make possible," muttered DaVinci.

Jillian bit her lower lip.

"Kidding," said DaVinci. "Just kidding. I'm sure he's a model Roman citizen or whatever, and I promise to play nice. I'll have to if I want to get him to sit for me."

"*Hmm . . .*" murmured Jillian.

"What? I'm not allowed to ask him to sit for me?"

"Oh, I don't know. He's very . . . it's just that he can be a little aloof."

"Caught that."

"He doesn't mean to be. I think he spends most of each day feeling super confused, if you want to know the truth. Can you imagine it? Waking up to a world that's nothing like the one you've spent your whole life in?"

DaVinci, who had been enjoying both the banter and the prospect of capturing Quintus's *gluteus maximus* on paper, was brought suddenly and harshly back inside her own reality.

"Yes," she said glumly. "I can imagine that."

"Oh, I'm so sorry," said Jillian. "I wanted you to have a break from all that—"

"It's okay," said DaVinci. "There aren't any . . . breaks. Not really. And I'm sure you're right about Mr. Gruff-and-Grim. I'll behave better the next time we meet." She gave Jillian a tired smile. "So give me a tour of your fabulous new home, already."

After hugging DaVinci tightly, Jillian did just that.

A Sword in Time

"It's very . . . *normal*," said DaVinci after the apartment tour. She plopped onto Jillian's sofa and stared up at the ceiling. At the *popcorn* ceiling. "Gotta say, I never imagined a world where Jillian Applegate and popcorn ceilings could exist in such close proximity."

"The rent is low," replied Jillian.

DaVinci's eyes caught on a trio of expensive, copper-bottomed pots hung on the wall beside the stove. "And you care about what things cost since . . . when?"

Jillian's cheeks tinged with pink. "I care."

"Says the woman who just flew me out here first class."

"That was on frequent flyer miles."

Frequent flyer miles? DaVinci frowned. Frequent flyer miles and not cash or gold ingots or whatever Applegates paid with? Jillian *had* changed. DaVinci's heart skipped a beat. What if this was because of *her*? What if the changes she'd made to the time line had . . . had altered Jillian, like it had altered things between Yoshi and Ana?

"If this is my fault, I will never forgive myself."

"If what's your fault?"

DaVinci groaned. "I told you that I changed some stuff. History stuff. But I also changed *people*. Like, actual personality-type things. Or, I don't know, choice-making things. In this time line, Yoshi got engaged to Ana."

Jillian frowned. "You're saying Yoshida *doesn't*, well, *didn't* get engaged to Ana in the time line you interrupted?"

DaVinci shook her head, mentally stumbling on

the word *interrupted*. It sounded so purposeful. "I didn't mean to interrupt anything except for the demolition of my house. And if I changed *you*, I . . ." She shook her head. "How do I begin to apologize for that?"

Jillian took her hand and smiled softly. "Dr. Littlewood and I were discussing things, and he agrees with me that it's unlikely your changes could cause any kind of ripple effect that would reach all the way out here. The changes are probably confined to you and your immediate family."

"You told Littlewood?" asked DaVinci, blanching.

"Of course. The repercussions . . . the implications . . . Of course he needed to know."

"Yeah. Okay," said DaVinci. "It's just so embarrassing. Or something."

"I didn't mean to make you feel bad. You shouldn't. It's not like there are textbooks you could have consulted. Up till now, none of us have made notable changes to *any* time lines, so it was perfectly reasonable for you to assume your changes would be limited in scope."

"Great. I'm blazing trails in space–time exploration."

DaVinci reached for a curl that had slipped down over her forehead and twirled it a few times before tugging it back behind her ear.

"I don't pretend to understand what you're going through," said Jillian, "but I'm here any time you want to talk." She hesitated. "In a way, Everett's been through something similar, and he said talking helped. And there's Quintus, too, but—you know what? Let's talk about something else *besides* bungled time travel."

DaVinci grimaced. "That's me. Bungler of Time."

"So," said Jillian, ignoring the remark, "how are the twins?"

It was classic Applegate: when someone exhibits distress, pretend you don't notice and change the subject.

DaVinci tugged at another errant curl.

"Are they planning to room together when they go off to college next month?" Jillian asked.

"*Um*, I don't really know," said DaVinci. "I haven't been talking to my family much. I've been sort of . . . out of it."

"Everett still talks about that volleyball championship game you took us to," said Jillian. "Although I think he liked the uniforms more than the actual sport." She smiled, shaking her head at some memory.

DaVinci felt confused. "I took you to a volleyball game? What volleyball game?"

"Klee and Kahlo's? The championship?"

When DaVinci didn't respond, Jillian's expression shifted. "The game that landed them the full rides to Santa Clara University?"

"Klee and Kahlo are going to UCLA." DaVinci spoke with conviction, but as soon as the words were out of her mouth, her stomach began to knot, as if it was getting to the truth ahead of her brain.

"No," said Jillian softly. "Santa Clara University."

"Why would they go to Santa Clara?"

"*Um* . . . volleyball?"

"They want to study architecture and urban design," whispered DaVinci. "Not volleyball."

"They're not 'studying' volleyball," replied Jillian.

"They're majoring in hospitality. You know, like for events or the hotel industry. Volleyball just pays for everything."

"I don't understand," whispered DaVinci. What she meant was I don't want to understand. I wish I didn't understand. I refuse to understand.

But she did understand.

She understood, and she wanted to scream, to demand that space–time give it all back.

Jillian spoke softly. "So this is another . . . change to the time line?"

"I've ruined my sisters' lives," whispered DaVinci. How could she have done this? It was one thing to speed up the Yoshida-Ana engagement trajectory. But to take away her sisters' dreams? How was she going to live with this? Her stomach filled with icy cold.

Jillian grabbed DaVinci's hand. "Listen to me. You did not ruin your sisters' lives. Things may be different than you were expecting, but Klee and Kahlo are . . . well, they're very excited about Santa Clara."

Jillian was saying it as if she needed to convince herself, and that was all DaVinci needed to know the truth. She felt sick to her stomach. "What did I do? How could I?"

A frown etched creases across Jillian's face.

"I'm not going to pretend it hasn't been hard for them. For your mom and dad, too. But . . . but according to what you told me, this was their . . . their chance to *escape*. Volleyball gave them that possibility."

"To escape? Escape what?"

"Well, your family's expectation that they would study art or teach art or make art or somehow devote themselves to art."

Now DaVinci frowned. "But that's what they want. To be architects. I helped them with their portfolios. They were so proud when UCLA accepted them both."

Jillian bit her lip. "I can only tell you what I know. I don't think you helped them with their portfolios. I'm pretty sure of it, actually."

"This is like a bad dream, only I don't get to wake up."

"You said . . . you told me they maybe wanted something different. Something that was, how did you put it? *Theirs* I think you said."

"I would never say that," said DaVinci. Except she must have said it. In the version of history Jillian—*this* version of Jillian—knew, DaVinci had said that. Slowly, she shook her head.

"I just can't imagine a world where Klee and Kahlo would have chosen something over art and architecture. A world where . . . where they didn't beg me for help with their applications and portfolios. I mean, *volleyball*? Really? My little sisters?"

It was like a radio station playing two different tracks at the same time.

It was like biting into an apple and tasting lemon.

"I don't know what I'm supposed to do with this," DaVinci said at last.

As DaVinci watched, Jillian bit her lip. Frowned. The time line might have changed, but her friend's habits hadn't changed.

"You're biting your lip and frowning," said DaVinci. "Why?"

"It's just . . . you're saying you don't know what to do about this. But I don't know if you *should* do anything. They're happy. You know? They say it all the time, how they don't know what they would have done without volleyball."

DaVinci felt her heart crash like a boulder rocketing down Cold Springs Creek in flood. Sure they didn't know what they would have done without volleyball—after losing the dream that had sustained them for years, her sisters were *consoling* themselves with volleyball. And it was all her fault, because for some unfathomable reason, *she hadn't been there for them.*

But *why?*

Was it because she'd quit making art? Oh no. She turned to Jillian, grief twisting her expression. "I didn't help them because I threw out my brushes and paint. Is that why?"

Jillian shrugged uncomfortably. Squeezed her hand. "Honestly? I don't know."

"Halley said I threw out all my art supplies. That I quit making art."

"That part is true," agreed Jillian. "You told us you were done with art."

"And if I said I was done, I wouldn't have helped Klee and Kahlo when they needed it most." She blinked back the tears burning her eyes. "How am I supposed to live with this?"

"Oh, DaVinci," murmured Jillian.

The two sat in silence for several minutes. The light inside the apartment began to shift, and Jillian rose, crossing to the front window and raising the blinds. "I picked this apartment for the great views of sunsets," Jillian said softly, returning to the couch.

Side by side, the two gazed out the front window at an evening sky on fire with flaming vermilions and fierce golds. It was raw and primitive, a cretaceous sky, meant for T. rexes, not humans. DaVinci reached for her cell, and even held it up to capture the vast sky on her screen, but she didn't press the shutter button.

"I wish I'd brought my paint box," she murmured, dropping her phone to her lap.

Jillian turned to her. "Oh, DaVinci—"

"Except . . . I threw out my paints." Tears spilled over her lashes and down her cheeks. "How could I have done that?"

As soon as the question was out there, she wished she hadn't asked it. She didn't want to know. She didn't want to hear one more thing about this messed up reality. This world where she would do something as *wrong* as throwing away her paint box or failing her little sisters.

Jillian spoke softly. "We never talked about why you did it. You said you didn't want to talk about it."

She hadn't even tried talking to her friends about this? And they hadn't . . . insisted? Tried to shake her by the shoulders or read her the riot act or whatever best friends were supposed to do when they saw you going completely off the rails? It was a knife to the gut. All of a sudden, she needed air. She crossed to the door and pulled it open, instantly reeling back from the heat.

Oh. Wow. *"Ugh!"*

She slammed the door shut and swore.

Jillian's eyes were anguished.

Maybe her friends *had* tried. Who knew what had really happened? Not DaVinci. That much was for sure.

DaVinci closed her eyes tightly. "I just . . . I

wanted some fresh air." She uttered a low, grunting laugh. "Which apparently Florida is sold out of." Another pause. "I'm sorry."

Jillian, who had risen and crossed to DaVinci, wrapped an arm around her shoulder. "I get it."

"I don't. I don't get *any* of this," said DaVinci. "How could I have tossed my art supplies? I don't know what I said to you before, but I want to talk about this. I *need* to talk about this."

"Okay," said Jillian. "What do you want to know?"

"Start from where I said I was done with art. Why did I say that?"

Jillian's brows furrowed.

"Wait. Don't start there," said DaVinci. Her friends wouldn't know *why* she'd said what she'd said. "How about this: *When* did I say I was done? What else was happening at the time?"

"Well, it all started when you didn't get into the UCSB's College of Creative Studies. You were really upset about that."

"I *am* upset about that."

"Yeah. Well, you attended UCSB for a while, but then you just . . . dropped out midterm."

"That's what Halley told me."

"Right," said Jillian. "After you dropped out, you painted that big angry mural on your house, and then you said you were done with art."

DaVinci's mouth dropped open. "I painted a 'big angry mural'?"

Jillian nodded. "Your parents left it there for a few months, but I guess the Van Sants said their kids were having nightmares, so Yoshi repainted the house."

"Some . . . big angry mural I supposedly painted is the reason my house is no longer blue?"

"I'm just repeating what you told me."

It was like being stuck in a hailstorm of bizarre where the hailstones kept getting bigger and bigger.

"I *loved* our aqua-blue house," she said, sinking back onto the couch. "We all loved it. I can't believe *I'm* the reason my house is the color of a peach margarita."

Jillian dug her teeth into her lower lip and then spoke. "I guess you don't remember suggesting the new color?"

"Oh my God. That color was *my* choice?"

Jillian shrugged but said nothing.

"I told my parents to paint our house puke pink?" DaVinci's throat tightened. She swallowed and then croaked out her friend's name.

"Jilly . . . I don't know who I am."

It was like being inside a wrong self. How was it possible to be alienated from her own self? And not only from her *self,* but from everyone she should have known best, who should have known *her* best. Her sisters. Her best friends. Her family. None of them knew her. None of them recognized who she was. They just kept talking about this stranger—this person she never, *ever* wanted to know, much less *become.* She'd never felt so isolated.

She stared out the window, watching as the sky shifted from ochre to amber to coral, and then finally to a dull pink and a duller gray, a sky grown defeated and tired.

When she finally spoke again, her voice sounded

just as defeated and tired.

"I don't understand what hiring a plumber had to do with me not painting."

Jillian gave her friend a squeeze around the shoulders. "You could start again."

"Start over? Like, do I try to paint everything again from memory? I don't even know what the last thing I painted *was*."

"The last thing you painted—before the mural, I mean—was the *Still Life with X* series. And for what it's worth, *Still Life with Lobster* is still one of my mom's favorite paintings."

DaVinci looked sadly at her friend. The lobster painting had been pathetic. She was capable of so much more. "It was totally derivative," was all she said out loud.

"That was what you said when you didn't get into the program," Jillian said softly. "That someone called your pieces derivative. In a *bad* way."

"There is no *good* way," replied DaVinci. "Besides, they *were* derivative. That's why I didn't include them in my portfolio."

Jillian looked puzzled. "What do you mean you didn't include them? The *Still Life with X* series *was* your portfolio."

DaVinci felt as if a giant hand had reached inside and squeezed her lungs.

"You're telling me I submitted *Still Life* as my 'work in evidence of talent' for the College of Creative Studies art program?"

Frowning, Jillian nodded.

This wasn't possible. DaVinci felt sick. The room was suddenly 190 degrees. "Can we have some AC in here?"

Jillian jumped up and crossed to the wall thermostat.

DaVinci whispered. "Why would I submit my still life series instead of *East Mountain 360*?"

Jillian, still tapping the thermostat temperature down, down, down, didn't respond.

East Mountain 360 remained, in DaVinci's opinion, some of her best work. She'd received prestigious awards for her murals since then, but she felt the murals weren't as interesting or provocative as the pieces in *East Mountain 360*.

So why would she have ignored them in favor of the *Still Life with X* series?

And then,

suddenly,

all the pieces fell into place.

She understood. She knew where everything had gone off the rails. She knew why she hadn't been in a position to encourage the twins, to mentor them through their application process. Why they'd left art for volleyball.

Why she was no longer painting.

It was because the dry rot in the floor of the downstairs studio never happened, which meant she'd never been forced to find somewhere else to paint. Which meant she hadn't spent entire months on the flat roof of her house, learning what the mountains looked like in every sort of light, learning how the sea had a personality expressed through color and reflective value. She'd never done any of it because she'd never climbed up to the roof when the indoor studio with its magnificent north-facing wall of windows was declared off-limits, because it had never been declared off-limits. DaVinci had never painted *East Mountain 360*. Her greatest work *ever* existed only in her memory.

29

· *DAVINCI* ·

Florida, July

It was after midnight, Florida time, and DaVinci lay on the sofa bed in Jillian's apartment thinking about the train wreck that was her life. Thinking about all the things she'd done the past two and a half years and then crashing into the horrifying realization she *hadn't* done them.

She'd never painted the eight large *East Mountain 360* canvases, encompassing the wraparound view from her family's rooftop "studio." *East Mountain 360* had been the project that had turned her from being a dabbler in many forms—textiles, sculpture, serigraphs—into a painter. It had been the project that taught her to *see*. The project that got her into UCSB's College of Creative Studies as an art major and into the elite Honors Program, with its included studio space and year-end exhibition. DaVinci had always known how lucky she was to land studio space and a show as a freshman. None of her awards, none of her funding, none of her teaching jobs or commissions would have been possible without that studio space and that year-end exhibition.

Except—

She hadn't won the awards.

She hadn't been hired to teach.

She hadn't received commissions from wealthy residents of Hope Ranch, or Alameda Padre Serra, or Montecito.

She'd done none of it.

She'd traded her painter's apron for an Enterprise Fish Company apron. She'd quit making art. But the problem was, the DaVinci who'd had *years* to get used to this reality was *not* the DaVinci lying on a hide-a-bed in Florida, eyes wide open after midnight.

She wasn't even close to sleepy; back home in California, it was only nine o'clock. Her stomach was growling. Complaining. Loudly demanding a snack before bedtime.

She hadn't painted the *East Mountain* canvases.

The thought seemed to empty her lungs. Three hours had passed since she'd learned the truth, but it still left her gasping for air. Since that first, awful realization, she'd been trapped, revisiting cause and effect, a contagion sequence where one thing led to another and another and another. "The law of unintended consequences," Jillian had called it.

For want of a leak, the floor did not rot.

For want of a rotten floor, the family did not turn to painting on the rooftop.

For want of painting on the roof, DaVinci never learned to see.

For want of artistic sight, DaVinci's portfolio sucked.

For want of a nonsucky portfolio, DaVinci didn't get into UCSB and said, Screw it—
And all for the want of a leak.

The bitter circle kept repeating in her head.

But how was she supposed to break it? Or more importantly, how was she supposed to break it without introducing a whole new set of unintended consequences? What if something even worse than her brother's early engagement or the twins' devastating change in college plans were to happen?

At least no one had died because of the changes she'd introduced. (She had Jillian to thank for that bright bit of encouragement.) Her current life *sucked*, but everyone she loved was still alive. If she tried to go back in time and chase off the plumber whom she'd hired, what else might change?

She was exhausted. The backs of her eyes felt gritty from dry airplane air and too much crying. And not enough sleep. She had to get some sleep. *Really* had to.

Shifting in bed, she succeeded in tangling her legs in the ankle-length nightie Jillian had loaned her. She should have said no to the stupid nightie. Yes, she'd forgotten to pack one, but she hated long nighties. They made her feel like her legs were in jail. Although, tonight maybe that was just the blankets trapping her. After kicking her legs a few times, she succeeded in freeing them. It wasn't like she needed a blanket in Florida.

Sighing, she attempted to settle back into Jillian's luxurious down pillows. DaVinci wasn't going to think about her problems anymore tonight. No, sir. No more. She needed to think about something else.

Something sleepy.

At least it was quiet.

Almost quiet.

If you didn't count the hum of the refrigerator. Or the sadistic tick-tick-tick of Jillian's desk clock. Why did people buy clocks that ticked so loudly?

Think about something else.

A bottle of Evian on the end table caught DaVinci's eyes. Why did Jillian only drink Evian water? She said she was trying to spend less. But if Jillian wanted to save money, why did she drive a car that smelled like top-shelf leather? And why didn't Everett live here to save on rent? And what time did the sun rise in Florida? And dear God, *why couldn't she please just fall asleep*?

DaVinci's stomach growled at an alarming decibel.

"Oh, good grief," she muttered, tossing back the 600-count pima cotton sheets.

She gave up on sleep and got out of bed. She crossed to the kitchen, her way illumined by moonlight spilling through the blinds. The light through the slats created a pattern of light, dark, light, dark that reminded her of her favorite canvas from the *East Mountain 360* paintings: *Moonlight Sonata*.

She crossed to the refrigerator, gripping the handle but not opening the door.

When she'd decided to paint by moonlight, she hadn't painted the ocean by moonlight—too obvious. Or the mountains by moonlight—nearly as obvious. She'd painted her driveway, and the bit of East Mountain Drive you could see when you looked down from the height of her roof. She'd captured the way moonlight rendered the recycle bins, the twins' bikes, the tilting mailbox—*everything* in sharp relief: *dark, light, dark, light.* It had been her best piece in the series.

Except . . .

Now it didn't exist. Her best work had simply . . . ceased to exist. Poof! Gone.

Her stomach clenched, but this time it wasn't from hunger.

Dropping her hand from the refrigerator door, she fought a tightening sensation in her throat. *No more tears.* And no food, either. Food wasn't going to fix anything that mattered. She turned from the fridge and gazed at the hide-a-bed, at the light spilling through the blinds. And then, before she could second-guess herself, she crossed to the door, stepped into a pair of flip-flops, and slipped her leather purse over her shoulder.

She needed to get out and drive somewhere. Or drive nowhere. It didn't really matter.

She opened the door.

Oh.

Car keys . . .

Back in Montecito, Jillian had always had a key caddy in her room, and sure enough, there was a caddy here on a shelf by the door.

Keys in hand, DaVinci slipped out of the apartment and into a black-and-white world drenched in moonlight. Five minutes later, she was driving past one of central Florida's ubiquitous lakes. The night air was warm, and it was tempting to grab a quick swim by moonlight. Except for the minor issue of Everett's grim warning as to the probable number of alligators in Florida's waterways.

She wanted to capture the lake, to preserve it on canvas, bright, and bathed in silver. Pulling across the oncoming lane, DaVinci parked beside the lake on the road's sandy shoulder. The moon, high overhead, lit everything in sharp relief. Across the lake, an old dock tilted into the water at an angle suggesting neglect. Two support beams had rotted away already.

Movement caught DaVinci's attention. Ripples on the lake. The air was still—heavy and hot, without any breeze. The disturbance might have been caused by reptiles, although DaVinci couldn't see any. The circles on the water spread outward, concentric rings bumping into one another and retreating, which then restarted the cycle. On this rippled surface, the reflected moon split into a hundred tiny moons, a meteor shower of luminous bodies.

Pulling out her phone, she rested it on the car door to take a picture of the broken moons so she could paint them later. She forgot to turn off the flash, and it flared in the dark, jolting and unanticipated. Her phone returned an eerie image: hundreds of glowing orange-gold dots spread across the lake. At first, she assumed the phosphorous dots were fragments of reflected moon, but then she realized what they really were. Dozens—hundreds, maybe—of glowing *eyes*. Freaking alligator eyes, rising stalklike just above the surface of the water. A shiver clambered along her shoulders.

What were they all staring at *her* for? Actually, she didn't need an answer. She started the engine again, spewing gravel and sand as she sped away.

Although she wasn't ready to admit it to herself, her drive wasn't entirely aimless. She began to note landmarks Jillian had pointed out earlier. The Piggly Wiggly. A Burger King across from a McDonald's. The Sun Trust Bank where Jillian had gotten cash. The corner where the food truck had sold them Cubanos. DaVinci was in downtown Wellesley, such as it was.

Flicking her blinker on, she turned down the road leading to Littlewood's lab, where she and Jillian had driven earlier in the day. Where Everett had said cheerful things about monsters in lakes and the possibility of things going worse if you tried to fix the past.

She was almost to the lab. What was she thinking, driving to Littlewood's lab in the middle of the night?

She knew what she was thinking. What she was doing here. Might as well admit it.

"I'm fixing things, okay? Do you hear that, space–time? I'm coming for you."

Saying it out loud made it real. She was going to do this. Continuing past the "No Trespassing!" sign, she drove well above the posted fifteen miles per hour. Why bother adhering to the laws of the land if you were about to trespass the laws of nature?

She couldn't let herself think about that. This was the right thing to do. Her life needed fixing, and Klee and Kahlo had made horrible messes of their lives thanks to her, and DaVinci wasn't going to just stand by and let things be.

There it was: the building with the large "42" painted on the side. The building housing Littlewood's basement laboratory. And a time machine that could change everything. She stopped the car. She was here. It was time to go inside and fix things.

She stepped out of the car, but then something

made her hesitate, and she stood frozen in place, one hand resting on the handle of the car door. What if Everett and Jillian were right? What if returning to "fix" things made something *else* worse? What if she fixed things so Klee and Kahlo could enroll at UCLA, but then a big earthquake struck the campus, killing them both? How would she feel, knowing she had put them there? But what if enrolling at Santa Clara University meant they got in a multicar collision, and she could have prevented it?

"Stop it!" she whispered into the quiet night. *"Ugh!"*

This was getting her nowhere. There were risks everywhere, no matter what twists or turns history took. You just did your best and got on with it. You couldn't stop to worry about every possibility or you'd end up . . . *paralyzed*.

"Says the woman standing still as a statue," muttered DaVinci. And then she let out a single gruff laugh. In her borrowed white nightgown, she must look exactly like a Grecian statue. Or Roman, perhaps.

But she wasn't a statue, and she refused to let her circumstances paralyze her. It was time to fix the mess she'd made. If she didn't go in there and do it now, she might not get another opportunity. She closed the car door, locking it just to be safe. It was a seriously nice car. She was about to put the keys in her bag when she remembered she needed the code printed on the key fob to unlock the laboratory door.

On her way to the stairwell, DaVinci noticed someone had left a light on inside. She shook her head. Arthur Littlewood was a classic absentminded professor. He was the *definition*—no, the *poster child* of absentminded professors. A tiny grin bloomed on her face. She'd actually missed the old guy. She was going to adopt him as her crazy uncle.

"Meet my crazy Uncle Arthur," she said, reaching for the keypad to unlock the door. "He's mostly harmless, unless your name is Mr. Space–Time—"

DaVinci broke off and stilled her hand in midair.

What was she thinking, betraying Arthur Littlewood's trust like this? What would he think of her after this?

"Ugh!" She groaned and covered her face with her hands, pressing her bowed head against the door.

The door that was . . . *vibrating*?

What the heck? Actually, it reminded her of the vibrating sensation caused by the time machine in action. Maybe Littlewood *was* still inside. She peeked through the window, but it wasn't Littlewood she saw. It was *Quintus*.

"Oh. *Duh.*"

Quintus who worked the night shift as security for Littlewood. Quintus whose presence meant she'd come for nothing.

The door vibrated more insistently. What was Quintus doing, up and burning the midnight Tesla coils? Eyes narrowing, she examined Quintus where he stood not far from the machine's travel platform. His calves were exposed, but the rest of his freaking gorgeous, *of-god-like-aspect* self was wrapped in a blanket. Who wrapped themselves in *blankets* in Florida, for goodness sake? He ran a hand through his hair—short, dark, and cut in a severe way only the very attractive could carry off. With that jawline and those high cheekbones, carrying it off was not a problem.

He was hovering over the podium that controlled the time machine. Was he bored? Experimenting? Planning a jaunt to the past to make use of the world's most generous ATM? DaVinci felt a chill running up her spine. What was it he'd said about retrieving Caesar to make America great again? No. He wouldn't. There was no way he would *actually* bring a duplicate Caesar here. Was there?

But what was he doing firing up the machine *by himself*?

She was jumping to conclusions. Quintus was probably doing something Littlewood had asked him to do. But why would Littlewood have Quintus time travel in the middle of the night? Wouldn't time traveling—which meant *leaving the lab*—be a little counterproductive to lab security?

DaVinci reached for the door handle and then cursed softly. It was locked.

Duh.

She keyed in the door code and waited for the mechanism to cycle through its unlocking protocol. And that was when she realized something important. Quintus wasn't wearing a *blanket*. He was wearing a cloak. No—*a costume*. He was dressed like some kind of Roman centurion or whatever they called themselves.

"Oh my God," she whispered. All at once, the pieces came together. Quintus the security guard really was secretly using the machine to send himself back to Rome to grab Caesar!

He stepped onto the platform just as she entered the lab.

"Are you freaking insane?" she shouted, running toward him.

Quintus, of course, couldn't hear her over the roar of the machine. She was going to be too late. Forcing herself to run faster, she waved her arms at him, which proved to be as useless as shouting.

What would Princess Leia do?

Leia would shoot him with a blaster. And if she didn't have her blaster . . .

Roaring like Han Solo bluffing the storm troopers, DaVinci ran straight at the security guard, aiming to knock him right off the platform.

30
·*QUINTUS* ·
Florida, July

Thus far, Quintus had watched Everett operate the controls of the time machine on fourteen journeys to the Ancient Library of Alexandria. Moreover, so often had Quintus read the instructions for the operation of the machine that he had committed large portions to memory. Some of the words still gave him trouble, but for these he'd brought his Latin-English dictionary.

Troublesome words aside, he was finally prepared to return to Roma where he would deliver the letter from Gaius Julius Caesar to Gnaeus Pompeius Magnus as he had sworn to do. Quintus knew he would need to act swiftly once he arrived—the journeys to Alexandria lasted for only six minutes. Fortunately, the device could be configured to transport him to any location in Roma. To gain swiftest access to the general, Quintus was going to send himself to Pompey's massive residence-*cum*-theater on the Campus Martius.

And, should he fail to meet Pompey on the first

journey, Quintus would repeat his journey until he *had* met him. Some of the visits to Alexandria had necessitated this approach. It required patience, and for patience, there was no one like a soldier who had served under Caesar.

Five hours remained until either Littlewood or Everett was likely to appear. Enough time for seven or more visits, should they be necessary. Tonight he would accomplish the mission Caesar had charged him with almost six months ago, by his reckoning. Tonight!

And after?

Caesar's charge belonged to a world now gone for more than two thousand years.

Quintus pushed the thought aside. It mattered not what he did *after*. Delivering his message faithfully was all that mattered.

With a soldier's precision, Quintus began to change from the garb of the Floridae to that of a soldier of Roma, an *immune* of the Eleventh Legion.

He knew only one way to dress: swiftly, as if an enemy had caught the camp asleep and out of uniform. How familiar the process of belting his tunic, of tugging the overly long garment above his belt to the height proper to his rank. He laced his hobnailed soldier's boots, recalling how Jillian, visiting his *domus*, his borrowed home, had mistaken his masculine boots for the sandals of a modern woman. She had remarked that she loved gladiator-style sandals. Quintus's offense at the remark was sharp and natural, but he had hidden it. No one in this age acknowledged the sacred calling of service to Roma, the sacredness of each leather lacing, each nail in his boot.

He was nearly done. He grasped the apron of

leather strips, his *pteruges*, upon which were displayed the decorative tokens of the battles he had fought in Gallia. Now his scabbard was ready to receive his gladius, and he secured both to his belt. With his sword in place, he felt once more like a true Roman soldier.

Lastly, he reached for his *sagum*, the woolen cloak that had kept him warm many a night in cold Gallia. The sagum, worn over his shoulders, was secured in place with a *fibula*, a pin from an age before buttons or zippers. It would be awkward to work the machine's controls while wearing his cloak, but he would not risk offending Pompey by presenting himself less than properly dressed.

Perhaps, though, he would stoke the fires of the great time travel engine before donning his sagum. Setting both fibula and sagum down, Quintus followed the written instructions, occasionally consulting his dictionary. As he labored, he felt himself entering a cool and collected space in his mind. It was like the minutes before a battle. Some of his fellows had emulated the *Celtae* or *Belgae*, driving themselves into an emotionally frenzied state before battle, but most tried to follow the example of their great general, who grew cooler and calmer in the hours before engagement.

Only when the machine was screaming its final cries did Quintus take up his cloak again, securing it by means of his fibula, an ornamental and impractical one given him by his wife. He checked one last time to be certain he still had Caesar's letter to Pompey. This done, he rechecked the coordinates on the screen one final time, experiencing a momentary fear that he might have mistranslated the word *longitude*. Hastily, he flipped his dictionary open to check the word.

While he was confirming the word was correct, he noticed movement in his peripheral vision. A person. Running toward him. Instinct took over and he dropped the dictionary, his hand swinging automatically to his gladius. His sword was already out by the time he registered, with shock, that it was the visiting girl from earlier in the evening. Weaponless, wild, and fierce, DaVinci ran at him, her green eyes flaming cold fire.

31
·QUINTUS·
Florida, July

On Quintus's third journey with Everett to the Ancient Library of Alexandria, something had gone wrong. Quintus and Everett had been ready to travel, standing on the platform dressed in first-century-BC clothing, when Littlewood had suddenly leaped toward them, pushed his way onto the platform, and made a last-minute alteration to the screen.

At least, as Littlewood later explained to Quintus, he had *meant* for the alteration to be last-minute. As it turned out, Littlewood didn't clear the platform in time and was unintentionally transported to the first century BC along with Quintus and Everett.

Littlewood, suddenly in Alexandria, hadn't considered the necessity of keeping quiet to avoid attention and had launched into noisy apologies (and considerable hand-wringing). Quintus's quick thinking saved the day, or at least prevented raised eyebrows among the Alexandrian librarians. Quintus threw his *sagum* over Littlewood's shoulders to hide the professor's odd clothing, while shushing him and secreting him behind a massive column.

This had left Everett free to retrieve Aristotle's long-lost writings on comedy. Discovery had been averted, and the three had returned home with Alexandria none the wiser.

But tonight, when Quintus Valerius found himself in first-century-BC Roma with a twenty-first-century girl, his next step wasn't immediately clear. Should he throw a cloak around her? Order her to stay put while he ran to deliver the message to Pompey? Things had worked out fine with Dr. Littlewood's accidental travel, but this girl was *not* Arthur Littlewood.

She was neither apologetic nor a wringer of hands. She was whispering loudly—*berating* Quintus, of all things—in such a constant stream of words that he had no chance to reply.

He had greater reason to berate, but he forced himself to ignore the girl's unceasing chatter and regroup, returning his sword to its scabbard.

He had to decide quickly: Should he abandon his mission for the time being or press on? He'd lost a full minute already, and his window of opportunity had been small to begin with. The girl was certainly a nuisance, and worse, had the potential to do what Littlewood had not done—draw unwanted attention to both of them.

Quintus glanced at her—she was still chastising him, albeit in a whisper. Quintus judged it might prove difficult to force her into silence, never mind into hiding. He had not studied war under Rome's greatest general without learning to distinguish between a time to press on and a time to withdraw and await better opportunity. This was one of the latter times.

He returned his attention to the girl, who was still addressing him.

"Assuming you have a plan, which could still misfire in a zillion ways, including our being seen *right now* by someone who shouldn't see us. And who knows what effect—"

"Silence!" commanded Quintus.

Even the crickets that had been chirping halted their song.

The girl, however, glaring at him, began again in her loud whisper. *"Have you even heard a single thing I've been saying?"*

"Against such an outflow of words, the very gods could hardly defend themselves," Quintus replied dryly.

At this, the girl fell silent. Her cheeks colored brightly, highlighting the tiny freckles sprinkled along the tops of her cheeks. She was distractingly pretty.

To better order his mind, Quintus turned from her. A breeze wafted the scent of lavender past them, forcibly reminding him of his home, of the herbs his wife tended and dried.

His jaw clenched; he had to focus on present safety, not nostalgia.

Naturally, the girl chose that moment to resume her tirade.

"You don't need to *defend* yourself from my words. You need to *listen* to them. There's a big difference. Besides, everything I said is true. You can't bring Caesar to Florida!"

That was her fear? This at least, he could allay.

"Caesar is not in Roma at present."

She glared at him.

"Nor have I any plan to bring him to your land."

At this, she made a grunting sound and crossed her arms over her chest, drawing Quintus's attention to the region. His face warmed and he looked away a second time, fixing his gaze on the structure surrounding them. It was solid Roman concrete, variously brick-faced, white-painted, or frescoed, and achingly familiar.

"You must not be seen," he said quietly to the girl. "And if you speak in a manner so . . ." He struggled for the English word and then gave up, using the Latin word in the hopes it would translate well. "So *assiduis*—"

"I am *not* the one behaving like an ass here, thank you very much!"

"You mistake my meaning. I was at a loss for the English word." Quintus paused. Recalled the word. "I meant *incessant*. If you do not cease speaking, you will draw attention to us, which has the potential for damaging the historical time line."

At this, the girl's eyebrows rose. "So you *are* aware that's a danger."

"*My* actions will not endanger the time line."

"Says *you*."

With this, the girl bent down and retrieved something from the ground, which was tiled in a patterned mosaic. "You might want to make sure no one finds this lying around."

Quintus frowned. It was his Latin-English dictionary. He recalled having dropped the book on the platform. Evidently, it had traveled along with them. Such an item—a bound book—was next to unknown in Roma, and certainly this format, with its brightly lettered cover and perfectly even printing inside, would have puzzled every scribe in the vast empire.

"Your caution is commendable," he said, watching her tuck the bound book into her handbag. "Our return should commence shortly."

He wasn't sure how much time had passed. Attached to his belt by a strip of leather, he kept a four-minute hourglass—one that he and Everett used during trips to Alexandria. Because of the girl, Quintus hadn't had an opportunity to start the timer, but he did so now, upending it and sending the sand rushing through the narrow funnel.

The girl seemed to have decided she'd said enough, and the two awaited the return journey in silence, giving Quintus an additional opportunity to observe her. In the moonlight, her fair hair seemed almost to glow. He had a sudden and melancholy remembrance of his wife, of her dark tresses as he'd lain with her, sleepless under a moon-bright sky following some fight or other. There had been many.

The girl beside him sighed. "How much longer?"

He consulted his hourglass. It was empty. The four minutes had passed. Quintus frowned. Something was wrong. Before he'd started the hourglass, many minutes had already passed. They should not still be in Roma. Something was wrong.

"Well?" demanded the girl. "How long?"

"I know not. Soon, I believe."

The girl shivered slightly. Quintus, seeing her state of dress was unequal to the nighttime chill, began to undo the pin securing his cloak.

"Listen. I don't know why you're here," said the girl, breaking the silence, "but since you didn't already defend your actions with some story about *Littlewood told me to*, it's pretty obvious you didn't ask permission to use the machine."

Quintus bristled. With such an object at stake, what need had he of *permission*? He had sworn an oath to Gaius Julius. Not that the girl would be capable of understanding what such a thing meant. He ceased attempting to remove his cloak for her use. She could shiver.

The girl grabbed several curls falling across her forehead and tucked them neatly behind her ear, which was tiny and perfect and pale as the moon itself.

"When we return," Quintus said coldly, "you will depart and allow me to proceed on my mission."

"It's a mission?" she asked.

Quintus nodded in reply. He was well aware she would assume he had received his "mission" from Littlewood. But this suited his purposes, so he did not specify differently.

"Why didn't you say so to begin with?" she demanded.

"I am not required to explain my actions to you."

"Hmmph," grunted the girl, as though she didn't believe him.

Absently, she reached for a curl and began to twine it round and round a finger. Quintus wondered what its texture would be, run between his own fingers, and then berated himself for the thought.

"Shouldn't we have been pulled back by now?" asked the girl.

Quintus's frown deepened. Both his own internal

sense of time and the hourglass said they should have, indeed, returned by now.

"Time seems this night to move at the pace of a stubborn ox," he said.

"You mean 'at a snail's pace'?"

Quintus shrugged, uncertain what manner of beast a *snail* might be. He did not care to request the return of his dictionary to consult it. Instead, he began counting the passing seconds. When he had reached 120, he could no longer hold out hope that the machine was preparing to return them. Something had gone awry.

At his side, the girl shivered again, more vigorously, and wrapped her arms around her torso.

"I understand not the nature of our delay," said Quintus. And then he added gruffly, "Would you like my cloak?"

She shook her head, sending the ruddy-gold strands in a shimmering dance across her shoulders and down her back.

"I fear something is amiss," he said, finally voicing his concern.

But before the girl could reply, Gnaeus Pompeius Magnus crossed into view.

And saw them.

And changed course, heading straight for them.

32
·NEVIS·
Florida, July

Special Agent Benjamin Nevis was wrapping up his Florida investigation and nearly ready to grant official approval to Arthur Littlewood, *PhD*, as a heavy-use consumer of electrical power. Nevis had run a series of unexceptional background checks on all the students employed by Dr. Arthur Littlewood. He'd met with the professor a second time, and even followed him clandestinely one night when he'd had nothing better to do. Littlewood couldn't have been more boring if he'd tried: dinner at Chick-fil-A, followed by an early lights-out at home.

Nevis's remaining task was to ensure the manager of the local substation liaised with Littlewood regarding his peak usage schedule. The substation manager, Ronnie, welcomed Nevis, ushering him into a stuffy office with faux-wood paneling and an in-wall AC unit that dripped noisily. Nevis gave the manager a schedule from Littlewood's USCF lab.

The substation manager examined the schedule,

scratching his balding head at the same time.

"Hang on a minute," Ronnie said. "Lemme check something."

He shook his ancient corded mouse and then clicked a few times. And then, frowning deeply, he made eye contact with Nevis.

"Well, when it comes to Arthur Littlewood's facility, sure looks to me like you're barking up the wrong tree."

Exerting considerable self-control, Nevis only raised an eyebrow at the colloquialism, uttered in a slow drawl. Nevis couldn't say goodbye to the South quickly enough.

Ronnie continued. "Whoever pinpointed Littlewood's USCF lab as a peak consumption facility didn't trouble themselves to do their homework."

Nevis bristled. *He* had pinpointed Littlewood's lab himself after being provided with only a name, a zip code, and an affected substation.

The manager scribbled a few lines on a sticky note.

"Here's the address you want in conjunction with Littlewood and stressors on the electrical grid."

Nevis examined the sticky note.

"That's a private address," said the manager, tapping the paper twice. "It's a unit in a former orange juice processing plant. Old military facility before that."

Nevis frowned. He didn't need a history lesson on greater Wellesley.

Ronnie continued. "The buildings have been turned into storage and light industry. Arthur Littlewood owns one of them, and *that's* where the high peak usage originates from. Not the university."

Nevis's pulse quickened. Why would a physicist of Littlewood's caliber fail to recognize the difference in electrical consumption between his two places of operation? It wasn't possible the professor was ignorant of the difference. So why hide the existence of the second facility? Suddenly Arthur Littlewood's nervous behavior made sense.

A smile bloomed across Nevis's pale face. The case had just gone from duller-than-dirt to interesting. Perhaps even . . . *incriminating*. This might prove to be the break he'd been looking for. Finally, a chance to do some real investigating. A chance to prove to the SAC *and* the bureau just what he was capable of, given the opportunity.

Arthur Littlewood, mild-mannered physics geek, was hiding something, and Special Agent Benjamin Nevis was going to find out what it was.

33

·*QUINTUS*·

Rome, 53 BC

In spite of his eagerness to deliver Caesar's letter to Gnaeus Pompeius, Quintus's first impulse on seeing the great general was to slip farther back into the shadows to hide the girl. Her presence complicated *everything*. He had no way of knowing why space–time had not yet returned them. And yet, he was here now, with Caesar's message, and Pompeius was here now, walking straight toward him. The too-perfect opportunity overruled his impulse to hide.

"Gnaeus Pompeius Magnus!" Quintus called aloud. Then he shoved the girl farther back into the alcove, whispering, *"Stay hidden!"*

The great man halted. "Quis es?" *Who are you?*

Quintus felt a moment's shock when he noticed himself mentally translating his native tongue into English.

"Est mihi, Quintus Valerius Posthumos," replied Quintus, stepping out from under the portico and into the moonlight.

"Iterem?" *Again?*

Quintus had to force himself to stop mentally translating.

"As you see, sir," replied Quintus.

"And did your commander order you to pester me until I delivered a different answer? One more to his liking?" asked Pompey.

"Forgive me, sir." Quintus bowed, his heart pounding. He must have already delivered the letter—already received the reply. Or rather, his other self had done so.

Which meant he'd come for nothing.

But as soon as the thought entered his mind, he banished it. So long as the delivery of the letter had lain in doubt, there had been no choice: it had been his duty to return.

"Well," said Pompey, "your general is as stubborn as a wild ass."

Quintus felt his hackles rise but held his tongue.

"I shall not take his wife's step-daughter's brat for my wife. Is the general grown so great that he thinks the leavings on his plate are to my palate?"

Upon hearing the insults, it took all Quintus's strength to regulate his features.

"Come, come," beckoned Pompey, his countenance softening. "You shall have a cup of wine for your trouble. I hold you not responsible for Caesar's obstinate nature. My own dear Julia was of such a temper . . ."

Here the great general broke off, paused, and swiped at his eyes. Pompey's former wife, Julia, Caesar's widely beloved daughter, was only recently dead. Quintus could easily believe no other woman, even one distantly related to Caesar, could take the place of Julia.

"Forgive me, sir. I intrude upon your rest. I shall depart," said Quintus.

"No, no. You do not intrude. I sleep poorly of late. Come along. We will share a glass of Falernian wine. You shall not bear reports that Pompeius Magnus sends Caesar's messengers away with parched throats."

Quintus was about to reply that he would not dream of spreading such a rumor when the general threw an arm around his shoulder and began marching him away from the girl. At this proximity, Quintus could smell wine on the general's breath; this would not be Magnus's first glass of Falernian tonight. Quintus was still considering how to extract himself from the invitation when the girl cried out, loudly, and in English.

"Hey! Where do you think you're going without me?"

Quintus turned.

Pompey turned.

The girl stormed out of the shadows, hands on her hips, the fire in her green eyes visible even by moonlight.

34

· DAVINCI ·

Rome, 53 BC

DaVinci had done what Quintus had asked. She'd stood there in the alcove, shivering to death, waiting for him to finish his conversation with Little Caesar in the toga (and no pizza to show for it, either), but when Quintus turned around and started marching off with the guy, there was no way in hell she was staying there, hoping he'd decide to come back for her the next time his calendar had an opening.

"Yes, you!" she shouted, after Quintus turned around. "Don't even think about walking off and leaving me here in the Coliseum to get eaten by lions or whatever."

Quintus stared at her.

Little Caesar in the toga stared at her.

And then Quintus smiled and, ignoring her, spoke in Latin to his new BFF wearing the bedsheet. The man asked a question. Quintus responded. The man laughed. Quintus laughed.

"I'm right here," she said. "I can hear you even if

I can't understand you. Seriously, Quintus, what the—"

"Silence," said Quintus, speaking to her in a tone she was already familiar with. And already hating.

"I'm not shutting up until you change your mind about leaving me here."

"Silence, *please*," said Quintus, an edge of desperation in his voice.

The little guy in the toga began talking to Quintus again.

She didn't know Latin, but years of Christmases and Easters with Grandma Shaughnessy, who loved a good old-fashioned Latin Mass, told her that Quintus's reply of, "Non, non," meant he was telling the toga-dude *no*.

Quintus stepped away from the man's side and spoke to her in hasty English.

"I've told him you're my slave—"

"You told him *what?*" demanded DaVinci.

"Cease speaking and listen!"

DaVinci, who had already opened her mouth to tell Quintus no *way* was she pretending to be his fantasy slave princess, now saw something in Quintus's eyes that made her shut her mouth. Quintus was worried. Like, *really* worried.

Quintus spoke in a hasty whisper. "If he thinks you're a slave from Caesar intended as a gift to my wife, then Pompeius won't assume you are intended as a gift for *him*."

"The old guy in the sheet thinks I'm a . . ." DaVinci held up her hand. "No. Just, no."

"Exactly," said Quintus. "I need you to behave like a slave—"

A Sword in Time

DaVinci, rolling her eyes, said, "You are completely delusional."

"Which includes *not* interrupting me whenever you feel like it and *not* staring at Pompeius with those luminous green eyes."

"Wait. 'Pompey-us' as in Pompey the Great?" Also, note to self: her eyes were luminous. *Luminous*. Who knew?

Quintus frowned. "Pompeius Magnus. You know of him?"

DaVinci shrugged. She knew of him if knowing of him consisted in maybe having heard of him once in some art history class when she was doodling instead of taking notes.

"Then you know—"

But DaVinci didn't find out whatever she was supposed to know because Pompey the Great was calling Quintus again.

"Stay here!" ordered Quintus. "And *stay quiet!*" Having given his orders, Quintus turned to rejoin the "great" man, who was actually pretty small of stature.

DaVinci scowled. And then tried to wipe the scowl off her face, guessing there might be disincentives in place for slaves scowling at their masters. Then she changed her mind and scowled anyway, because if she had to pretend to be a slave, she sure as heck didn't have to pretend to be a dutiful one.

After another few exchanges, Pompey approached her. She scowled harder. This, for some reason, made him laugh. He reached out like he was going to grab her hair, which was so not happening. She was just about to block him with some serious jujitsu, but then Quintus shouted something and Pompey the Great withdrew his hand. More like, jerked his hand back. DaVinci thought the correct term might have been *recoiled*, but she'd doodled her way through vocabulary lessons, too. In any case, Pompey-of-the-Great-Bedsheet walked rapidly away from her and seemed to be saying his goodbyes.

As soon as Quintus returned to her side, she muttered, "Finally."

He was fiddling with a piece of jewelry holding his cloak together, and then, before she could say she was fine, thanks, he'd whipped off his cloak and thrown it over her shoulders. The relief was immediate. The cloak was delicious with Quintus's body heat and even smelled faintly like him—leathery, which made no sense because the cloak was wool, if the itch factor was any indication.

"You didn't have to do that," she grumbled.

"Your garb is alien," Quintus replied. "This serves to hide it. Also, you are plainly shivering with cold."

"Hmmph," she grunted, conceding the point. Plus, it was nice of him to give up his cloak. She was thinking about saying thanks when he grabbed her by the elbow, steering her to a tiled walkway.

"Hey!" she said, "*Ix-nay* with the arm-gripping."

She jerked her arm free, and Quintus grunted at her, evidently exasperated, but he didn't grab her arm anymore. Instead, he steered her with a gentle touch between her shoulders at each of the dozen or so turns it took to get out of . . . wherever they were.

She was less sure by the minute it was the Coliseum. She *had* paid attention in Ancient Roman Architecture, sketching rather than doodling, and this place—while impressive and containing a high, rounded wall—looked more like a palace than gladiator central.

"What building is this?" she asked.

"It is a great villa Pompey *claims* to have built to glorify Venus Victrix." He made a sort of derisive noise that was possibly related to Pompey's claims.

"Is Venus . . . *whatsit* related to regular Venus, goddess of love?"

"Venus Victrix is that aspect of the goddess responsible for victory."

"*Huh.* Never heard of her."

For a brief moment, Quintus looked shocked, but then his face relaxed, like he was making an effort to hide his shock. Using a voice DaVinci associated with speaking to small, ignorant children, Quintus continued.

"Pompey seeks to aggrandize himself by creating religious associations in the minds of Romans between Venus, the goddess mother of Rome's founder, Aeneus, and himself. However, Pompey is too shrewd to have attempted to build his great palace within the *pomerium*."

"The pom-what-ium?"

"The sacred boundary of Rome."

"Oh, *that* pomerium," DaVinci said, recognizing the term. And then she remembered something else. "The first theater in Rome! I know about this building!" She looked excitedly around her. "Pompey built the first permanent theater outside the pomerium," she said, automatically repeating a phrase she'd once memorized for a test.

"To build it on the *Campus Martius*," continued

Quintus, "the Field of Mars, is also an act of hubris." And then, lowering his voice, he added, "The gods will have the last word, I think."

"Won't they just," murmured DaVinci. From what she remembered, Caesar was going to kick Pompey's bedsheeted butt right out of Italy.

They had just rounded a corner when Quintus gripped her elbow again. A group of men who were not just drunk, but *stupid* drunk ran crookedly toward them. She shrugged Quintus off, roughly.

"I can take care of myself," she muttered, glowering at him.

He raised one eyebrow, not bothering to contradict her.

Which made her even angrier.

In spite of her bravado, her heart was pounding, and she felt far more vulnerable than she was letting on. What was she doing here in ancient Rome? Why wasn't she *home*? The drunkards seemed to size Quintus up and decide it wasn't worth messing with him. They turned down another alley.

"Just so you know," DaVinci said, feeling braver now that the immediate danger had passed, "I totally would have *decked* Pompey the Great if he'd tried to kiss me or grab my hair or whatever the heck that was. And the same goes for you, buddy."

Looking at his muscled arms, she was struck by the fact that she probably couldn't deck him, but he wasn't going to hear that from *her*.

"I do not know . . . *decked*," Quintus said in reply.

"Punched. Struck. Knocked upside the head."

"You intended to strike Pompeius?" Quintus's eyebrow rose. "Then it is most fortunate I had the presence of mind to tell him you had . . . *pediculi*."

"What's that supposed to be?"

Quintus seemed to struggle for the English word but then found it. "Lice."

"You told Pompey the Great I had *lice*? Okay, seriously? That is so insulting!"

Although it certainly explained the recoiling.

"Indeed?" said Quintus. "I judged you would take it as a greater insult had he touched you."

DaVinci scowled. For the millionth time tonight. It was a facial expression she'd ditched when she'd left age fourteen behind, but Rome was apparently bringing it out in her again.

As they stepped through a perfect Roman arch and onto a new path, her situation came slamming back down on her.

"Oh my God," she murmured, her heart racing again. "We're still here. We shouldn't still be here. Quintus, why are we still here?" And then, in spite of her ban on arm-gripping, she grabbed Quintus's arm, which, not surprisingly, was firm as steel. "Seriously, what does it mean that we are *still here*? In ancient freaking Rome?"

"I know not," replied Quintus.

"That is not an acceptable answer!" She shouldn't still be here. She should be back in hot, sticky, twenty-first-century Florida. "In fact, *I know not,* has got to be the least acceptable answer ever spoken in history."

"I have no other answer to offer," Quintus said.

"Wait. So, like, what are we doing about this?"

Quintus said nothing, but he had increased his stride. Ahead of them was nothing but fields to one side and to the other . . . *Rome*. She was looking at

Rome. Which was wrong on so many levels.

"I asked you a question," she said to Quintus. Her voice had gone from angry to quavery. She hated when it did that. It was even more embarrassing than usual, contrasting as it did with Quintus's steady, deep voice.

"I do not know why the machine malfunctioned," said Quintus.

"Okay," she said. "Okay. Malfunctions can happen to anyone. Littlewood's a genius, right? I'm sure he'll fix it. Any minute. Right?"

Quintus didn't answer. Which was even less acceptable of an answer.

"So . . . what are we going to do?" she asked. She had to keep it together. "Where are we going?"

"Home," said Quintus.

"Whose home?"

"Mine. The home of my wife and child."

Hot Roman Dude had a *wife and child*? Wow. She had not seen that coming. But then she saw what *was* coming if the two of them showed up *chez* Quintus Valerius.

"*Um*, Quintus?" DaVinci felt her heart sinking. "You already exist here. You can't go home."

At which point Quintus stopped in his tracks. Even by moonlight, she could see he'd grown pale. And while she didn't understand a single thing exploding out of his mouth, she would have bet her *Janson's History of Art*, sixth edition that Quintus Valerius was making his way through every Latin swear in his dictionary.

35

·*QUINTUS*·

Rome, 53 BC

In his initial euphoria at finding himself still in Roma, Quintus had not considered the implications of a second Quintus already living here. Well, he had vaguely wondered whether this second Quintus had successfully delivered Caesar's message, but that was different from taking in the awfulness of the fact that another Quintus existed here and now.

Until the girl spoke, Quintus had been planning to return home, kiss his sleeping son, and lie with his wife. But none of this was possible. If his second self had already begun the two-week journey back to Caesar's camp in Gallia, Quintus could scarcely return to his wife and child. And if his other self was lying with his wife right now, he had even greater reason to avoid his home.

He uttered another curse.

"I'm so sorry," the girl said softly.

Pity changed nothing. He schooled his features, hiding his distress behind a mask of calm.

"It is unfortunate," he said. He turned to examine the girl. Her friends had spoken of her before she had arrived, and from their description, he had expected someone of more . . . *Amazonian* dimensions. Not this slip of a girl who looked like she might blow away in a strong wind.

"I can't believe I'm here," said the girl. "I, *um*, used to be an art student. There are art students who would give their dominant hand to visit *actual* ancient Rome." As she spoke, the girl looked about as cheerful as Proserpine on her annual visit to the Underworld. "Anyway," she continued, "we can assume that once Jillian and Everett and Littlewood figure out we're stuck here, they'll figure out a way to rescue us."

There was determination in her voice, but her nervous habit of winding her hair around her fingers belied her confidence.

"Perhaps," said Quintus. "But Littlewood has assured me space–time retrieves those who journey *every time*. This irregularity seems more likely to be the work of the god who controls space–time."

The girl did not appear to derive comfort from this suggestion. She shivered, frowned, and grasped another strand of her hair. His sister had had a pretty friend who did the same thing when she was upset.

His sister . . . They could go to the house of his sister.

But as he considered the idea, he realized it had no more merit than his earlier idea. In fact, it would bring the same potential complications as visiting his own house.

The weight of his situation settled heavily on his shoulders. If the gods had meant this as a reward for his prayers and sacrifices, there was much they had not taken into account. How like them.

"How long have you been gone from home?" the girl asked. Her voice was soft, and filled with more sympathy than she had extended thus far.

"I was a soldier in Gallia for four years before Jules Khan stole me from what you call Rome. During that time, I was sent thrice to deliver letters to Roma. The final time was seven months ago, by the reckoning of the time I have been in Florida. It was two days ago by the reckoning of this time, here in Roma."

"You must miss them very much. Your wife and your kid, I mean."

"Ours was no love-match," replied Quintus.

"Still, I'm sorry for, *um* . . . your loss?" The girl spoke as if asking a question.

Quintus had heard Pater Joe speak such words to the bereaved, and he believed the correct form of reply was to offer thanks, but the girl was already speaking again.

"I had to say goodbye to all the most important things in my life recently," the girl added. "So I get how hard it must be for you."

This, Quintus doubted very much, but he managed to grunt out a *thank you* anyway.

"How old is he? Your son?"

"Two years," replied Quintus. He felt a dull sort of ache in his throat. He wished he had been a better father to the child. "He is a beautiful boy. He takes after his mother, not me."

DaVinci laughed and then covered her mouth with her hand. "Oh. Sorry."

"Why do you apologize?"

The girl frowned. "I don't know. It's just something you say. I laughed because 'takes after his mother' is such a . . . *modern* thing to say, but we're in flipping ancient Rome. And you still said it."

Quintus felt a small smile tugging at one side of his mouth. "I have found that people express much the same sentiments in your time as in mine."

"*Huh.* Maybe. Although . . . your English is super formal. Just saying."

Quintus frowned. "I have acquired it through podcasts recorded in *Britannia*—in Great Britain."

"Well that explains a lot. If you really want to know how to speak English in America, you should watch more TV and movies."

"So I have been informed by your friends Everett and Jillian."

The girl laughed again. Her laugh was surprisingly deep. He would have called it *mannish* compared to that of his wife or of the camp women who followed the soldiers in Gallia.

"Dawn will break soon, and we are in Roma now," Quintus said aloud. "My soldier's cloak, worn by you, will draw attention. As will your garment, worn without the cloak. We must find you something more suitable."

"Hello," said the girl, flipping back the cloak and holding out a corner of her gown for inspection. "Long, flowy white dress. No sleeves. Totally Roman."

"You are *not* dressed as a woman of Rome."

"Whatever," muttered the girl. But she also wrapped his cloak more tightly around her garment.

Besides suitable clothing, he would have to find

lodgings. Somewhere safe to keep the girl. She could not be allowed to wander, that much was obvious. Her mannerisms, her attitudes, her lack of ability to speak Latin, and her exotic appearance . . . she would end up in the hands of slavers before the midday meal.

"It will be best," said Quintus, "if you are fitted with the clothing of a slave, lest you appear to be a runaway slave."

"That makes zero sense. If I'm not dressed like a slave, who's going to think I *am* a slave?"

"Everyone," replied Quintus, surprised at her ignorance. "You look like one of the *Celtae*, who dwell in Rome only as slaves."

"I *look* like a slave, so I must be one?" Her green eyes were full of fire once more.

Quintus, seeing she was not taking in the danger of her situation at all, attempted to explain it more clearly. "You will be safer dressed as a slave because others will assume you are under the protection of a Roman family and will hesitate to harm you. Or steal you," he added.

The girl muttered under her breath and then spoke aloud. "Fine. Let's get me some 'slave clothes.'"

For this, Quintus needed money. He glanced at the *fibula* holding his cloak around the girl's thin shoulders. He would have to sell the pin, as he had no other source of income or money. Fortunately, it was made of gold, except for the bronze clasp.

They made their way to the cluster of goldsmiths in the Forum where Quintus was able to find a dealer in jewelry who bought his ornate pin. With a small portion of the proceeds, Quintus purchased a cheap replacement *fibula*, and from a less prosperous part of the city, suitable used garb for the girl. This left him with only a handful of *sesterces*, which would pay for no more than two nights' lodging. He was going to have to find employment, and quickly.

As DaVinci accepted the used garment, she muttered, "If I get . . . *pedicures* from wearing this thing, I'm totally killing you."

Despite their gloomy circumstances, Quintus barked out a single laugh.

"What?" demanded the girl, brow furrowed.

"I believe you meant *pediculi*."

She glowered at him. "Whatever."

A smile pulled at Quintus's mouth, and he would have sworn she, too, was near smiling. She was a puzzle, both funny and fiery in a way not common among the women he had known.

They were now quite close to his family's *domus*, the home he had inherited from his father. It was not a fashionable part of town, but neither was it much frequented by thieves and thugs, and most importantly, it was a part of town where he knew he could find lodgings quickly. But first he must get the girl to change her clothing.

Quintus guided her to a quiet place where he knew the ground floor vendors would still be closed. Between the shuttered *tabernae*, the food and wine vendors' one-room shops, there were many small recesses where Quintus had hidden from his nurse when he was a child. One of these would serve as a private place to change.

He took the girl to one of the deeper recesses and handed her the slave tunic.

"I shall stand guard," he said, "although the street

A SWORD IN TIME

will be empty this time of morning."

"Are you sure?" asked DaVinci, her golden brows drawing together.

"My home lies hereby. I am sure."

"Fine," she muttered. "Absolutely no staring. Turn around." Placing both hands on her hips, she glared at him, waiting for him to turn.

Quintus turned his back to the girl, and *if* he wondered how much of her pale skin was freckled like her nose and cheeks, in his defense, it could be argued that he had lain with no woman for half a year and more.

The girl grumbled nonstop as she donned the woolen garment, calling down curses on any *pedicurelles* that might be hiding in the seams. Her abuse of the Latin word for lice did at least have the effect of diverting Quintus's thoughts from her milk-colored flesh.

And then, with a final curse, she shoved Quintus's right shoulder.

"I'm done. Satisfied?" she asked, a dour scowl on her face. "Do I look *Roman* enough for you now?"

In truth, if there existed a girl less suited to pass for Roman, he had not seen her. He swallowed, trying not to stare at her legs, which were longer than he would have expected for one so short in stature.

"Well? Am I slave-y?"

"Your resemblance to an unexceptionable slave has greatly improved," Quintus said.

"My resemblance to a *what* kind of slave?" Then she held her hand up, palm out. "You know what? I don't need to know. I don't even *want* to know. I. Don't. Care."

She punctuated each final word by shoving her former garment inside the same bag in which she had placed his dictionary. He considered asking to have his dictionary back, but decided it was best kept hidden. Besides, if they were to find themselves permanently settled in this century, the book would do her more good than him. She could study it for occupation once he'd settled her safely behind the closed door of whatever lodgings he could find.

He was about to tell her his plans for the remainder of the morning when he saw something that made the words catch in his throat. It was his son, racing ahead of his nurse, and laughing as only a two-year-old outrunning a guardian could laugh.

36
· DAVINCI ·
Rome, 53 BC

At first, DaVinci assumed Quintus was staring at the small boy like anyone would have done, given the decibel of the kid's shrieking laughter. She was just trying to decide if she should help the poor lady chasing after the boy when something unexpected happened. Without a word, Quintus turned to face her and then pinned her against the wall, pressing his body to hers and burying his face in her curls. Every point of contact between them crackled with electricity—and not the kind that meant time travel was about to happen.

"*I must not be seen*," he said. His breath was warm beside her ear. A shiver ran through her.

At least three responses ran circles in her mind, with *What the heck?* and *How dare you!* first in line. These utterances were, however, facing major competition from *What was that you said about finding a private room?* Because, *wow*. She could feel heat pouring off his body. She shivered. This was intoxication. Unstoppable, contagion levels of intoxication.

"*Quintus*," she said, but then she stopped, unable to remember what she'd been planning to say next. Even to her ears, her voice sounded warm and throaty. He was nuzzling his mouth along her throat. *Oh, dear sweet gods of Rome!* His pectoralis major pressed into the hollow along her breastbone, and *wow*, he was *built* . . .

He was also speaking again.

"*I must not be recognized*," he murmured into her clavicle. This time she caught what might have been anguish in his voice.

Anguish, it turned out, was a good antidote for intoxicating man-touch.

"*You know them?*" she whispered, suddenly alert to their surroundings.

In place of answering, he nodded and wove his fingers into her hair. Now he was clasping the sides of her face like he was going to give her a kiss, and not a *nice* kiss. So much for that antidote . . .

But he didn't kiss her after all.

"*Have they gone?*" he whispered. His lips brushed her ear as he spoke.

Which. Just. *Wow*.

She would have answered if speech had been a possibility, but her words had clocked out for the day.

"*He is my son*," Quintus said softly.

This information provided another inoculation against Quintus's hunk-magic. (This was totally a thing: Hunk. Magic.) She gave herself a mental shake and checked to see if the kid and the woman were there.

"I can still see them," she reported. The boy had paused to examine a stone.

"Tell me when they've gone," said Quintus. With his face buried in her hair like that, DaVinci couldn't see his expression, but she could hear pain in his voice.

His son. His *kid*. Laughing and running, here in Quintus's home town but totally out of reach. It must be killing him.

And then something happened. The boy stumbled as he tried to stand and sent up a wailing cry that would have made anyone with an ounce of compassion turn to look.

"No!" she whispered sharply, grabbing Quintus's head so he couldn't turn. "If he sees you and starts crying 'Daddy' or whatever, your wife is going to notice you making out with me. So. Not. Good."

At that, the fight seemed to go out of him. His head sagged until his forehead was resting on her shoulder. She could feel his muscles clench with each of the child's howling cries. Finally, the crying stopped, and the woman gathered the child in her arms and retreated.

It was safe now for Quintus to release her, but DaVinci didn't let go. She needed to hold *him*—and for a completely different reason than what she'd felt moments ago. She wanted to tell him she understood. That she got it. Or that she got some small part of what he must be going through, losing what mattered most. So she held tight for another few seconds, like she could use those seconds to pass courage from her innermost self to his. To tell him it would be okay.

Of course, it wouldn't be okay. And she got that, too.

Finally letting go of him, DaVinci spoke. "They're gone."

Quintus stepped back and released her, drawing a slow breath.

She followed his gaze. He was staring at the exact corner where the pair had disappeared. Of *course* he was. He would have known where they were going. *Home*. DaVinci's heart pinched for him.

"*Tata*," said Quintus.

She stared at him, not understanding.

"Tata is what Roman children call their fathers," said Quintus. "At least, where affection is strong. You asked," he added.

Had she? Oh yeah. She'd warned him that he didn't want his kid seeing him and calling him whatever Roman kids called their dads.

DaVinci didn't know what to say, which was a rarity, but she decided silence was the best course, which was even more of a rarity.

Quintus didn't seem to expect her to say anything. He was now busying himself tugging at his . . . *dress*, or whatever it was called. He seemed to be purposefully avoiding eye contact.

"Your wife's got beautiful eyes," said DaVinci, trying to dispel the massive amount of *awkward* that was now filling all the space between them. Filling the entire street. Possibly filling the Roman Empire.

Quintus, however, looked amused. Or . . . something. "Did you mistake the boy's nursemaid for his mother?"

"Oh. Nursemaid," said DaVinci, giving her forehead a slap. "Of course Roman toddlers have nursemaids."

Her companion frowned. "Not *all* children have nursemaids. Ours is a slave I was awarded in the victory over the *Usipetes*. She bore a child and has been in milk ever since, so she is nurse to the boy."

"*Huh.* Go figure. So *not* your wife then."

Quintus shook his head and then settled his hand on his sword. "We must find lodging for you. You will await me there while I seek employment." Hot, hunk-magic Quintus was gone. Anguished, devastated Quintus was gone, too. He was back to business.

Well, if he wanted to get back to business, she could handle that. "I can seek employment, too," she said. "I mean, if we're going to be stuck here awhile . . ." At the thought, something in her throat pinched, and she had to take a slow breath. No matter how hot Quintus was, she did *not* want to be stuck here *awhile*.

"You cannot seek employment," said Quintus.

She set her hands on her hips, ready to argue the point all day if she had to. She *knew* she was a hard worker, and she was not about to be babied by some hulking Roman soldier.

"You are already employed, in the eyes of Rome," said Quintus.

"What do you mean?"

He raised an eyebrow and gestured to her garment.

Oh. Right.

She'd forgotten.

She sighed heavily. "Got it. I'm your fantasy slave princess. Forgive me, oh master of masters. It slipped my mind."

Quintus's face reddened at her words, and she wondered if maybe he'd stumbled across something *besides* podcasts of conversational English on the internet.

"I'm kidding," she said.

He gave a curt nod. "Let us depart."

She had to take long steps to keep up with Quintus, and around every bend, there was something else demanding her attention, which honestly was making it harder to stay freaked out about being stuck in ancient Rome. She *was* freaked out, but the freaking was continually allayed by compelling examples of ancient art and architecture. A painted wall, a sculpture of a Roman god or goddess, a building fronted with fluted columns—it was all so fresh looking, not worn and chipped as she had imagined ancient Rome. Of course, it wasn't *ancient* at the moment. Her internal pendulum swung away from *totally Zen-with-being-here* and back to *terrified-to-be-here*. She really should have paid better attention in that meditation class.

The first two places Quintus tried to get a room were full, but the third had a single room on the fourth floor. As they traipsed up narrow, rickety stairs, DaVinci consoled herself that at least the view would be good from up top.

But as it turned out, there was no view.

"Hey," she said to the innkeeper, who was setting a tiny oil lamp on a shelf. "There's no window." She turned to Quintus. "We need a window. Not staying without a window."

Quintus, ignoring her, paid the innkeeper, who also ignored her and started trudging back down the stairs.

"Wait a sec," DaVinci said to Quintus. "Make him give us something better. I need a window."

"*Insulae*—that is, 'apartments' in Rome have no windows."

DaVinci stared at him, openmouthed. "No windows as in . . . *none*? Ever?"

Quintus ignored the question "You will stay here."

In fairness, he'd already answered the question. DaVinci sighed. No fourth-floor views. No *anything* views. Crossing her arms, she made a *hmmph* noise.

"I must find paid labor or we will starve," continued Quintus.

Her stomach growled. She could definitely use some pizza or pasta or whatever else ancient Romans ate when in Rome.

Examining the room, she saw there was only one mattress, shorter and narrower than a twin bed.

"I get the bed," she said. And now that Gruff-and-Grumble Quintus was back, she wasn't inclined to share it.

"It will have *pulices*," said Quintus.

"What is that supposed to mean?"

Quintus shrugged. "I do not know the English word."

DaVinci reached into her bag and pulled out the Latin-English dictionary, flipping to the *P*s. "How do you spell it?"

"P-V-L—no—P-U-L—"

"Found it. *Ewwww!* Fleas! Disgusting." She looked up from the dictionary. "Fine. *You* get the bed."

Quintus seemed to be attempting to hide a smile. "I must depart."

"Okay," said DaVinci. What else could she say? "So . . . I guess if space–time decides to start behaving, we don't have to be in the same place or anything, do we? Space–time won't care, will it?"

Quintus shrugged. "I know not."

Again with the unacceptable answers.

Having said this, he left the room and thudded down the stairs.

"Great," said DaVinci. She flopped on the bed. Then remembered about the fleas and jumped up, crossing to the far side of the room.

She surveyed her cell. There was nothing interesting about the room. Not even graffiti. Okay, there was one interesting thing. The oil lamp, which looked handmade.

"*Duh*, it's handmade," she muttered to herself.

She examined it, noting the hasty construction. She could knock out forty of these a day if Quintus couldn't find gainful employment. Of course, she'd need a good source of clay . . .

"*Ugh!*" she grunted. She was *not* planning to settle down and make clay lamps for the rest of her life. Space–time had better get its shizzle together, and fast.

"You hear that?" she said, tipping her head to the ceiling with the reprimand. Then, settling in the corner farthest from the flea haven, she tried to entertain herself by looking up a handful of words she remembered from the outdoor graffiti. The individual words were intended to convey highly insulting messages. She also remembered one three-word sentence. When she looked up the words, it turned out they announced to the world the amazing news that *Titus crapped here.*

"Oh, good grief!"

She closed the dictionary and shoved it back inside her purse, jostling her phone in the process. This, she pulled out and turned on.

"Hello, relic of the modern age," she murmured.

The glow was about three times brighter than what the pathetic lamp could manage. She adjusted the screen brightness to save her battery and then fumbled around in her purse for her portable charger, which turned out to be completely drained.

"Awesome."

She had 43 percent battery remaining. No charger. No *window*. And no idea when Quintus would be back. And she wasn't even tired, which ruled out sleep as a way to pass the time. She *should* be tired. She hadn't slept for a day, except on the plane from LA to Miami.

"How can I not be sleepy?" she asked her empty room.

The room had nothing to say to this, and after another minute of muttering to herself, DaVinci made a decision. She might be stuck in ancient Rome, but she sure as heck wasn't going to stay stuck in this dismal room without a view.

Standing, she dusted herself off and tromped down the stairs to check out Mr. Quintus's Neighborhood.

37

· *DAVINCI* ·

Rome, 53 BC

Taking a deep breath, DaVinci departed the *insula*. She wasn't going far. Getting lost in a city two thousand years in the past had pretty much zero appeal, but sitting in her windowless cell was only making her worry about whether or not she was stuck in Rome. She needed something more distracting than looking up dirty words in the dictionary. What she *needed* was her paint box. Or a redo button for several of her life choices in the past week. Yeah, a redo button would be excellent.

Moping sure wasn't going to help. DaVincis were made for action, not moping. What was it Halley used to call her? A "force of nature"? So she didn't have a paint box. Fine. Did she have a pen and paper? She checked her purse, shoving her phone out of the way. No pen. Or paper. Of course not. But then, in a head-desk moment, she realized what she *did* have. Out came her phone. She knew precisely what use she was putting that 43 percent of battery life to. Pictures *now* could be turned into paintings *later*.

She gazed up and down the street. There was only one way to go; to the left the street dead-ended into a cluster of empty wooden tables. To the right, then. As she strolled, everything begged to be photographed, from the interesting faces passing by to the stone carvings over doorways to the freshness of the colors in a Rome that hadn't yet faded from glory.

She felt her breathing softening and deepening while she took in the sights and smells and sounds of the vibrant city. The street she walked down now looked nothing like the quiet, empty, shuttered street of an hour earlier. She hadn't noticed the narrowness of the passageway before, but at this time of morning, the street was so crowded it almost felt like the surrounding walls were pushing inward.

She joined the moving river of humanity, shuffling slowly forward, a stranger in a strange land. And to think, this was Quintus's home—this was his *normal*.

She stood aside for three men carrying bleating lambs over their shoulders, shouting what DaVinci assumed meant, *"Get the heck out of our way, already!"* Although it might have been, *"Last chance to get lamb at these prices!"* Her Latin vocabulary was practically nonexistent, other than the handful of graffiti insults she'd looked up. Happily, no one was showing any interest in a young woman surreptitiously snapping pictures with her iPhone.

There were men and women dressed like her, in short tunics that looked like they'd been worn day and night for years on end. Which they probably had; Quintus hadn't said anything about getting her a pair of "slave pajamas" to sleep in. A few children dressed in nicer (well, *cleaner*) clothes were tossing bits of flatbread to pigeons. One of the girls was trying and failing to catch a pigeon.

"Good luck with that," murmured DaVinci. When Klee and Kahlo were little, they had devoted hours to elaborate schemes for catching seagulls at the beach, resulting in similar levels of success.

Turning from the children, DaVinci examined the faces of the adults rushing past. Almost everyone she saw looked exactly like her idea of *Italian*. Glowing olive-toned skin, brown or hazel eyes, and extremely healthy heads of dark hair. It made her feel slightly anemic. It also made her wish she had some paper and a box of Conté crayons. She was buying some as soon she got home. And new paints and brushes and—

It hit like a punch to the gut: she was *assuming* she would get home. But what if she didn't? Her stomach knotted. What if she was stuck? She thought she'd felt alone before, in her own time surrounded by people who didn't share her memories, but what if she never made it back? It would be a completely different kind of alone, trapped here. What if all she had was a phone full of images of her friends and family? Hastily, she turned her phone off. Then turned it back on to check the battery. Down to 41 percent. She supposed if she were stuck here, she could get some paints and paint pictures of her friends and family from her phone photos. At least that way she'd have *something* to remember them by.

At the thought, she had to swallow back tears.

She would *not* let herself think like this.

Littlewood was a genius. He would be hard at

work figuring out what had gone wrong and how to fix it. She had to keep her fears at bay. Stay busy. Keep occupied. Her phone had lots of battery left. She decided to stay the course with *Project Capture Ancient Rome on Camera*. More pictures. Less worrying.

She began retracing her steps from earlier in the morning, thankful for her pathologically accurate sense of direction. Soon she was passing graffiti she recognized and crossing a wide street that had been empty earlier. Now it was filled with people hawking goods, gossiping over cups of wine, and rushing off to do . . . whatever Romans did. She turned into a quieter side street, realizing she'd made it all the way back to the street where Quintus had seen and recognized his son. The street where he'd pretended to make out with her. The memory sent a warm shiver through her. What would it have been like if he'd actually kissed her? She felt a tug in her belly and immediately rolled her eyes at herself.

As if.

Quintus might be a veritable Apollo—well, whoever that translated to in the Roman pantheon, but he was also rude and patronizing and, hello, *married* with a kid.

The thought brought back her memory of the look on his face when he'd seen his son but couldn't do anything about it. Talk about a kick to the cojones. Talk about *loss*.

And then she had an idea.

If she could find Quintus's house, maybe she could hang around and snap a picture of his boy. With her own fresh fears about never seeing her family again, she had a pretty good idea how much a picture would mean to Quintus. And as soon as she got home—because she was totally getting home again—she could print it out or even paint a miniature for him to carry everywhere. It was a genius idea.

As long as she could figure out how to ask, "Where's Quintus's house?"

Reaching for her dictionary, DaVinci felt a swell of purposefulness. It was refreshing; purpose had been hard to come by this past week. She wedged herself into a recess like the one where she'd changed clothes earlier, and in the privacy of that nook, she looked up a couple of Latin words: *ubi* for *where* and *domus* for *home*. These two words, in combination with Quintus's name, ought to get her where she needed to go.

She approached the first respectable mom-type she saw—well, mom or wet-nurse, it was impossible to tell which—and asked her the question.

"Ubi . . . domus . . . Quintus Valerius?"

From the woman's raised brow, DaVinci knew she'd mispronounced the words or put them in the wrong order or something equally awful. Or maybe slaves weren't supposed to speak to nicely dressed women. She tried repeating the words, but the woman said something that sounded like *ignorant* and pushed forward. After a few more tries and a few more *ignorants*, DaVinci consulted her dictionary again, where she learned *ignoro* meant roughly, "I have no clue."

She tried asking a few more passersby, who ignored her or said, "*Ignoro*," but then her luck changed. A stocky sixteen- or seventeen-year-old boy sporting classic bedsheet attire approached her, asking her something that included the words *domus* and

Quintus.

"Yes!" she replied excitedly. *"Si! Da!* Whatever! *Ubi domus Quintus Valerius?"*

The guy smiled and gestured toward a narrow alleyway overhung with upper stories that made it considerably darker than the street she'd been on. Just as her spidey-senses started tingling, toga-youth seemed to change his mind about showing her where Quintus lived. Shoving her into one of Rome's ubiquitous alcoves, he pinned her against the rough wall and slipped a sweaty hand under her tunic.

Her heart rate tripling, she shouted, "Hey! *Not* okay! Non!" Pushing against him, she tried to spin free, but he shoved her hard, slamming the back of her skull into a wooden shutter.

Automatically, she shouted, "Ow!" but there was no one to hear her in the empty alley. How could she have been so stupid! Deftly, the young Roman pinned both her arms with his hands while trying to wedge his knee between her thighs. She struggled to get a hand free—anything free—but it was a losing proposition; her legs were trapped between his legs and the wall. The Roman scum knew what he was doing, like he'd done it before.

Rage and some self-defense training kicked in, and DaVinci took a deep breath to shout at the top of her lungs, but the boy, sensing what she was thinking, slapped a heavy hand over her mouth before she got the chance. His knee parted her thighs. Instinctually, she screamed, but her voice was muffled beneath his hand.

This wasn't happening this wasn't happening this wasn't happening.

But it was. What would Leia do?

DaVinci's mind skittered, and then she realized that by covering her mouth, the youth was forced to hold both her wrists with one hand, which gave her better odds for freeing an arm. She wrenched a hand free and then reached sideways, bent her elbow, and delivered a sound strike to his nose with the heel of her palm. The hand covering her mouth slipped, and she shouted, "*Back off,*" managing at that moment to wriggle free and dash back into the adjacent crowded street. Chasing her, the boy shouted one of the obscenities she'd looked up earlier. She wished she could remember one to shout back. Turning, she saw him. A bloom of bright red streamed from his nostrils as he squared off in front of her. She braced herself for a solid knee-to-the-groin, but a few heads were already turning their way, and her assailant seemed to be having second thoughts.

Backing away, he shouted, *"Servum nequam,"* spewing blood and spittle at her, and then dashed away into the crowded street.

He was gone. She was safe.

He was gone he was gone he was gone.

Shaking, she rearranged her tunic, which had slid halfway down one shoulder. She was safe. This was a *victory*, so why was she shaking like a leaf? Leia would *not* be shaking, dammit! Tears welled in her eyes, and she blinked them back, furious at herself.

It was at this moment that a woman carrying five flat loaves of bread approached her. DaVinci, still blinking back angry tears, met the woman's eyes. DaVinci couldn't understand a single word the woman was saying to her, but, with a start, she recognized the wide-set eyes, the strong nose, and the determined chin. It was the nursemaid from earlier. It was the compassionate face of someone who seemed to guess what DaVinci had just been through, and *that* made it the face of a friend.

38
· DAVINCI ·
Rome, 53 BC

It took a few more Latin sentences from the nursemaid before DaVinci heard any words she recognized, but she was pretty sure *vino* meant the same thing in ancient Rome that it meant in her time. While she felt more like throwing back a sugary black coffee, something told her neither sugar nor coffee were making their way to Italy for a millennium or more. And honestly, maybe something with alcohol would be more settling at the moment.

"*Vino,*" she said to the woman. "*Vino, si.*"

The woman laughed and murmured, "*Vino, sic. Vino, sic,*" and a whole bunch of other things DaVinci couldn't understand.

But she could follow the woman to the *vino, no problemo*, and hopefully to a place where she could sit down a moment and let her heart rate return to normal. The back of her head was throbbing slightly. Was wine an analgesic? It couldn't hurt.

Besides, she'd gone to all this trouble to get a

picture of Quintus's offspring, and this woman knew the answer to the combination of *ubi* plus *domus* plus *Quintus*. DaVinci sure as heck wasn't going back without the toddler's picture, not after what she'd been through.

On the way to *domus Quintus Valerius* or whatever it was called, DaVinci managed to dig out her dictionary and flip it open to a page with "to speak" on it. She then informed her companion, "I no *dicere* Latino," which was apparently a butchered enough version of the sentence to convince the woman of its truthfulness. From that point on, the woman began to add hand gestures to everything she said.

Some of the gestures made sense: miming taking a sip from a cup. Others left DaVinci baffled, and could have meant anything from "hunger" to "menstrual cramps" to "when's the baby due?"

The woman repeated the gesture, tapping her belly again and then tapping the loaves she carried.

Hoping her new BFF was asking her if she wanted one of those fresh loaves of bread, DaVinci mimicked the belly gesture, following it by pointing to her mouth and nodding vigorously.

This made the woman laugh, but to DaVinci's disappointment, the nurse didn't offer her any of the bread she was carrying. Maybe it was rude to eat in the streets. They reached what she took to be Quintus's *domus*, and the nurse brought her to the back and into a kitchen. Or . . . *possibly* a kitchen. Without a dishwasher, fridge, or stove, it was hard to be sure.

DaVinci was instructed to sit on the floor, which was tiled in a black-and-white geometric pattern. She *hoped* "sit down" was the instruction, at least. She sat—

collapsed, really—and sighed heavily. This was *so* not the morning she'd planned for herself.

The woman reached down to hand her a piece of bread. Very dry bread. Not the fresh stuff she'd been carrying. Well, beggars couldn't be choosers, and all that.

DaVinci lifted the hunk to her mouth, but the woman flapped her hands, saying, *"Non, non, non,"* which didn't take a lot of imagination to translate. DaVinci set the bread down in her lap and awaited further instruction.

Was she supposed to say grace first? Wait for the nurse to sit down beside her and take the first bite? She felt the vastness of the cultural knowledge she was missing. She had absolutely no idea how to be Roman. The thought, or maybe just the entire horrible morning, brought a lump to her throat. That *vino* would be really nice right about now. How much *vino* would it take for a 110-pound weakling to drink herself into oblivion?

The woman was now speaking in a softer tone, which DaVinci felt pretty sure was meant to calm her. She swallowed and tried to look self-composed. The nursemaid, fussing with an *amphora* like those in DaVinci's art history books, had the look of someone who'd seen it all. Someone who'd beat up a few groping backstreet thugs herself. DaVinci felt a rush of gratitude. How did you say *thank you* in Latin? As soon as the woman's back was turned, she peered into Quintus's dictionary. *Gratias tibi ago* seemed like the right thing to say: *I give thanks to you.*

"Gratias tibi . . . uh . . . ahh-go," murmured DaVinci.

The woman turned and beamed at her, presenting her with a cup of wine. She then mimed dunking the bread in the wine.

"Oh," replied DaVinci, smiling. This was how you conquered dry bread. Genius. "Got it," she said out loud, dunking her bread.

"Gottitta," said the woman, nodding and smiling. *"Gottitta!"*

It took DaVinci a moment, but then she realized the woman was repeating a version of what she'd heard DaVinci say.

Out of sheer gratitude, DaVinci said, "Got it," two more times, nodding, smiling, and dunking her bread.

While she was chewing her bread, DaVinci heard the shrill laughter of a child from another part of the house. This seemed to be a cue to the nursemaid to run out of the room, leaving DaVinci to the pleasures of her daily, day-old bread soaked in vinegary, watered-down wine, and seasoned with peace, quiet, and safety.

"I will *never* take safety for granted again," she murmured, dunking her bread. If she were stuck here, she couldn't afford to take her safety for granted. If she were stuck here . . . It didn't bear thinking of. She wouldn't think of it. Lifting the sopping crust to her mouth, she focused on not thinking about it. Focused on chewing. Swallowing. Getting rid of the lump in her throat that kept popping back to say hello every time she thought of home. Fortunately, the wine had begun to warm her belly. Maybe she could ask for an escort back to the apartment . . . Of course, Leia wouldn't have demanded an escort. She would have simply kept her wits about her and not allowed dubious youths to lead her into dark alleys.

Today would have been a lot easier with a blaster, DaVinci thought gloomily.

The cries of the child had been quickly silenced, and now DaVinci could hear the voice of another woman. By peering around the threshold, DaVinci could *see* the other woman. She was unmistakably the boy's mother. Quintus's wife. Mother and child had the same eyes, the same eyebrows, the same rosebud mouths. Quintus had been right about the kid not looking like him at all. And, wow, his wife was young. Like, younger than Klee and Kahlo.

A moment later she heard a man's voice, calling, "Mucia!"

The young wife looked to where the voice was coming from.

Mucia, huh? The name wouldn't win any popularity contests in America.

The man called again. His voice didn't sound exactly like Quintus's, but she supposed that Quintus wouldn't sound exactly like Quintus after so many months spent speaking another language. Or possibly *this* Quintus had a cold.

The nurse and Mucia continued to converse. The man in the other room continued to call until Quintus's wife, looking in the direction of the voice, set her son beside the nurse and strode away.

When the little boy toddled into the kitchen, DaVinci felt the same flutter of purposefulness from earlier. She was here to make sure Quintus had something to remember his son by. Something to hold on to when they got back where they belonged. Well, where DaVinci belonged. She felt a pang of sympathy for Quintus. For him, going "home" wasn't the same thing at all.

Maybe she should record a short video . . .

The toddler, mumbling in what DaVinci assumed was baby-Latin, sat down next to her and accepted a piece of the newer, softer bread from his nurse.

In between bites, the child babbled to DaVinci, showing her various treasures he carried in a small straw basket. A seashell, a piece of saffron-yellow yarn, and some rocks. Lots of rocks. Which apparently needed lots of description. Possibly, he had named them all. DaVinci smiled and laughed and nodded and hoped the nurse would leave so she could take a picture.

After five or so minutes, the nurse turned to Quintus's son, pointed a finger and said something in Latin that probably meant: *Stay put, you.* The boy grinned and nodded and began talking to DaVinci about his rocks all over again.

DaVinci, wasting no time, snapped several pictures before starting to record a quick video of the lecture on rocks and their praiseworthiness. She'd recorded a full minute when she noticed a noise. A . . . *familiar* noise. Or rather, a couple of familiar noises. Of the variety made by couples who were, well—

"Oh my gosh. Seriously?" she whispered to the boy. Should she cover his ears?

He didn't seem to notice.

"Well, that's ruined," she murmured, stopping the recording. Pretty sure Quintus would not want to hear the sound of his other self and his wife getting it on in the back room.

The little boy, not at all bothered by the noise, continued to babble with his mouth full of bread. Swallowing his food, he held out a rock for DaVinci's inspection.

"*Hmm*, exceptional," she said, nodding gravely. The boy laughed, and they "discussed" several more rocks in his collection, which was a nice distraction because the moaning was getting hard to ignore. *Wow*, was it going to be a challenge to look at Quintus with a straight face the next time she saw him.

"So," she said to the little boy, "are Mommy and Daddy always this enthusiastic?"

The little boy's answer to her question was to hold his piece of saffron-yellow yarn up to DaVinci's hair.

"Hey, you nailed it," she said. "That is totally the color of my hair."

(It totally wasn't.)

The noise in the other room crescendoed and then, mercifully, stopped.

The little boy laughed and pointed to where the sound had been coming from.

And DaVinci laughed, too, because really, what else could you do?

At this point, the boy's nursemaid returned, muttering under her breath, shaking her head, and then sighing as she looked at Quintus's son. The nurse ruffled the child's hair and chucked him under the chin.

DaVinci stood up. While the *goings-on* had been going on, she'd searched the dictionary to find the Latin word for *depart*. She was just about to put the new word to good use when the little boy shouted and jumped up, crying, *"Tata!"*

The little guy ran out of the kitchen and straight into the arms of a hunky-looking Roman, who was rearranging his toga and was followed by Quintus's wife, rearranging her dress.

"Tata! Tata! Tata!" shouted the little boy.

It was the word Quintus said Roman kids used for *Daddy*.

The problem was, the man with Quintus's wife wasn't Quintus.

39
·*DAVINCI*·
Rome, 53 BC

DaVinci left the *domus* of Quintus Valerius feeling sick to her stomach. Why had she gone to Quintus's house? Why hadn't she just stuck to admiring the buildings and fending off assailants?

She never should have gone inside. She hadn't asked to see any of that. Or *hear* any of that. *Ugh!* She didn't want to know about the personal life of Quintus's wife. His lying, betraying, getting-some-on-the-side wife. Of course, she wasn't, technically, the wife of the Quintus *DaVinci* knew, but that hardly mattered.

She tried to push the whole thing out of her mind. She was in Rome. Everything she'd heard and seen was in the past. Like, the really ancient, dead-and-buried past. She shouldn't think about it.

The list of things she needed not to think about was getting long.

Her eye caught on a tiled mosaic set over a butcher's shop door, intricate and strangely beautiful considering the subject matter was, well, butchering. Down the walls on either side, she saw scrollwork painted in red and ochre, done with a tiny but confident brushstroke. The next shop she passed, and the next, and the next, were each painted and tiled with similar levels of detail, of care, of beauty.

But in spite of the beauty surrounding her, she kept finding herself drifting back to the sights and sounds of Quintus's *domus*. The Quintus she knew might not be affected by it like the Quintus she didn't know, but she wasn't stupid enough to think her Quintus wouldn't care. *Of course* he would care. So much for showing him the video. She should have just stayed put in her fourth-story, windowless jail cell. *Ugh.* How could Mucia have done that? And on top of the affair, she was apparently passing off another man's child as *Quintus's* child.

It really drove home the fact that there was no place for Quintus, *her* Quintus, here in Rome. He was as much a person without a place as she was, back home. More so, even. At least she hadn't landed in a strange new life where her closest friends and family members were engaging in illicit liaisons.

She sighed. Poor Quintus. He might be an oafish soldier, but he was a person, too. She could never breathe a word of what she'd witnessed. That, on top of everything else he'd lost? No. She wouldn't say a thing.

Compared to his life, her life back home was practically perfect.

Back home.

Her stomach twisted.

Not. Thinking. About. It.

She tried one last time to work up a decent level of enthusiasm for the perfect Roman arches and fountains with *S.P.Q.R.* carved above them, but it was no good. Her brain kept returning to the events at *Domus Quintus*. All the visual cues had been there to confirm the kid wasn't Quintus's kid. That little boy looked like Mucia, but he also looked like the man the kid had called *Tata*. Similar moles, the same hairline, identical ears—all things DaVinci had been trained to examine, categorize, and put to good use in portraiture.

There was no doubt that the man Mucia was sleeping with was the boy's real dad, and even though DaVinci hadn't even *known* Quintus twenty-four hours ago, she couldn't shake her feelings of sadness.

Only when a group of idle Roman men wolf-whistled and called after her, did she find something she could focus on and *stay* focused on: her safety. Back home, she would have responded with the finger, but here she was nobody. She was a slave. A slave who was eager to get back to the dullness of her windowless cell unharmed.

As she reentered the room, her lips drew tight and thin. It really was a horrible little room. She was tired now and contemplated napping on the bed, but . . . *fleas*. She considered her surroundings gloomily, but then she noticed someone had brought a few more things into the room. On the table that held the oil lamp, there was a flask and a small lump of . . . something. And on the far side of the room was a bowl. Ah. A piss pot.

"Lovely," she said, turning to investigate the flask instead.

It was full of the same watered-down, vinegary sort of wine the nurse had given her. The lump turned out to be a small wrapped packet of olives. She wondered if the offerings were an ancient Roman version of a hotel wet bar, handy and overpriced. But she was hungry. Starving, actually. She gobbled the olives—surprisingly salty—and drank the wine, which was much more appealing now that the olives had made her thirsty.

But vinegary wine turned out to be not so great for quenching thirst, so she decided to go back out again in search of one of those public spigots with clean running water. At least, she hoped it was clean.

She carried the now-empty flask downstairs and found a spigot where she got in line behind other people filling waterskins and amphorae. Once hers was full, she traipsed back toward the *insula* only to see Quintus returning. He looked tired and dejected, like he, too, had discovered the truth about his wife and son.

DaVinci had just cleared her throat to greet him when he looked up and saw her. As soon as he made eye contact, his expression changed from dejection to anger.

He shouted something at her in Latin, then closed his eyes and exhaled, muttering one of the salty graffiti words before addressing her in English.

"Upstairs with you. *Now.*"

DaVinci blinked. The imaginary Quintus she'd been feeling sorry for all day had vanished to be replaced by the real-life Quintus who was addressing her. Rudely, forcefully, and like he owned her. DaVinci bristled, the tenderness she had felt for him obliterated.

"It's lovely to see you, too, Quintus. Hard day at the office?"

Her sarcasm apparently made no impression on him. He grasped her by the arm and started hauling her up the stairs.

DaVinci's response was visceral and automatic, her free hand instantly balling into a fist. Although she stopped short of actually popping him one, she did yank her arm free while shouting, *"Not okay!"* Her heart was pounding. If he touched her again like that, she *would* pop him one.

Quintus made a noise that combined growling and exhaling but didn't try to grab her again. However, as soon as they reached the fourth-floor apartment, he launched into a lengthy chastisement.

"How could you *think* of going outside? Did you not understand my instructions? Were they not plain enough for even a simpleton to understand? Do you have any idea how dangerous this city can be for someone with your appearance?"

He glowered at her as they crossed the threshold.

She glowered right back. "Just because I agreed to wear slave clothing does not mean you are in charge of me. I choose what I do. And if I feel like taking a stroll outside, I will. Whenever and wherever I please. And without consulting you!"

"You cannot do as you please here. Someone like you could cause irreparable damage to the time line—"

"I don't see why the same isn't true for *you*!"

"Because I'm not a . . . a . . . *pulchra* young woman."

"Oh, now I'm *pulcrous*," shouted DaVinci. "Well

let me just grab my dictionary so I can figure out whatever the hell that's supposed to mean." She flipped angrily through the *P*s, went too far, and had to start over. She flipped past the *P*s a second time. And a third. "Dammit!" She threw the book down and glowered at Quintus.

The room was thick with the silence that followed.

"Beautiful," Quintus said at last. "It means *beautiful*. It is the most dangerous gift of the gods. Have you not heard of Helen of Troy? Men would fight to possess you and . . . and . . . do the sorts of things men desire to do with beautiful women."

DaVinci's green eyes widened. Did Quintus just call her beautiful? She blinked. Hadn't seen that coming. Crossing her arms, she attempted to glare at him, but being compared to Helen of Troy was taking some of the wind out of her sails.

"It is your unusual appearance," Quintus said in a softened tone. "What is rare and beautiful will always be desired by many and taken by the unscrupulous. Carelessness here is far more dangerous than carelessness in your own land."

His words struck home more than she wanted to admit. She *had* been careless. But hearing him say it restored some of her indignation at being bossed around. "Well, I *did* go outside, and I'm *fine*, thanks all the same." She wasn't fine, not entirely, but that was none of his business.

"You should have stayed here."

Up till now, Quintus had been pacing the room, back and forth. He paused, turned back toward the table, and pulled three lamps from a leather pouch. He lit them, bathing the room in warmer tones. It was a genuine improvement. Having completed this, Quintus spoke again.

"I arranged for food and drink to be brought to you," he said. "And even a personal . . . *latrina*, so that you would not need to use the public ones."

"Thank you," said DaVinci, begrudgingly.

"But I told you to stay here," said Quintus.

"Yup. Heard you the first three hundred times—"

"A child of five years would have displayed more sense," Quintus continued.

"Wow. Thanks." Her voice dripped sarcasm.

"An uneducated slave would have known better."

Anger roiled inside her. "You've made your point—"

"Even the most pampered and sequestered of Roman matrons would have consulted—"

Something inside DaVinci snapped.

"Well, unfortunately for you, I'm not a five-year-old." She paused, breathing hard. She was done with sarcastic responses that didn't convey her sentiments. It was time for clarity.

"You do not get to boss me around. Understand? You need to recognize that I *am not* your wife, and I am definitely, positively, *not* your property."

"That much is plain," Quintus shot back. "My slaves and my wife would not question a simple directive—"

"News flash: your wife and slaves don't tell you everything that goes on when you're not around."

As soon as the words were out, DaVinci knew she shouldn't have spoken them. Her eyes widened slightly, and her hand crept to her mouth.

Quintus frowned at her, but he seemed to decide that getting the last word in was more important than questioning her about what she'd said.

"A simple directive," he said. "I asked you to stay here. That was all I asked."

She sat as still as she could, wishing she could drop through the floor. Hoping he would continue ranting at her instead of asking her what she knew about his wife and slaves. How could she have said that? She shouldn't have let him get to her like that. She shouldn't have let it slip. She *was* acting like a child. Heck, maybe she should have stayed put like Quintus said. It was his time and place, not hers. He'd basically called what had happened to her out there, not to mention, she wouldn't be stuck hiding his dirty laundry if she'd just stayed inside.

Quintus, silent at last, must have decided he'd said enough. He reached for the flask DaVinci had just filled at the fountain. Finding it contained water and not wine, he cursed in Latin. After that, he gripped the table with both hands and leaned on it, seeming to focus on the empty olive packet. He took several slow breaths, in and out, his forearms rippling with tension. The table creaked ominously, and he straightened himself. And then, in much calmer tones, he turned and spoke again.

"With regard to my household, you ought not to speak ill of those whom you do not know."

DaVinci gave a short nod, ready to agree to anything so long as he changed the subject. All the fight had gone out of her. She was even willing to imagine a world where she wouldn't get into a shouting match with Quintus the next time he asked her to stay safe.

But Quintus, examining her face, seemed to sense that something was off.

"What is it?" he asked quietly.

"Nothing," she said quickly. And completely unconvincingly.

Quintus's brow furrowed. "You know something. What did you see when you ventured forth?"

DaVinci shook her head. Tried to match his gaze. Tried not to blink. Blinked anyway. Blinked a lot.

After examining her with his clear eyes for a full minute, Quintus spoke. "Caesar employed me as a messenger for several reasons. I learn languages with ease. I travel swiftly and can fight to defend what I transport. Most importantly, however, he employed me because I am a good judge of when a man is lying or telling the truth. You are hiding something."

DaVinci swallowed uncomfortably. Tried to avoid eye contact. But Quintus stepped closer.

"What are you hiding?"

"Trust me—you don't want to know."

"If it concerns my slaves or my wife, I have no wish to remain in ignorance."

DaVinci winced at the conviction in his voice. Her stomach knotted.

She took a slow breath.

And another.

And told him everything.

40
· *QUINTUS* ·
Rome, 53 BC

What the girl told him was impossible. His *wife*? To dishonor herself so? To dishonor *him* so? It was unthinkable. The girl must be lying. How could she be telling the truth? But her face . . . In her face he had detected none of the signs that betrayed liars. His stomach sank. A memory returned—his wife whispering to one of her friends at a party, pointing to another man. Refusing to repeat what she'd said when Quintus had asked, saying it was nothing. He had known her for a liar from that evening.

There had been rumors when he struck the marriage bargain, too, but he had ignored them. The alliance had been a good one for the Valerii.

"I'm so sorry," the girl was saying. "I shouldn't have said anything."

Quintus had almost forgotten DaVinci was there.

How could Mucia have been so false? And for so long? To have lied about their son? A dangerous rage began to fill him. The child was not his son. He felt the truth of it. Had he always known? Always turned a blind eye?

"I shouldn't have told you," the girl said, speaking again. "You should just try and forget I said anything."

"Forget? *Forget* what you have told me?" Quintus struck one of the lamps from the table. It made a satisfying thud before breaking into pieces. He needed an entire *room* of pottery to smash. "I shall divorce her."

"You can't do that—"

"I shall castrate her lover and *then* divorce her."

"You *know* you can't do that," said the girl.

Quintus glared at her, his fists clenched. "I can and I will."

The girl, who had been seated in a corner of the room, now stood. She crossed toward him until they stood toe to toe. Her jaw quivered.

"No. You. Will. *Not.*" DaVinci's green eyes sparked like pale flames. "I made a mistake telling you, but I will *not* allow you to make an even bigger mistake."

Anger roiled inside him. Summoning the tone that had once brought the leader of the *Averni* to tears, he spoke. "Do not presume to instruct me."

The girl, though plainly shaken, nevertheless presumed.

"If you take revenge," she said, "will it end there? Will Mucia's family and her lover's family just *drop* it? Or will they come after you next? And of course, they won't know *you* are here—they'll come after the *other* you. Is that fair? Bringing a fight down on the head of someone who doesn't even know you exist?"

"He would be in agreement with me on this

issue—"

"That doesn't matter, and you know it. *You*, this you, does not belong here doing . . . *things*."

"Perhaps the gods brought me here for the purpose of cleansing the name of the Valerii."

"Maybe, but until Venus herself shows up with printed instructions, you have to let the Quintus Valerius who lives here fight his own battles. Anything else would be a colossal mistake."

"The only mistake would be to allow the whore to continue parading her bastard as a Valerii."

"That is not the worst thing that can happen. It isn't your problem, Quintus. Not anymore. It may not be fair, and you may not like it, but it stopped being your problem the moment Jules Khan yanked you out of your time and place."

"I will castrate Khan and then castrate Mucia's lover and then divorce her," growled Quintus.

The girl opened her mouth to protest, but then shrugged, as if changing her mind. "That first idea has merit."

Quintus crossed his arms over his chest. "You mock me."

"Uh, no. I don't."

Her expression was gentle, even compassionate. "I think what happened is terrible," she said softly. "And I, for one, one hundred percent agree your wife has it coming, and so does that jerk who won't even stand up and claim the kid as his own."

Quintus grunted. The girl spoke truth in this matter, at least.

"But you can't go around meting out justice. It's not your battle to fight."

"Do not tell me," said Quintus, his voice growing louder with each word, "what I already know!"

Suddenly, he felt he could not remain in his lodgings for another minute.

"I need air." He swept from the room, ignoring the girl's protests. And when she followed him, he didn't try to stop her. Let her try to keep up with him.

The air outside was hot and still, a stifling Roman afternoon. The streets were at their emptiest while Rome took its ease for an hour or two. His wife would be at home. Napping, perhaps. He would rouse her and march her back to her father's house, announcing the divorce then and there. He would strongly suggest her father exercise his right as *paterfamilias* and kill the unfaithful wretch before she brought further dishonor to her family.

Vaguely, he was aware the girl DaVinci was still following him and that she had been calling after him for some time.

"Cacat," he swore under his breath.

As if he didn't have *enough* to worry about. He turned onto the street where he had lived, his purpose firm as ever. But no sooner had he taken three strides than he heard the girl screaming, and this time it didn't sound like she was shouting at him to wait for her.

Cursing again, he halted and retraced his steps. Rounding the corner, he saw the girl being hefted like an amphora of wine over the shoulder of a burly man while his drunken friends cheered, shouting among themselves over who should have her first.

41
· NEVIS ·
Florida, July

Special Agent Nevis mopped his brow and continued scanning the files on Arthur Littlewood. *Mopped his brow*: there was a phrase he'd never understood until this past month.

About forty minutes earlier, he'd called the front desk to say his AC was malfunctioning. He'd called, again, thirty minutes ago. And twenty minutes ago. On each occasion, he'd been assured someone from maintenance was coming. Even though he was on his way out of Florida and wouldn't be sleeping in the hotel tonight, Nevis had arranged for the FBI to pay for one last night so he'd have an "office" in which to work until he left. Having paid for it, he was damn well getting some AC.

He was under orders to catch a red-eye tonight to Louisville, having already extended his stay in Florida by a day, against his SAC's wishes. He'd tried to get his stay in Florida extended by another two days, hinting at possible malfeasance—Littlewood operated on government money—but HQ had denied the request. So now Nevis was spending every last minute in Florida combing every last record he could access on Littlewood. Nevis wasn't giving up yet. And he for damn sure wasn't leaving the state without a visit inside Arthur Littlewood's secret facility.

He'd cased it yesterday, after getting the address. Upon descending the stairs to the basement entrance, Nevis had noted a security camera. He made a point of staring into its lens. Let Littlewood fret about *that*.

The lights had been on inside, giving Nevis a decent view of Littlewood working away in a lab not so different from the one on campus. Nevis had been on the point of knocking to ask Littlewood some questions, but something told him he should gather a little more intel first.

He'd spent last night getting exactly *nowhere* with the investigation, but today his luck had changed. In the past two hours, he'd turned up two interesting links connecting Littlewood to a man who had died under questionable circumstances.

And now here was a third link—a very *compromising* third link—to connect Dr. Arthur Littlewood with Dr. Jules Khan, formerly employed at the University of California, Santa Barbara. Nevis *knew* he'd been on to something with Littlewood. Oh, he was definitely questioning Littlewood about this former colleague. He typed out a few notes.

A knock at his door interrupted his thoughts. He heard someone call "Maintenance" from outside in the hall. Swearing at the timing of the interruption, Nevis closed his laptop and rose to open the hotel room door. For the eight and a half minutes it took the maintenance man to unscrew a panel, do something that seemed to involve banging on whatever was behind the panel, and then replace the panel, Nevis paced back and forth, back and forth, awaiting the moment he could resume his research.

"That oughta do you for now," said the man from maintenance.

Nevis thanked him and practically pushed him out the door. He had a mystery to solve. Khan and Littlewood had both been presenters at a physics conference in Santa Barbara in 2001. The two had corresponded in 2006 and 2007, disagreeing about something technical that Nevis couldn't understand. After that, there had been nothing to connect the two, until a year ago.

One year ago, Littlewood had written a substantial personal check to Jules Khan. After this, there had been no further checks, but there was something even more damning. Littlewood had withdrawn cash from his bank in amounts identical to that check on the first of every month until December of last year: the same month that a death certificate had been issued in California for Khan. The body had never been recovered.

That same December, Littlewood had traveled to Santa Barbara. Things got stranger at this point. Following the trail, Nevis turned up a mention of Khan *after* his death. A bizarre incident involving a man who'd stolen a car from the estate of Jules Khan after an apparent attempt to impersonate Khan.

So why was Littlewood paying off Jules Khan? And what was the connection between Littlewood and Khan's death? Or between Littlewood and the would-be impersonator? He compiled his findings and wrote out his questions and then called his SAC, prepared to demand additional time in Florida. His SAC didn't take his call.

Cursing, Nevis sent an email requesting permission to pursue the investigation of a possible wrongful death involving Arthur Littlewood.

42

· *QUINTUS* ·

Rome, 53 BC

"Put her down *at once*," Quintus roared to the four men who surrounded DaVinci.

One of the drunkards, seeing a Roman legionnaire, detached himself from the group and ran away.

Another, his hand on a dagger at his side, addressed Quintus in Latin. "Say that again in the language of Rome, *cunne*!"

Quintus had done it again: he'd used the wrong language with the wrong person.

Running at the men, now down to three, Quintus called out in Latin.

"I said, put her down, son of a dog!" Having said this, he drew his sword on the *filius canis*.

The trick was to threaten with the sword while avoiding actual harm to the girl.

The girl, however, had ideas of her own.

DaVinci—upside down—pulled hard enough on

her captor's toga that it slid off his shoulder. The young man's friends laughed and made lewd comments, one about disarray and the other about the eagerness of the girl. The man himself was either such a tidy dresser or so fearful of Quintus's approach that he dropped the girl.

From her position on the ground, DaVinci kicked the youthful captor's legs so hard that he stumbled, inciting more insults from his companions.

Thus, by the time Quintus was within reach of the three, one of them was on the ground, and the other two were laughing uproariously at the sight. This was all the invitation Quintus needed. Extending his sword arm, he brought the pommel of his gladius into resounding contact with the jaw of the first dissolute in his path. The man went down on one knee, clutching the side of his face and screaming obscenities. The other remaining man, however, had a trim physique and was removing his toga in preparation for a fight. He raised his fists and taunted Quintus.

"Afraid to face me without that sword, *mentula*?"

Quintus assessed the eager fighter and then calmly replaced his sword in his belt. A second later, Quintus's leg shot out as he tried to land a kick in the man's gut. His opponent sidestepped the kick, coming back with a fist aimed at Quintus's face. Quintus blocked, and the fighter swung his toga, wielding it like a shield. The swinging toga also served to block Quintus's view of the youthful abductor DaVinci had tripped. By the time Quintus could see the abductor again, he was rising to join the fray. Quintus now found himself fighting two opponents at once. Well, it was better than fighting the original four at once.

Roaring like an angry bull, Quintus delivered a face punch to the youth, using the momentum of the blow to crash into his second opponent. The two tumbled to the ground, Quintus's fall softened by the body underneath him. Without missing a beat, Quintus rolled out of the fall and grasped at the hem of the opponent still standing. The opponent fell to the ground, knocking his head soundly on the cobblestones.

Quintus rose to check on the third attacker, who was still rubbing his jaw and running through a litany of Roman obscenities. DaVinci, however, got to him first and delivered a sound kick to his groin. The obscenities pinched off into a painful wheeze.

Where had the girl learned to fight like that? The thought, unfortunately, distracted Quintus from the movement behind him. The fighter with the soldierly physique had risen again. He landed a solid kick to Quintus's kidneys, and now Quintus was wheezing, too.

But Quintus Valerius hadn't trained with the greatest warriors in Rome's vast empire for nothing. Ignoring the dull pain, he spun and landed a quick pair of jabs to his opponent's jaw. The fighter went down, eyes rolling back in his head.

"Quintus!" shouted the girl.

He spun left, swerving just before the girl's abductor, dagger outstretched, aimed a thrust at Quintus's hamstring. It was not a bad move, but Quintus dodged it easily, pulling his own sword from where it rested.

"You want a fight?" roared Quintus.

A pair of shutters on the ground floor slammed shut, distracting DaVinci's abductor.

"For shame," Quintus shouted at the abductor. "Brawling while decent citizens take their afternoon rest. Come on," he said, left hand beckoning to the youth. "I dare you, you son of a flea-bitten dog!"

Once again, he'd uttered his insults in English, but either the tone in which he uttered the threat or the obvious pleasure he took in the prospect of a blade fight made his opponent turn suddenly pale. Throwing the dagger at the girl, who successfully dodged it, the would-be abductor fled down the street, toga in utter disarray.

"You sons of dogs! Anyone else?" roared Quintus.

The last two men remained on the ground, one insensate, the other whimpering in pain. Quintus centered himself, preparing to deliver a knockout blow to the whimpering one.

"Enough!" shouted the girl.

Glowering, Quintus met her eyes. It would be much more satisfying to leave *both* of his opponents unconscious.

"You've proved your point. You're a badass. Now let's *go*," the girl said.

He met her eyes, flames of green in her flushed face. *Gods below*, but she was beautiful. And she was also right. He had defeated his opponents. There was no honor in kicking the fallen. It was time to leave. He satisfied himself with an ungentle, booted nudge that rolled the moaning man over onto his face and into a puddle of doubtful origin.

"I said, *let's go*," said DaVinci, fisted hands

jammed onto her hips.
> Swearing under his breath, Quintus followed her.

43
·DAVINCI·
Rome, 53 BC

DaVinci's legs were shaking as she climbed back up to the fourth-floor apartment. In the week since she'd saved her house and wrecked her life, she'd stopped exercising. She was out of breath, although possibly some of the shaking was due to escaping that ugly bastard who'd run off without his dagger.

It had been the same repulsive youth who'd groped her earlier in the day. *Ugh!* If she was stuck in Rome, maybe it was time to relocate. Move to the coast. Or to New Zealand. She had no interest in looking over her shoulder every time she went out to fill a water jug. Although she *had* taken her attacker's dagger for her own. This put a grim smile on her face.

This time he'd had friends as back up. She may not have understood the words they heckled her with, but she had definitely understood their intentions, and the odds had not been in her favor. If Quintus hadn't come back . . .

But Quintus *had* come back. And she was safe.

And unhurt. Well, there was a bruise blooming on her forearm and one of her knees felt wonky.

She grabbed the pitcher of water from the table and took a long drink. Out of the corner of her eye, she saw Quintus wiping his forehead. Although the lamplight was dim, it cast enough illumination for her to see his forehead was bleeding.

"Forehead cuts are the worst," she murmured, reaching inside her purse for a Kleenex. But when she went to place it on the cut over his eye, Quintus snapped at her.

"I require no aid."

"You're bleeding," DaVinci said, standing her ground.

"I wouldn't be bleeding if you hadn't followed me."

DaVinci, holding out the Kleenex, glared at him. "I'm *trying* to be helpful."

"It would have been *helpful* if you had stayed put as I instructed you."

That, again? She threw the Kleenex down and folded her arms. "Okay, first of all, covering ground we've already been over, I do *not* take instructions from *you*. And second, maybe I would have stayed put if you'd bothered to get us a room with a freaking window and not some jail cell!"

"Roman insulae don't have windows!"

DaVinci glared at him. Quintus glared back. The man was impossible. In fact, now that she thought about it, maybe his wife was the injured party in the relationship.

"None of this would have happened," Quintus said, "if you hadn't tried to attack me on the platform of the time machine."

A flush of heat rose from her neck. "None of this would have happened if you treated space–time with some respect, instead of like it was some . . . some *toy* invented to amuse you."

"You have no idea the importance of the mission for which I came—"

"No, I don't, but I know this much: You're going to have to accept the fact that you don't have a place here anymore. You can't reclaim your old life; it's gone. Rome is no longer your home. Your wife is no longer your wife."

Her heart was pounding, and she could tell the flush that had started at her neck was probably turning her whole face tomato red, but she didn't care. She wasn't here to look pretty for Quintus, that was for damn sure. She held his gaze, daring him to look away first. Daring him to tell her she was wrong.

Unexpectedly, Quintus broke eye contact first. "You are cruel to speak such things," he said, "though they be true."

She hadn't meant to be cruel. She was just telling the truth. If only he knew the irony of what she'd just said about his old life being gone. She might just as easily have been lecturing herself.

Quintus sank onto the protesting bed, squatting to pick up the tissue from where it had landed on the ground.

"No! Don't let that touch your wound!" DaVinci leaped forward and snatched the Kleenex out of his hands. "Bacteria, hello!"

God only knew what kind of filth was on the floor of this disgusting room. She pulled a clean tissue from her purse and offered it to him.

Quintus took it and dabbed at his forehead.

"You're missing part of it," she said, sitting beside him and moving his hand to the right place. His skin was warm, and when they touched, something tugged inside her belly. Something it would be a lot simpler if she ignored. She released his hand, lacing hers together in her lap.

"By the way," she said. "thank you for coming back to help me."

As soon as the words were out, the memory of the assault hit her like a car crash. She sucked in a breath, trying to swallow back her terror. It didn't matter that she knew she was safe; her body knew she'd been in danger. Real danger. The muscles running along the insides of her arms seized violently, and a moment later her thighs seized, too. And then every muscle in her core contracted, and suddenly she was shaking, everywhere, an inexorable, teeth-chattering, head to toe tremble that felt like it would never stop. She'd seen Yoshi's rabbit shake like this after a hawk had landed on the rabbit's cage and then flown away. She was that rabbit. The hawk was gone, but her body shook and shook and shook.

At some point, Quintus had placed an arm around her, and gradually she realized he was murmuring softly to her, half in Latin, half in English.

"You are safe now. I will allow none to harm you. You are safe."

She felt the safety of him, the strength of his arms, his muscular chest pressing into her shoulder, comforting her. The shaking began to die back, her arms calming first, and then her legs, and finally her torso, until all the tremors had passed. She was safe. *She was safe.* She could feel Quintus's calm pouring into her, steadily washing over her, surrounding her. She shifted to settle into his arms, but Quintus, misunderstanding her movement, started to release her.

"No," she murmured.

He obeyed.

She didn't want him to let go. Up till now, her arms had been hugged tightly around her chest, but now she slid one arm around Quintus's broad back, resting the other on his forearm. She held her breath, waiting to see how he would respond. He didn't pull away. She took a slow breath. Leaned into Quintus. She was safe.

Safe, and . . . something more.

She felt a tug in her belly, like she had when he'd grasped her early this morning while hiding from his son. But he'd been pretending to embrace her that time, and this, whatever this was, wasn't pretend.

She felt his breath on her hair, warm and steady. She felt the heat of his chest, its rise and fall where their bodies touched, the warmth of his arms enfolding her. The tug in her belly shifted, becoming a flutter, whispery and soft. It was the dance of a hundred fireflies, of pulsing light and gentle dark.

Yeah. She was in for it now. She needed to move. She needed to pull away. She needed to let go. Her body, however, didn't care what her brain thought she needed to do.

She was familiar enough with desire—it was impossible to avoid as an art student who spent hours sketching sleek and muscled specimens of nature's finer efforts. But this was different. Or, it was . . . *more*. It was desire and . . . and . . .

Her mouth tugged into a smile.

. . . and gently blinking fireflies pulsing in her belly.

Oh, DaVinci . . . She licked her lips and instantly found herself thinking of *his* lips, full and red. Wondering what it would be like to kiss those lips. Would he kiss her back? The fireflies sparked and swirled. *Oh, DaVinci* . . .

The feeling in her belly shifted into a stab of desire, hot and insistent. She tipped her head to find his mouth—and felt a drop of something hit her hand: *splat*.

A drop of blood from his forehead had splashed onto the back of her hand.

"Oh," she said, frowning. Talk about a way to kill the moment. She pulled back.

Instantly, Quintus released her.

"You're still bleeding," she said, leaning away to examine his forehead. "Okay. I see it. Hold still." She folded a section of tissue in half and then in quarters, pressing it to a spot over his left eyebrow. "Hold this," she said.

He pressed the tissue to his forehead. She dropped her hand.

"Thank you," said Quintus. His voice was low and gravelly, and DaVinci felt a sudden certainty she hadn't been the only one thinking about kissing.

Which was just . . . a million kinds of stupid. What was she thinking? She was stuck in ancient Rome, not vacationing in Cabo. This was not a time to be hooking up, no matter what the fireflies in her belly said.

And then, while she was trying to reason with imaginary bugs, she felt the sharp sting of a real bug. Biting her. For real. Swearing, she launched herself off the bed. *Ugh!* What had she been thinking, sitting on that flea-infested mattress? What had she been thinking about *everything*? Especially *all things Quintus Valerius*.

She glanced at him. He looked awful. Well, as awful as a person that good-looking could look. He'd been wandering the streets since dawn, followed by getting shouted at by her and learning awful things about his wife and kid, followed by fighting off street thugs. She tried to think what Leia would recommend. Stay hydrated, maybe?

She reached for the water pitcher and handed it to Quintus.

"Here. You should drink some water."

And kiss me. You should kiss me.

Okay. No. She seriously needed to stop that line of thinking. The fireflies in the belly thing needed to stop. Now.

He accepted the pitcher and downed the remainder of the water, looking at it disappointedly when it was empty.

"There's a fountain really close," DaVinci said. "I'll, *um*, stay inside if you want to fill it up."

"It was unkind of me to demand that you remain here, alone in a strange place," said Quintus.

Darned right it was, thought DaVinci. But this time she kept her thoughts to herself. Quintus had only been trying to keep her safe from, well, the kind of thugs he'd ended up helping keep her safe from.

"Come," said Quintus. "We will go together."

"Okay," said DaVinci, a tentative smile blooming. "Together."

She liked the feel of the word. Her fireflies flickered and whirred. They liked it, too.

She followed him down the stairs, legs more or less steady, although she sensed her quads were going to be screaming at her tomorrow.

Tomorrow.

The thought of *tomorrow* hit her hard; she had no idea if they were actually going home again or if they were stuck in the Eternal City forever.

They reached the ground floor and stepped out into the street. DaVinci was just about to ask for a refresher course on the Roman aqueduct system when she saw Quintus stiffen and draw his sword.

Across from them, at the bottom of the dead-end street and lounging at a *taberna*, were five Romans with a variety of weapons displayed on the tables they occupied. One of the men, DaVinci recognized. It was the guy who'd first attacked her, and later thrown his dagger at her. He was back, with a few more of his apparently limitless supply of *friends*.

44

· NEVIS ·

Florida, July

Special Agent Nevis was trying to keep calm on the phone with his SAC, who had finally deigned to return his call, only to lecture Nevis on doing his job. *"Doing his job?"* What did the SAC think he was doing, exactly? Nevis hadn't been this angry in a long time. Not since the disappearance of his former brother-in-law Lewiston with those stolen millions.

"Sir, with all respect, there is something here. I'm convinced of it—"

"And I'm not," snapped his boss. "So unless you've got a signed confession you haven't mentioned yet, I expect you to get on that flight to Louisville tonight."

"What if I could get one?"

"A signed confession?"

"Littlewood is nervous. He's got a secret facility that he attempted to hide from us. And I strongly suspect he's the key to uncovering the disappearance and death of Jules Khan—"

A Sword in Time

"I took an hour out of my day—my *very busy* day—to look into Arthur Littlewood. If there is a man less likely to contemplate an act of terrorism, I would like to shake his hand. Littlewood has his head in the clouds, not on jihad."

"But sir—"

"*And* I looked at Khan's death. I am satisfied it had nothing to do with Arthur Littlewood."

"I think you're wrong, sir—"

"Well, it wouldn't be the first time, would it, Nevis? Remind me who's in charge here? Oh, that's right. *I* am. And I'm telling you to stop pursuing this imaginary case and get on that plane tonight."

Nevis fumed in silence.

"Do you think this is some kind of goddamn vacation you're on?" demanded the SAC.

"No, sir," replied Nevis.

"Good. Because neither do I. I want you in Louisville tonight."

Silence.

"Understood?"

"Yes, sir."

"And Nevis? If I find out you aren't on that plane, you can consider yourself unemployed."

The phone made a clicking noise.

"Sir?"

Silence.

The SAC had hung up on him.

Nevis grabbed one of the hotel's complimentary plastic bottles of water and hurled it at the opposite wall where it exploded, splashing the nightstand and one of the queen beds.

There was something going on with Littlewood,

or there had been—Nevis was sure of it. And he sure as hell wasn't going to drop the whole thing, fall in line, and stay out of trouble. Not when he had a chance to crack a case like this. It was the opportunity he'd been waiting for: a way to advance his career so that his next move was upward instead of the lateral crap he'd been saddled with since Lewiston's disappearance.

He had the rest of the day at the Wellesley Hampton Inn. After that, the bureau expected him to be in Louisville for a week. Fine. That gave him another six hours. He would make the most of them. One last visit to chat with Arthur Littlewood at his off-campus location. One last chance to crack things wide open.

One thing was for sure. This time, Nevis was getting some answers.

45

·*QUINTUS* ·

Rome, 53 BC

Quintus took the measure of the five men seated at the taberna. Two were slaves who kept their eyes on their masters. The slaves were burly and armed with clubs, but based on the sloppy manner in which they held their weapons, it was not likely they had been trained to fight. The third and fourth, both freemen, were removing their togas and folding them with care. At least one of them had been drinking.

That left the fifth—a youth. Quintus frowned. It was the same youth from the group who had earlier attacked DaVinci.

Cursing under his breath, Quintus felt a flash of anger at himself as he examined his surroundings. He had rented an *insula* from which there was only one escape route—the road to the right. And there, cutting off their retreat, were four more men who had spaced themselves across the passageway, making clear they were the companions of those seated at the tavern. Quintus swore. Where had his soldierly instincts been when he'd chosen this residence? He knew where: in Florida, in a land where such instincts were not needed.

The street yawned before him, lazily inviting him to take his chances.

Of the four blocking the road, one was armed and dressed to fight, clearly a freeman, but Quintus wasn't certain from the dress of the others whether they were slaves or paid servants. The freeman looked vaguely familiar, but Quintus could not place him. It mattered not. The man and his bulky companions had murder written in their glances.

"*Excrementum*," muttered DaVinci, pointing to the four waiting down the street.

She'd seen them, too.

Excrementum, indeed.

Nine to one. Even with one of them drunk, and slaves who might not fight well, the odds were distinctly bad.

Without removing his gaze from the street, Quintus murmured to DaVinci, "If I ask you to return inside, will you comply?"

She shook her head, filling Quintus's periphery with a shimmer of red and gold.

"These men are bent on a fight," said Quintus.

To Quintus's great surprise, DaVinci laughed softly, producing a dagger.

"Maybe that son of a *canis* came back for this," she said, hefting the dagger the youth had thrown at her.

Quintus did not correct her as to what the son of a rabid dog had returned for.

"Your instincts in the last fight were good," he

said, "but you have not the strength to resist the larger or more sober of this group. I beg of you to reconsider and return inside."

"I won't," replied the girl at his side. And then, more softly, "I won't leave you alone."

A door to the right of the tavern opened briefly as an elderly man began to step out. But after assessing the situation in the street, the old man retreated, slamming the door and sliding the bolt home.

Quintus swallowed. The girl would resist him if he tried to force her back inside; he saw it in the stubborn set of her jaw. By all the gods, he had never felt for any woman what he felt for this fierce girl.

"Hold your blade thus," Quintus said to DaVinci, indicating the grip on his gladius. "And strike to injure, not to mortally wound. The punishment for a slave who kills is . . . unspeakably grim."

The girl nodded. Hefted her blade. Swept her shining hair behind her shoulders. *Gods*, she was glorious.

And then, together, the two stepped into the street.

46

·EVERETT·

Florida, July

Everett, arriving at the lab at eleven on Saturday morning, was the first to notice something was wrong.

Jillian's car was parked outside the lab, but neither Jillian nor DaVinci was there. Hands on his hips, Everett surveyed the lab. All was quiet. Empty. Not even Quintus was there, which in and of itself would not have troubled Everett; Quintus was only scheduled to stand guard until sunrise. But the presence of Jillian's car, in combination with the absence of, well, *everyone*, was odd.

Most members of the twenty-first century would have cleared everything up with a quick text or phone call. But while Everett owned a cell phone, using it was rarely his first impulse. Jillian teased him mercilessly, calling him a Luddite. He didn't *mean* to be backward, but having grown up without constant connectivity, he had trouble remembering it was there for him when he needed it.

In his defense, the first resource he turned to *was*

A Sword in Time

technological in nature. He crossed quickly to Quintus's desk to check the monitor records of entries and exits at the laboratory building. Someone had entered at 1:44 a.m. He checked the video record. It was DaVinci. If Jillian's car was still out front, DaVinci must still be nearby. Hastily, Everett scanned forward past 2:00 a.m., 4:00 a.m., 6:00 a.m., and up to the present. The door hadn't been opened again until his own arrival. There was always Littlewood's spare office, through the little-used door at the corner farthest from the basement stairs. Perhaps for some reason DaVinci and Quintus had chosen to enter it, but upon checking, Everett found the tiny room as empty as the basement.

There was only one other way to leave . . .

Frowning, Everett strode to the time machine, checking for recent usage.

He found it: the machine had been used, but it had been hours ago, and no one had returned yet, which could only mean one thing—their trip must have been plotted to the very recent past.

Who would want to travel to the recent past? His heart skipped a beat as the pieces fell together.

DaVinci.

Oh, heavens . . .

Everett typed in commands to bring up the exact configurations for the machine's last time and place settings, but at that moment, the computer decided to run a series of self-checks prior to reporting the information.

"Now?" groaned Everett.

DaVinci *had* talked about visiting the recent past to alter the changes she'd made. She must be attempting it. Could she have persuaded Quintus to assist her? She must have; Quintus hadn't left the building.

As the machine continued its diagnostics, another possibility occurred to Everett: perhaps Quintus had been transported accidentally in an attempt to stop DaVinci.

The machine beeped and Everett glance at the display showing the last transport configuration. He blinked to clear his eyes. The destination setting hadn't been recent. Not remotely recent. Two persons had used the machine to travel to ancient Rome—to *Quintus's* time—at 1:45 a.m., which was over nine hours ago. It made no sense. They ought to have returned just before two in the morning, and it was nearly eleven. Everett searched again for a record of their return journey, but there was none. It was as if the machine was malfunctioning.

This was the moment Everett realized he should be placing phone calls.

Seizing the phone Jillian had given him, he texted Littlewood that something was wrong with the singularity device, that Quintus and DaVinci appeared to have used it, and to please come to the lab immediately. Then he called Jillian.

She answered, sleep slurring her voice.

"Hello?"

"Goodness. Were you sleeping?"

"DaVinci kept us up late. West Coast time."

"Of course, of course." Everett took a deep breath. "Jillian, I'm terribly sorry to tell you, but DaVinci took your car last night and drove here to the lab, where I am at present, and it would appear she and Quintus used the time machine to travel to Rome in 53 BC."

"Wait—they did *what?*"

Everett could hear the rustle of bedcovers thrown hastily aside.

"They traveled to ancient Rome," Everett repeated. "What is more, while I can see the record of their outbound journey, I can find nothing indicating they returned."

"Well, give them a couple of minutes—"

"They've been gone nine hours."

"That's not possible," whispered Jillian.

"I texted Dr. Littlewood. Oh—I beg your pardon. He is replying. One moment, if you please." Everett read the text and returned to his call. "He is on his way."

"I'll be right over." Jillian hung up before Everett could remind her she had no car to drive "right over." Seconds later, she texted him: *Calling a taxi.*

Four minutes later, Littlewood arrived with a worried expression on his face. He strode straight to the time machine podium, murmuring to himself about his terrible capacity for distraction.

"What is it?" asked Everett. "What's wrong?"

"This is all my fault," said Littlewood. "It must be . . ." He broke off, fingers flying over the podium screen. "Oh dear. Oh *dear.*"

"What is it?" asked Everett.

Littlewood met Everett's gaze. "I, ah, well, I had an idea for changing the duration of the temporal— that is, it wasn't *my* idea. Well, the idea was mine but not mine *per se*. Credit where credit is due, you know—"

"Out with it!" cried Everett. "What did you do?"

"I . . . ah, that is, a *me* from the future came up with a method whereby travel into the past might be extended. And I . . . well, I may have modified the frequency generator to operate at the third harmonic."

"And that means what, exactly?" said Everett.

"It means the singularity device was configured for an extended journey."

"An . . . *extended* journey?" Everett's eyes grew wide. "Is that even possible? Have you tested it?"

"Well, now . . ."

"You haven't tested it."

"Well, no, not me, personally, although it would appear a test is underway . . ."

Everett paled. Neither DaVinci nor Quintus would have any idea what had prevented them from returning. From returning *hours* ago. They must be terrified. Everett turned to Littlewood.

"How long will their stay have been extended, exactly?"

Littlewood grimaced. "Ah. Yes. Without having tested things properly—"

"And you didn't think to mention this to anyone?"

Littlewood, worrying the collar of his jacket, shrugged miserably.

As Everett stood, silently taking all of it in, Jillian arrived.

"Where are they?" she cried, striding across the room. "Why aren't they back yet? Are they okay?" She turned to Everett. "You didn't answer my texts."

Everett patted his pocket, where his phone should have been but wasn't. Jillian crossed to his desk to retrieve it and then handed it to him without a word. He felt his face flushing. Jillian had sent seven text messages, all variations of *Are they going to be okay?*

"I apologize most sincerely," he murmured, taking Jillian's hand. "I can't seem to remember to keep it with me."

"I know," Jillian said quietly.

Littlewood looked up from the podium screen. "They should return late this afternoon." He raked long fingers through his untidy hair. "If my calculations are correct. That is, if my, ah, *future self's* calculations . . . Of course, I haven't actually tested it yet, to know with certainty."

Everett turned to Jillian and explained that the professor had been experimenting with length of stays and had forgotten to put the settings back to normal.

Jillian shook her head in disbelief. "But Quintus and DaVinci won't have any idea what's wrong. They probably think they're stuck forever."

"And we have no method whereby to communicate with them," Littlewood added morosely. "We could try traveling to their last known location, but without knowing the customs and language, or where they might have wandered to in five hours—"

"We'd never find them," said Jillian.

"I meant to run tests, but I became distracted," Littlewood said glumly. "I planned to use an animal as a guinea pig, you know."

"An animal as a *guinea pig?*" said Jillian.

Littlewood nodded. "I considered purchasing an actual guinea pig, but then I thought about the tortoise that likes to sun itself along the north wall of the building—"

"Not Alistair," murmured Jillian. "Tell me you didn't run an experiment on poor Alistair."

Everett thought it was a better idea than running an experiment on Quintus and DaVinci, but he kept the thought to himself.

"No, I didn't have the chance," said Littlewood. "I recalibrated the settings on the singularity device, but when I went outside to look for, ah, for *Alistair*, he was nowhere to be found. And then I . . . well, I became distracted and, oh dear . . . This is all my fault."

Everett and Jillian exchanged glances. Littlewood's forgetfulness was legendary.

"No one could have foreseen what DaVinci and Quintus would do," said Everett.

"It's not your fault," said Jillian, placing a gentle hand on Littlewood's shoulder.

"An experiment might be helpful, though," said Everett. "Not on Alistair," he added. "But it would give us something to do, while we wait."

"Something to do would be good," Jillian murmured softly, nodding.

"Yes," nodded Littlewood. "There are contingencies for which one ought to be prepared . . ."

"We could run a test on a plant specimen, perhaps?" said Everett, gazing at a potted jade plant Quintus had brought inside.

"Ah, well, I think it needs to be something more . . . alive than that," said Littlewood.

"Plants are alive," said Jillian.

"But they won't die without oxygen," replied Littlewood.

"Why is that a problem?" asked Jillian.

"Because of concerns to do with the length of the return journey?" asked Everett, looking to Littlewood.

"I'm not certain, of course," replied Littlewood, "but it did occur to me that if the duration of the stay is extended, the duration of the return journey might also be somewhat lengthened."

"Oh no," said Jillian. "So that part when we time travel back home, and we can't move or breathe for half a minute—"

"I'm not certain," said Littlewood. "So I wanted to see how the tortoise fared."

"Tortoises can survive without oxygen for much longer than humans," said Jillian. "Branson had a tortoise," she added by way of explanation.

At that moment, Littlewood's cell phone rang.

He stared at the caller ID as if puzzled and then excused himself to take the call in his adjacent office.

Everett spoke, addressing Jillian. "I believe we must experiment using a living creature."

"It would help to have something . . . *active* to do," she said, worrying her hands, "but if we discover bad news . . ."

"All the more reason to test," said Everett. "If we discover bad news, we bring in emergency medical assistance." Everett broke off. "Hang on," he said, swiftly capturing a moth that had been resting on the wall.

"A thousand apologies," murmured Littlewood, returning to their conversation. "Had to take it, though. Unavoidable. Important business."

The fax on Littlewood's desk began printing. All three turned toward the noise.

Littlewood nodded and murmured, "Ah. There it

is. Good, good," before turning back to Everett and Jillian. "That document can wait. My apologies. Where were we?"

"We need to prepare," said Everett.

"We need to figure out what we might need to prepare for," clarified Jillian, "by sending something, but a tortoise wouldn't have worked—they can hold their breath a long time."

"I captured a moth," said Everett. "Will that suffice?"

Littlewood nodded. "Yes. Excellent. Now then, if we wish to, ah, learn the probable fate awaiting our friends, we must choose a destination for our moth that will allow it to return ahead of our friends."

Everett had already thought about this. "I suggest we try setting the outbound journey for the moth using the *second* harmonic, which will extend the moth's stay in the past but still return it ahead of Quintus and DaVinci, who traveled using the third harmonic."

"Ah yes," said Littlewood, brows raised. "The second harmonic. Faster. Good thinking."

"And I know a place and time where we can send the moth so that no one will notice its appearance or disappearance," said Everett.

"Indeed?" asked Littlewood.

"To my bedroom, in 1919," Everett replied. "After my . . . well, after the death of my other self, my parents shut the door and allowed no one to open it."

"We read about it online," said Jillian softly.

Everett felt a pinch of guilt. He knew it hurt Jillian to remember that death. Himself, he'd only ever felt gratitude for being given *two* chances at life.

"Right," said Littlewood. "Let's get underway, then, shall we?"

Everett nodded.

"It's better than sitting around doing nothing while . . . while . . ." Jillian broke off, her eyes filling with tears.

"I'm sure everything will be fine," said Everett, taking her hand in his. He wasn't sure, not at all, but this wasn't the time for speaking doubts aloud.

Littlewood, apparently, didn't share his compunction.

"Well," the professor said grimly, "if our little moth asphyxiates, that will certainly clear up our questions."

It took Littlewood a while to satisfy himself the experiment had been properly calibrated, and what with one delay and another, it was not until after four in the afternoon that the moth returned, whole, asleep, and apparently none the worse for wear.

"They're going to be okay," said Jillian, her eyes squeezed shut in relief.

Everett threw an arm around her shoulder. "We've nothing to worry about."

"Such a relief," murmured Jillian. Then she turned to Littlewood. "So how much longer? Forty-something minutes, best guess, right?"

Everett was about to say yes when he noticed that Littlewood was *hmming* and *ahhing* to himself while examining his phone.

"What is it?" asked Everett.

Littlewood looked up, a frown creasing his brow. His free hand clutched a clump of his hair.

"Tell us," said Jillian.

"It's just that, ah, while our experiment confirms the amount of additional time provided by the use of the second harmonic, it would appear . . . how shall I put it? Our friend the moth, here, is capable of living without oxygen for quite some time. For days, studies suggest."

"Oh," said Jillian. "So we still don't know . . ."

"I'm afraid we won't know until . . . well, ah, until they return."

The color drained from Jillian's face.

"Perhaps we should call an ambulance," suggested Everett.

Littlewood was back to muttering to himself. "No time to run another experiment with the tortoise . . . I don't say the return journey *will* be extended beyond the usual thirty or so seconds, of course."

"We're back to where we started," said Everett. "We don't know."

"I know CPR," said Littlewood.

"We could end up needing a lot more than CPR," murmured Jillian.

"We can't risk paramedics standing by in the lab when Quintus and DaVinci return," Littlewood said firmly.

"We are *not* risking their lives," began Jillian, but she was cut off by a noisy thumping at the door to the laboratory. "Are we . . . expecting someone?" she asked softly.

Littlewood, who was now tugging his hair straight up, shook his head.

"I'll get rid of them," said Everett, crossing the room.

He peered through the window and saw a man holding up identification of a sort he'd seen on television. Everett's heart sank. This visitor wouldn't be so easy to chase off. Although Everett had been away during the FBI agent's visit to Littlewood's campus location, Everett felt certain the visitor was Special Agent Nevis.

47

·*QUINTUS*·

Rome, 53 BC

Quintus's mind and body shifted into a familiar state of high alert. He had faced terrible odds before, but never with a girl by his side, let alone one so . . . *beloved*. It filled him with an unfamiliar dread. He attempted to set his feelings aside. To analyze the men before him. That was his task. That was all he had to do. Of the two opponents who had removed their togas, the one *not* drunk was clearly at ease with his gladius. And carrying a shield, he was prepared to fight. Quintus would have to subdue him first.

"Your slave struck a citizen," the youth called in Latin from his table. "She must be punished."

DaVinci whispered, "What is he saying?" Quintus could hear the tension in her voice. Before he could answer her, though, the trained fighter stepped forward, shield hand beckoning, the other gripping his sword.

"You will be compensated for her," the man said. "Just hand her over, and we can avoid bloodshed."

A Sword in Time

"Not entirely," grunted the youth, leering. "Virgin or not, I think she will bleed before we are done with her."

Thinking fast, Quintus, grabbed DaVinci roughly by the arm. "Take her. She is too much trouble anyway." He swung her around in front of him, placing her between himself and the trained fighter.

The men at the table broke into lascivious laughter, making rude gestures Quintus feared DaVinci could not mistake.

"What's going on?" she demanded in English, trying to break his viselike grip. It would suit his purposes better if she appeared fearful, the gods forgive him. Ignoring her question, he stepped forward, still gripping her forearm. Then, lowering his sword, Quintus shoved DaVinci forward toward his opponent, at the same time addressing DaVinci in hasty English.

"Beloved, *drop low!*"

The moment the fighter lowered his sword to take DaVinci, Quintus sprang. It was a less than honorable attack, but the deception gave Quintus the advantage he sought. His blade bit deep into the sword arm of the unprepared fighter, who dropped his weapon from his now dangling and useless arm. DaVinci, who had indeed ducked low, had unfortunately spun out of Quintus's view. He couldn't track her; the next several moments would be decisive. The fighter Quintus had attacked was bleeding heavily and had let go of his shield to staunch his wound. Swiftly, Quintus grabbed the discarded shield and brought it down heavily on his opponent's head, leaving the man unconscious.

Next, Quintus had to subdue the slaves and reach the other two freemen in the tavern, all before the men down the alley were able to close in on him or DaVinci.

Quintus rushed the slaves. The first, unprepared, fell under the hammerlike blow of Quintus's stolen shield, blood streaming from a head wound. The second slave, clearly in fear of his life, attacked Quintus with his club. From his periphery, Quintus noted the youth and the drunkard had risen and taken up weapons. Quintus fought the second slave giving no quarter, and the poor man, reconsidering his chances, fled, ignoring his master's cries to return.

Whirling, Quintus spun just in time to meet the onslaught of the drunkard and the youth. He parried the youth's blade, knocking it from his hand, but as he did so, the drunkard managed to stab Quintus's shield arm, gashing his bicep. Ignoring the pain, Quintus turned and thrust his gladius into the drunkard's belly. When he was certain his foe would not rise, Quintus spun to face the youth.

It was then that he heard DaVinci's cry. The youth, instead of recovering his lost sword, had used the moment of Quintus's attack on the drunkard to seize DaVinci by the hair and was now trying to steal the dagger from her. When his first attempt earned him a slash across the forearm, the youth yanked hard. Shrieking, DaVinci stabbed wildly. Quintus ran toward them just as they both stumbled over the downed body of the first fighter. The youth recovered more quickly, and this time, he managed to disarm DaVinci, holding her before him as a human shield.

"Coward!" cried Quintus. "Dog!"

In that same moment, Quintus felt a gentle rush of air behind him followed by a soft intake of breath. Spinning from DaVinci, Quintus saw he was under attack by one of the four men from down the street. His eyes followed the arc of his attacker's sword and instinctually, Quintus hefted his own sword upward to block the blow, but he was late, and the attacker's sword grazed Quintus's brow, glancing through hair and skin. Quintus tried to return to DaVinci's aid but quickly determined the swordsman engaging him wasn't going to let that happen.

With a jolt, Quintus realized he knew this attacker. The man was a former soldier, Titus Machus, who, unable to repay gambling debts, now hired himself to protect wealthy patrons.

Quintus swallowed heavily. Titus Machus might have failed to take him by surprise, but Titus would have more than one surprise up the sleeve of his tunic.

Engaging Titus with a loud cry, Quintus simultaneously tried to work his way to DaVinci. He heard her shriek, and turning to the cry, he saw why.

The youth held a knife to her throat. Grinning, the dog was now retreating with her, hauling her toward the three men at the top of the road.

48

· EVERETT ·

Florida, July

Everett held the door open for the federal agent.

"Good day. How can I be of service, sir?" Everett asked politely.

The agent brushed past Everett, beelining for Littlewood.

"Arthur Littlewood," said the FBI agent, his badge thrust out.

"Ah. Hello, again. Did we have a meeting?" asked Littlewood, gazing at his watch and frowning. "I must have misunderstood," he added with consternation. "It's, ah, not really a convenient time."

"Agent Benjamin Nevis," said the agent, flashing his badge at Jillian, the only person in the room who hadn't yet seen it.

Everett crossed to Jillian's side, and he murmured, "This is the agent Littlewood kept your information from. Play it cool."

Everett nodded and swallowed hard, hoping he would not be asked to produce ID. There had been other inquiries into the credibility of his identification, but none had yet been with an officer of the law.

"Sorry for dropping in unannounced," Nevis said, not looking at all sorry. "Quite a place you have here. You hold it privately, I believe?"

Littlewood stuttered, making a few false starts before simply nodding yes.

"I thought so," replied Nevis. "Odd that you didn't mention it to me already. I, on the other hand, *did* mention to you that I'm performing a review and approval process for heavy-use consumers of electricity to prevent acts of terror against the United States. Any particular reason your extremely heavy electrical usage for this facility escaped your mind in our previous conversations?"

"Ah," said Littlewood, pasting a thin smile on his face. "Yes. It didn't occur to me. But here you are. Now you know. I'm, ah, afraid I can only offer an abbreviated tour this morning. Expecting the arrival of friends, you know. Mustn't keep them waiting."

Nevis's eyes remained fixed on Littlewood through the entire nervous speech. The agent didn't say anything for a slow count of five, after which he walked toward what Everett referred to as the dining table.

"I think you'll find you have time for this," said Nevis, seating himself. He settled in as if for an extended visit.

"Well," said Littlewood, "that is, ah, I'm not at liberty at present to . . . well, you know, and since I already received your kind—"

"Let me tell you an interesting story," Nevis said, cutting off Littlewood's nervous ramblings.

Littlewood shook his head. "I really am *very* busy just now—"

"Your visitors will have to wait, I'm afraid," replied Nevis. "I'm here on a matter of national security. I'm sure your guests will understand."

Everett tried frantically to think of a safe means whereby to explain that, no, these particular guests could *not* wait, would *not* understand. He glanced at his phone, checking the time. If everything went as Littlewood had predicted, Quintus and DaVinci would return in thirty-one minutes. But approximately four minutes prior to their arrival, the machine would begin warming up, and there wasn't a snowball's chance in Hades Nevis would ignore *that* level of noise, which meant getting him out soon was critical.

"Please," said Nevis, gesturing grandly, "have a seat."

Littlewood sank into one of the chairs.

"My story concerns you, too," Nevis said to Jillian. "And as for you," said Nevis, looking at Everett, "I don't believe you showed up on the list of students Dr. Littlewood gave me. What did you say your name was?"

"Everett Randolph, sir."

"*Hmm.* We'll talk later. Please. All of you. Take a seat."

Everett's heart began to pound, but when he saw Jillian sitting, he joined her.

Nevis began his tale.

"As you know, I've been tasked with assessing threats to the power grid and with reviewing persons known to be heavy consumers. Your operations at the university seemed unexceptionable, Dr. Littlewood, but then I learned of this facility—which you neglected to disclose—and began to make further inquiries into your background and associations."

"I believe you mentioned my background was above reproach," said Littlewood. "On our *first* meeting."

"On a casual review, it was," said Nevis.

"Well, then, seeing as I've already received—"

Nevis cut him off. "But when I dug a little deeper, I stumbled on a name: Jules Khan."

Littlewood exhaled at the same moment that Jillian, at Everett's side, inhaled softly.

Nevis's eyes flashed in Jillian's direction, but he didn't address her. Instead, he returned his focus to Littlewood, who had just begun to fiddle with a napkin ring lying on the table.

"Jules Khan, interestingly, was declared dead at the close of last year. The Santa Barbara Police Department issued the certificate." Nevis turned to Jillian. "You lived most of your life in Santa Barbara, I understand."

"Yes." Jillian's tone was clipped. Everett took her hand beneath the table.

"Imagine my surprise on learning you were a neighbor of Jules Khan," continued Nevis, addressing Jillian. "What are the odds? I don't suppose you were friends?"

"I met him one time," said Jillian. "At an art gallery." She was composed, her expression neutral.

At this point, Nevis brought out and examined a small, spiral-bound notepad.

"The gallery owner was one of the last people to speak to Khan prior to his disappearance." The FBI agent looked up from his notepad. "Inga Mikkelsen and her daughter Halley Mikkelsen were the two others. Isn't that interesting?"

Jillian's hand clutched Everett's in a death grip.

Nevis leaned forward. "I had to ask myself, what are the odds two people who knew Khan at different times in his life ended up all the way out here in Florida, working together? And one of them the best friend of Halley Mikkelsen."

Everett tried to squeeze Jillian's hand, but her grip was so tight he doubted she even noticed.

"You *are* a close friend of Halley Mikkelsen, aren't you?" asked Nevis, flipping between pages of his notepad without actually looking at Jillian.

Everett took this to mean Nevis didn't have to observe Jillian's response because he already knew the answer to his question.

"Is there something you'd like to charge me with?" asked Jillian. Her tone was cool. She released Everett's hand and adopted a pose even more upright than her already enviable posture.

Nevis, ignoring her question, turned to Littlewood.

"Dr. Littlewood, have you had any contact with Jules Khan, deceased, in the past twelve months?"

Littlewood shook his head vigorously. Everett knew that, in a way, this was true; Littlewood hadn't met the *dead* Khan, even if he'd employed the duplicate *living* Khan.

"Can I have a verbal response, please?" Nevis asked.

"Unless you intend to charge someone here with something," Jillian said coolly, "Dr. Littlewood needs to prepare for his next appointment."

Everett checked his watch. Fourteen minutes.

Nevis ignored Jillian and repeated his request for a verbal response.

Jillian leaned forward. "Dr. Littlewood—"

"Yes or no?" demanded Nevis.

Littlewood ran a hand through his thinning hair and then, as though aware his gesture signaled distress, settled both hands in his lap.

"No," said Littlewood.

Nevis smiled. It was a cheerless sort of smile and reminded Everett of an illustration from a childhood storybook with the "smiling" crocodiles of the Nile.

"How curious," said Nevis. "Because I have here a record of your having written a check to Jules Khan that he cashed in Florida at a local credit union. Rather strange that the two of you would find yourselves in a transaction such as this, in the same town, without meeting."

Littlewood's face paled. He checked his watch, causing Everett to do the same. Eleven minutes left.

Jillian stood and crossed to Littlewood's side of the table. "Dr. Littlewood," she said quietly, "you need to ask this man to leave. You have the right to do that."

Nevis slammed his notebook on the table. "Let's stop playing games, right now."

"I believe Jillian is right," said Littlewood softly. "This isn't a good time. I'd like to, ah, consult an attorney before answering any more questions."

"You know Jules Khan!" said Nevis, his voice rising. "You wrote him a check. You had repeated contact with the man beginning nearly twelve months ago."

Littlewood had risen and was crossing to the door, Nevis at his heels.

"You not only wrote him a substantial check, which he cashed," accused Nevis, "but you then proceeded to withdraw cash in thirty-day intervals in the exact same amount right up through the month of December of last year—the month Khan was declared deceased."

"I must ask you to leave," said Littlewood, indicating the door.

Everett had followed the pair of them, professor and agent, as had Jillian.

"He's asked you to leave," said Jillian to Nevis. "If you're not charging us with anything—"

"At this point, Miss Applegate," said Nevis, "I am engaged in two serious criminal investigations, with the pair of you front and center. We're talking murder and acts of terrorism against the United States."

Everett had a vague recollection of Jillian explaining the Patriot Act to him. Could Nevis arrest all of them on mere suspicion of terrorist connections? Everett didn't know, but with a sinking feeling, he realized that there might be things nearly as bad as Nevis witnessing the appearance of Quintus and DaVinci out of thin air.

49

·*QUINTUS*·

Rome, 53 BC

Parrying Titus's blows, Quintus cried out in Latin to the youth, "Release her, dog!"

The girl's captor smiled. "I have other plans for her," he called.

Fury boiled inside Quintus. He was losing his focus.

Titus, seeing Quintus's shield sagging, responded swiftly. He leaped forward and drove the point of his sword over the top of Quintus's shield, enlarging the earlier gash to Quintus's bicep.

Quintus cursed at the pain and at his own inattention. It was the mistake of a raw recruit, letting his shield drop. He was out of practice. He was distractible, something he hadn't been for years, and he was vulnerable because of it.

Titus, having exacerbated the weakness on Quintus's left side, began training all his attacks on that weaker side, hammering blow after blow on Quintus's shield, which now began to droop dangerously. A scratch had opened over one of Quintus's eyes—he didn't know when—and blood trickled down from it. He could not risk swiping his forehead with hand or forearm, but the blood was threatening to blind him on that side. He shook his head violently, clearing his vision, but for how long?

The youth who held DaVinci, meanwhile, continued his taunts from up the street where he stood with Titus's three bulky companions.

"She shall be bathed with my hounds," he called to Quintus. "To cleanse her from the reek of your stench."

Bathe her? The wretch would not *touch* her!

Roaring with fury, Quintus charged, but Titus was there to prevent him from reaching the youth.

Quintus's foe drove him back farther and farther, lengthening the distance between him and DaVinci. His left arm was losing strength, his shield felt as if it had doubled in weight. Titus slammed Quintus's faltering shield with his own, a massive thing soldiers would have sneered at and mockingly asked Titus what he was trying to compensate for.

Quintus, however, had no time to deride his enemy. Something was wrong with his left arm. He heard rather than felt the moment his arm gave. There was a noisy thud as his shield hit the street. He could no longer lift it. For a count of two, he kept his grasp through the shield's grip, dragging the rectangle of wood and leather along the cobbled street, but then, cursing, he abandoned it.

As it fell, Quintus heard DaVinci crying out, but he kept his focus on his enemy's sword, flashing, darting, seeking his life's blood. Then, in a single instant, the scales tipped once more. Titus's right foot landed hard on the corner of Quintus's abandoned shield. The shield had fallen with its curved side facing up, so that Titus's foot seesawed unexpectedly and, for a moment, his balance was lost.

Quintus leaped forward, raining blows with both edges of his sword. He regained some of his lost distance and pushed back toward DaVinci, who was now hurling mangled Latin insults at her captor. Quintus regained another meter. And another, pushing his enemy back, back, back, closing the distance between himself and the girl for whose sake he battled.

Quintus now held a slight advantage; free from the weight of his shield, he was nimbler than Titus, whose shield was not only massive but also decorated with metalwork, further increasing its weight.

Close enough to observe the expression on the youth's face, Quintus noted the exact moment it changed, blanching as Quintus drew closer, as he drove Titus backward again and again. One of the bulky men Titus had brought muttered that he hadn't signed up for this and fled. The youth hurled threats at the retreating man, and, while the youth's attention was diverted, DaVinci seized the moment. Slamming her foot on his instep, she then drove her elbow into his diaphragm, snatching his dagger as he wheezed and doubled over.

She spun and turned on the two men remaining by the youth. Hoisting a bench by one of its legs, she struck the man nearest. The man, staggering and seeing her upraised dagger, followed his fleeing companion. Quintus had heard gossip that Titus never joined company with able fighters, whom he would have to pay well. Evidently the rumor was true.

Quintus's attention was pulled back to his opponent, who had apparently decided to abandon his weighty shield, hurling it missilelike at Quintus. Quintus spun clear, but his useless left arm didn't respond to the sudden move in concert with the rest of his body and he nearly lost his balance. In the time it took Quintus to regain his footing, Titus had replaced his shield with a knife, so that Quintus had to be wary of attack from two blades instead of one.

From his periphery, Quintus saw that DaVinci, meanwhile, had leapt onto a table and was taunting the wheezing youth and remaining hired man. She was Diana, fierce and fearless. She was Justitia, casting down judgment from on high. She was Venus Victrix conquering her enemies. *Gods above and below,* but she was glorious.

Quintus, his gaze on her, had lost focus once more, giving Titus an opening that nearly ended the fight. Just in time, Quintus raised his sword to parry the blow aimed at his abdomen. In an instant, Titus switched tactics, diving with his dagger to slash the tendon behind Quintus's left knee. Quintus turned in time to save his leg, but the turn, again, was clumsy, off-balance. Titus smelled victory, and, roaring, began a two-handed rain of blows that Quintus knew he could not withstand for long.

Instead of engaging each blow, Quintus now sought to avoid his enemy. Titus grew angry, calling him a coward, but Quintus held his course, dodging just out of reach again and again until Titus, piqued, threw his knife at Quintus.

Time seemed to slow as the blade sang past his

ear.

At the same moment, all of Quintus's muscles flagged, becoming as lethargic and unresponsive as his left arm. It was as if the connection between Quintus's mind and muscles had been severed. He couldn't even move his eyes to observe how DaVinci fared. He could only gaze in dismay at the approach of Titus's sword, a blade sent to cleave Quintus's soul from his body, to fulfill that final appointment Quintus had so many times escaped. Sight failed him, and his ears filled with a roar like that of a hurricane. As he fell into oblivion, Quintus's last thought was a prayer to Venus Victrix that the fair-haired girl might triumph where he had failed.

50
· *NEVIS* ·

Florida, July

Nevis was enjoying himself. He had the three right where he wanted them. *Someone* would spill the beans, and probably in the next few minutes. If only he could Skype his boss in for this triumph.

"Are you going to charge us?" asked the young woman, Jillian.

A joyless smile spread across Nevis's face. "You know, I think I might simply shut you down instead. Unless someone starts talking, I can guarantee you won't be getting approval to continue operating"—he gestured to the equipment—"whatever the hell this is. Alternatively, someone could start answering my questions."

"I am not a threat to the government or the people of the United States," Littlewood said, his voice rising. "The government funds my research. I depend on this funding. To suggest I'd bite the hand that feeds me is . . . is . . . *preposterous*."

"If you're not going to charge us," began Jillian,

but the professor cut her off.

"And as far as your threat to shut down my facility," said Littlewood, "you can't. I received approval status from your office just a few hours ago. And I categorically *insist*—"

"That's not possible," said Nevis. The professor had to be bluffing. He must be desperate. "That's impossible," Nevis repeated with more conviction. "It's my investigation, and I haven't signed off."

Littlewood was walking to a desk. "Someone from your office, name of . . . The name escapes me, but perhaps you'll recognize it . . ." He broke off, snatching a piece of paper from a fax machine.

"Here you are," said Littlewood, triumphantly. "Now I really must insist you leave."

Nevis grabbed the fax from Littlewood's hands. As he read through it, he frowned.

"Something's wrong," he muttered. Scowling at the signature he knew all too well, he pulled out his cell phone and dialed the SAC.

"Are you at the airport?" asked his boss. "Because that is the only place you should be calling me from right now."

"No, sir, I . . ." Nevis turned away from the group, suddenly wishing he'd made this call outside. He lowered his voice. "I was just shown a faxed document purporting to come from you to Arthur Littlewood—"

"Damned straight it came from me. I gave you very clear orders to drop that case and get your ass on a plane to Louisville. Are you informing me you're *not* at the airport?"

"No, sir, I'm with Littlewood now, and I'm telling

you—"

"That's it, Nevis. This is the last straw. I have given you chances when no one else would have, but enough is enough. You are in direct contravention of my orders, and I want your gun and your badge on my desk Monday at 7:00 a.m. sharp."

"Sir, you can't fire me—"

"Oh, can't I? Did I just forget my job title? Oh, look, here it is right on my door. *SAC.* I guess I *can* fire you. You're fired."

A jarring noise crackled in Nevis's ear—his boss had slammed the receiver down. Nevis felt the vein over his left temple begin to throb. This was outrageous. It was unfair. It was *humiliating!* And he'd be damned if he was going to take it lying down, skulking out with his tail between his legs like some flea-bitten dog.

He needed that confession from Littlewood. The SAC had said badge and gun on his desk by Monday at seven. Fine. Today was Friday. He had the law on his side for another forty-eight hours.

"Right," said Nevis. He placed his hands on his hips, flaring his jacket to give everyone a nice look at his shoulder holster and its contents. "I'm shutting this facility down and confiscating all property herein, effective immediately. Everyone out of the building."

The three assumed identical expressions of disbelief.

"Now!" said Nevis.

"You can't do that," said Jillian.

"I just did." He pulled out his phone. "And I'm placing a call to cut your power, so it's about to get really dark in here."

"Now, see here," began the professor.

Whatever protest he'd been planning was cut short because, at that moment, Everett rushed Nevis, grappling for his phone, which flew through the air to crash spectacularly into the painted cinder-block wall. Ignoring the ruined phone, Nevis focused on the young man. Nevis might have been caught off guard, but he'd had twenty-one years of training in scuffles like this, and it looked like Everett's only training had been with some hoity-toity boxing instructor. In under a minute, Nevis had him restrained and cuffed.

"Everett Randolph, I'm taking you in for assaulting a federal officer."

God, he'd missed moments like this.

Littlewood blustered over and said, "You've been fired. You can't arrest my student if they fired you."

"Well, that would be true," said Nevis, "except my change in status isn't effective until Monday. What day is it today? Oh, it's Friday. I guess I *can* arrest your student." He half despised himself in that moment for imitating his boss, but it was surprisingly satisfying.

The professor, jaw hanging open, now whipped out his phone.

"Calling a lawyer? On a Friday afternoon?" asked Nevis. "Good luck with that." He frog-marched his captive to the stairs.

"Everett!" It was the young woman. "Think of the time!"

"I know," replied Nevis's charge.

"No more talking," snapped Nevis. What was *think of the time* supposed to mean? The time the kid would do for assault? Who knew. Who *cared*. Nevis opened the door and, shoving the young man ahead, stepped out into the sweltering heat of a Florida summer afternoon.

As soon as he reached the top step outside, Nevis realized he ought to have made everyone march out in front of him. Still, what were they going to do? Start cramming equipment into their stockings? Fine. That would give him a reason to lock up all three of them. Three separate interrogations? Three associates second-guessing who would turn first? He could live with those odds.

After stuffing Everett in the back of the car, Nevis remembered that the vehicle was a rental and not designed for transporting criminals. Well, his arrestee didn't know that. Crossing to the front of the vehicle, Nevis activated the door's child safety lock—better than nothing. Damn, but it was hot in the car. During the time he'd been in the lab, the car's interior had warmed to the approximate temperature of freshly brewed coffee. Nevis frowned, and then he turned the car key far enough to activate the front windows, dropping them down several inches. Heat exhaustion wasn't going to make the kid more talkative.

"Excuse me, sir?"

The young man's eyes were a little wild. Panicking, possibly. Panic was good. Nevis could work with panic.

"Might I have a moment of your time?" asked Everett.

Hearing an insectlike buzzing, Nevis swatted the air near his exposed neck. All he needed from Florida was another of those yellow fly bites.

"I believe you'll wish to hear what I have to say, sir," said Everett.

Nevis paused, keeping the stairwell in his sights. Was the young man going to spill the beans on Littlewood and Khan? That would simplify his weekend. Not to mention improve his Monday morning. The bugs, meanwhile, were getting noisier. A damned bug convention. He should maybe slip inside the car. Turn on the AC while he was at it.

Swatting the air again, Nevis turned back to the driver's side door, entered the vehicle, slammed the door shut, and cranked the AC. Then he faced Everett.

"Well?"

51
· EVERETT ·
Florida, July

Everett had understood Jillian's hasty warning. Not that he'd needed a reminder of what was coming. He'd been thinking of nothing *but* the time and how to get Nevis out of the way before the officer saw people appearing out of thin air.

Although ordinarily the machine's noise was damped outside, Everett could hear it plainly. Probably as a result of operating at the higher harmonic. If the machine had fired up, everything was resting on Everett's ability to keep Nevis outside for the next several minutes. Fortunately, Nevis had been intrigued by Everett's seeming willingness to speak and had entered the car. Even more to Everett's purposes, the officer had turned on the noisy air conditioner.

"I would like to know," began Everett, "that is, well . . ." He paused. He needed to draw things out, but for how long?

"Any time now, son," said Nevis, checking his

watch.

Time. *Yes*, that was what Everett needed to know. "I should like to know the time, sir."

Nevis chuckled. "You want to know what time it is? What, so you can tell your Facebook friends the time of your arrest?" Nevis held up Everett's cell phone, which Everett did not recollect surrendering. The officer must have obtained it following that embarrassing episode of fisticuffs.

"Going to be tricky to use Facebook without your phone. Sorry, son."

"I regret that I have no Facebook friends," replied Everett, "however I should very much appreciate knowing the time. The *precise* time, if you please."

After giving Everett a strange look (probably for his polite speech—Jillian was always warning him to tone that down), Nevis consulted his watch, checking it against his phone.

"The *precise* time is 18:07, Eastern."

Everett nodded. Four minutes. The machine had fired up a minute earlier than they'd estimated. Not entirely unexpected given the experimental nature of the journey. Very well, then. To allow his friends to clear the first hurdle, Everett needed to keep Nevis here another four minutes.

"Thank you," said Everett.

"You got anything else to say?" asked Nevis.

"Yes. Yes, I certainly do." Three minutes and fifty seconds to go. That was . . . 230 seconds. He began to tap the seconds out by tens using his fingers, conveniently cuffed behind his back and out of Nevis's view. "What I should like to know is this." He paused. *Stretch the conversation for all it's worth.* He kept his eyes on Nevis, and the moment the officer's brow signaled irritation, Everett spoke again. "In the case of an individual who has identified himself or herself with falsified documentation, what is the severest punishment awaiting such a person, if convicted?" Another fifty seconds down.

"You want to know how long someone does time if they use a fake ID?"

"I believe the charge would be *for criminal possession of a forged instrument*," clarified Everett. Two minutes and fifty seconds to go: tap, tap, tap, tap, tap.

"Yes, I believe it might, depending on the circumstances and the state in which such a person was convicted," replied Nevis. "So what can you tell me about this purported individual? Does he or she have a name you can give me?" Nevis fumbled in a pocket and withdrew the notepad Everett had seen earlier in the lab. "A little cooperation goes a long way, son."

Everett frowned as though considering his options. Two minutes to go.

"Okay," said Nevis after only twenty seconds had elapsed. "There's not a whole lot of cooperation happening. So are we done here?" he demanded. "Because as fun as this has been, I've got a laboratory to shut down." He pocketed his note pad.

Another minute and three-quarters to go.

"This isn't easy for me," said Everett, his tone desperate. He had no need to fake that, at least.

Nevis rolled his eyes. "By all means, sit here and do some thinking about what *is* easy for you," said Nevis, turning off the AC. "Now if you'll excuse me, I've got work to do."

"Wait!" cried Everett.

"Time and tide, young man."

Nevis cut the engine, and with the decrease in noise, it became immediately apparent that something was going on down in the lab.

"What the hell?" muttered Nevis.

This time he didn't bother to acknowledge Everett's requests for further conversation.

Stepping from the car, Nevis slammed the door.

Nevis had to be stopped. Whatever the cost. Desperately, Everett tried to wriggle his wrists from the manacles, but his hands were too large to pass through.

Nevis meanwhile, his hands on his hips, seemed to be trying to decide if the loud thrumming noise indicated actual danger. Removing his jacket, he threw it onto the hood of the car, partially obscuring Everett's view in the process.

"You there!" shouted Everett. Nevis didn't even flinch.

If he could get himself out of the automobile, that would grab the officer's attention. Everett tried the back door, but it was locked. The front might not be locked, though. Stretching, he slid one long leg toward the front-door handle. He just needed to hook the handle with the toe of his shoe . . .

As the machine's screaming reached its pinnacle, Everett realized he'd lost count of how much time had passed. He had to get outside, and fast. He toed the door handle. Nothing. Nudged it again. Missed again. He was wasting time. Shimmying, he squirmed his way between the two front seats until he landed awkwardly in the passenger front seat. He couldn't see Nevis at first, but then he realized it was because the officer was already at the bottom of the stairs.

No!

Twisting, Everett turned from the door so that his hands could reach the handle. *Got it!* He wrenched the door open, pushed with his back, and then spun to kick it the rest of the way open.

The door squawked angrily, but the noise from the time machine masked the sound. With his arms still awkwardly cuffed behind him, Everett stumbled out of the car and called to Nevis.

"Sir, I have escaped and am no longer inside your vehicle."

Nothing.

"*Sir...*"

What was wrong with Nevis? The FBI agent, still in the stairwell, had gripped the banister rail and was walking, slowly, *backward,* up the stairs.

Everett's heart sank. Had Nevis seen something? He barely had time to ask the question before he saw Nevis reaching for the gun in his holster.

"*Wait!*" called Everett.

And then the basement door flew open and all hell broke loose.

52
· *LITTLEWOOD* ·

Florida, July

It had taken Littlewood an agonizing three minutes to be connected to Howell, Nevis's SAC, and that was only after he'd shouted at Howell's administrative assistant that *Yes, this was a matter of life and death!*

That had gotten her attention. What was more important, it had gotten Howell on the line, and Howell had given Littlewood what he needed. After a hasty goodbye, Littlewood scrambled out of the tiny office and into his laboratory. The time machine was now screaming at top decibel. Any second now Quintus and DaVinci would return, but in what state? Should he call an ambulance after all?

Jillian, wringing her hands, shouted, "Well?" upon seeing Littlewood.

"We don't have to obey Nevis. He has no authority," Littlewood called back. "Howell's sending the county sheriff immediately."

"Here?" Jillian's eyes grew wide.

"No help for it," said Littlewood, reaching again for his phone. "Might as well call an ambulance, too."

But at that moment, blue light arced through the room. A second later, their worst fears were realized: Quintus and DaVinci reappeared in awkward, crouched stances, and then, within a moment, both collapsed to the ground.

53

· *DAVINCI* ·

Florida, July

DaVinci felt the tug of space–time wrenching her from the Roman Republic, and then, after a familiar swell of heat and noise and confusion, she felt herself being dropped into the twenty-first century. She fell hard to her knees, tumbling off the platform of the time machine, feeling as always that she would never rise, never recover. But none of that mattered. Had Quintus made it? Forcing her eyes open, she stared. Her vision swam, but she could see enough to tell she was alone. She was facing the back corner of Littlewood's laboratory, and she was alone.

"Quintus! No-*oooo*!" Her cry became a howl of despair.

"DaVinci! You're alive!"

DaVinci tried turning to the voice—Jillian's, but nausea sent her back to her knees.

Jillian ran to her, throwing her arms around her.

"It's okay," said Jillian. "You're back. You're safe."

"*Quintus—*" DaVinci's throat had tightened so much that she couldn't speak. What had gone wrong? Was Quintus dead? Her stomach heaved. If he wasn't here, he was dead, either way. If not by the thugs, then by the passage of two thousand years. A drawn-out moan escaped her throat.

"I am here, beloved," said a deep male voice.

"Quintus?" DaVinci looked around wildly, feeling her stomach heaving again. She ignored it. Quintus was alive! Leaning heavily on Jillian, DaVinci reached for him. "You're *alive!*"

Half a second later, it was Quintus's arms around her. Quintus's damp, bloodstained toga pressed to her cheek. Quintus's voice murmuring comfort as he pressed his mouth to her forehead, kissing her hair and the top of her head.

"You're *alive*," murmured DaVinci.

"You're both alive," said Jillian, "but we're all in trouble."

DaVinci wanted to laugh. "You want to hear about trouble? Let me tell you about—"

"Everett may be in imminent peril," Littlewood shouted above the dying wail of the time machine.

"What's wrong?" asked DaVinci, confusion and nausea fighting inside her.

"An FBI agent with a gun just hauled Everett off in handcuffs," said Jillian.

"Seriously?" said DaVinci. "I leave you guys for *one day*, and this is what happens?"

"I need both of you to hide," Littlewood was shouting to Quintus and DaVinci. "You can't be seen. The sheriff is on his way, and Nevis is outside. My back office, maybe?"

DaVinci, staggering only a little, turned for the back office, but Quintus must have had other ideas. With one of his bring-the-thunder roars, Quintus took off across the room for the exit leading outside, sword drawn.

"Quintus, no!" cried Jillian.

"You mustn't be seen," called Littlewood, running after him.

DaVinci groaned. "Yeah, that's not gonna happen." And then, armed with the dagger she'd stolen off a douchebag a minute earlier—or two thousand years earlier—she took off after Quintus.

54

· *NEVIS* ·

Florida, July

There was a madman in a Roman gladiator costume. The madman had . . . *appeared* in the basement, and then he'd run out of it brandishing a sword. He was shouting in some language Nevis didn't recognize and—good God—he wasn't listening to Nevis's repeated orders to *Freeze—right there!*

Nevis raised his revolver, steadying his shaking right hand with his shaking left hand. Just aim. Just hold it steady.

"Freeze!"

And then, *wham!* The flat of a sword hammered his left forearm. Nevis uttered a choked cry and dropped his weapon. Cradled his arm. It wasn't responsive. Had the idiot broken his arm?

"You are in a lot of trouble," shouted Nevis. His arm felt numb, which meant it was probably going to hurt like the devil soon.

"*Servum nequam!*" shouted the costumed giant. "Dog! Cur!"

Nevis took a closer look at the madman. He was . . . *bleeding*. In fact, he was *covered* in blood. *Fresh* blood. And that was the moment Nevis decided to run for his car.

He was nearly there when the giant tackled him from behind. Nevis fell with a thud, partially breaking his fall with his good arm. Now a whole chorus was shouting at him, but whether they were trying to call off the giant or trying to egg him on, Nevis couldn't tell.

And then Nevis noticed the sword at his throat. There was blood on the sword. He registered one voice rising above all the others, calling shrilly: *No, Quintus!*

Nevis lifted his eyes from the sword to see a young woman wearing . . . Nevis didn't even know what to call it. She had interposed herself between Nevis and his attacker so that she was leaning over Quintus's weaponed arm and could look him in the eyes. She was telling the costumed giant in no uncertain terms to back off.

The sword disappeared. Nevis coughed. Thought he might be sick. Noticed something in the gravel, inches from his face. A thumb drive. Without thinking, Nevis grabbed the drive, pushed himself up, and ran like hell for his car.

55

· DAVINCI ·

Florida, July

As Nevis sped away, Littlewood addressed Quintus and DaVinci. "Take my keys and drive to Father Joe's. Wait for me there. Do you understand? You need medical attention. Forget hiding in my office. It doesn't even have a lock, and we can't risk you being seen here looking like that."

DaVinci examined Quintus, whose toga was more red than white by a long shot.

"Is your own safety certain?" asked Quintus, gripping Littlewood's shoulder to stop him in his tracks.

"Yes, yes," replied Littlewood. "I'll be fine as long as you're gone before the sheriff arrives. Everett—you stay here. We'll need the sheriff's help with those handcuffs. Go on! Off with the rest of you!"

"We're taking *my* car," Jillian said to Littlewood, handing his keys back. "It will be better if your car is here and not mine. Besides, mine has tinted windows." She turned to Quintus. "In the car. Now. Explanations will have to wait."

DaVinci grabbed Quintus's uninjured arm and pulled him toward Jillian's car. "If Littlewood says he's safer with us gone, then he *is* safer with us gone. Let's go!"

She had the presence of mind to join Quintus in the back seat so she could treat his wounds.

Jillian had the presence of mind to open her glove compartment and toss a first aid kit to DaVinci.

"Buckle up," said Jillian. "We're not taking the slow road."

DaVinci opened the first aid box and located a pathetically small roll of gauze. She looked at Quintus's bleeding forehead. At Quintus's bleeding left bicep. At Quintus's bleeding collarbone. And knee. And shin.

"Where do I even start?" she muttered.

She was trying to triage more blood than she'd seen in a lifetime of sibling hijinks. The whole situation was ridiculous. Five minutes ago, she'd been fighting for her life, and now Jillian was driving them *who knew where* while DaVinci tried to decide which freaking wound needed gauze the most. They *all* needed it the most!

Jillian cornered hard, zipping past the Piggly Wiggly. A woman in the parking lot waved, and Jillian, never too busy to be polite, returned the wave. The ordinariness of the gesture snapped something inside DaVinci, and she felt laughter welling up inside. Half a second later, she was chortling, and then laughing, and then unable to stop laughing.

"So . . . sorry," she said to Quintus, attempting to stop. But then, seeing Jillian's astonished face in the rearview mirror, DaVinci nearly doubled over with laughter. "So . . . inappropriate," she said, gasping. "But I . . . can't . . . stop."

Quintus seemed amused at least. And his bicep, to which he'd pressed a torn strip of his tunic, seemed to be bleeding less. Maybe laughter *was* good medicine.

But when Quintus, his voice ragged, requested a Band-Aid from the first aid kit, DaVinci's laughter turned a corner and became tears. And not delicate, shining tears glistening in her pale green eyes, either, but genuine ugly crying. Tears. Snot. Wailing.

"I thought they were going to ki-*ill* you," she said to Quintus between sobs. "And I was trying so hard." She sucked in a deep breath. "I was doing everything I could think of, but those guys were really good at not getting stabbed."

Here, Jillian released a delicate snort of laughter. "Sorry, sorry—*so* sorry!"

"She fought bravely," Quintus declared. "We were simply outnumbered."

"We totally were," agreed DaVinci. "I'm sorry, you guys. I don't know what came over me. Shaughnessy-Pavlovs are *not* big crybabies. *Ugh.*" Attempting a smile, DaVinci swiped at her tears using the now-soaked roll of gauze.

"No one is going to mistake you for a crybaby," said Jillian.

"What is . . . *crybaby*?" asked Quintus.

With a grunt of laughter, DaVinci reached into her purse and wrenched out Quintus's Latin-English dictionary. "Here," she said, handing the book to Quintus. "Looks like you're going to need this more than me after all."

And then she proceeded to tell Jillian what an amazing swordsman Quintus was, how movies like *Gladiator* and *300* could learn a lot from watching him in action. "I mean, the *movies* can't learn or whatever, but the, you know, the guys that make up the fight scenes totally could."

"Fight directors?" offered Jillian.

"Them. Yes. They've got nothing on Quintus Maximus here."

"*Valerius,*" corrected Quintus.

"Quintus Valerius *Maximus,*" insisted DaVinci, wiping the last of her tears from her face.

"These 'directors of fights,'" said Quintus gravely, "could learn much from observing DaVinci in action. She is most resourceful."

Tears filled DaVinci's lower lids. "Really?" She blinked the tears away. "That might be the nicest thing a guy has ever said to me."

"You have associated with men of poor imagination," Quintus said. He tucked a stray curl behind her ear. And then gathered more of it in his hand, smiling softly at it. *At her freaking hair.*

A warm, tingling sensation awoke in her belly—her fireflies, back again. They swirled and twinkled and fluttered, and it felt as if she were being bathed in light, from the inside out. She tilted her head up to gaze at Quintus.

Hunk. Magic.

"Even covered in blood," she murmured.

Quintus's mouth pulled into a questioning smile.

Yeah. She needed to kiss that mouth. And then, just as DaVinci was about to go in for a kiss, Jillian announced, "We're here."

Here appeared to be the parking lot of a Catholic Church.

"Pater Joe will be most pleased to meet you," Quintus said softly.

DaVinci attempted to straighten her slave tunic, and then, grunting, gave up and simply followed Quintus and Jillian. As they rounded a corner dominated by the world's largest bird of paradise plant, DaVinci got her first view of the church proper. She blinked twice. And smiled. The house of worship where this Father Joe person was apparently to be found was painted blue. Appallingly, unbelievable, eye-soreness-inducing *aqua blue*.

56
· *DAVINCI* ·

Florida, July

It was the X-ray of her metacarpal that settled things for DaVinci with regard to which time line she preferred to live in. As soon as Jillian noticed how purple and swollen DaVinci's left middle finger was, there had been a trip to the ER, and an X-ray, and a call home to say she was fine (but she was in the ER), and her parents expressing concern that she'd broken her left middle finger for the *second* time in less than six months.

Which, according to the physician in Florida, she *hadn't*. DaVinci had grilled the doctor, asking him if he was really, totally, *120 percent sure* her left middle finger had never been broken before.

"Not according to the X-rays," said the physician.

Her finger was still the same finger from the original time line. Well, what had she expected? That it would have broken and healed itself to match the current time line? Of course not. Her body had been *with her* the whole time. It was like the paint on her shoes from working on her commission. The commission might have vanished, but DaVinci's shoes, which had been *with her* the whole time hadn't lost their paint spots any more than she'd lost her original memories. If her paint spots and her memories hadn't vanished, and if her body was still her same body, then her muscles must still . . . know their stuff. It stood to reason she still knew how to paint. At least, she hoped she did. In any case, it was time to find out.

And so, on the drive from the hospital back to Father Joe's, where Littlewood had insisted everyone stay until the sheriff sent word Nevis was locked up, DaVinci did some hard thinking.

The question was this: Could she live in this time line? The fact that this time line had *Quintus* as a part of her life made the answer pretty obvious, but she wanted to make her decision free from the intoxication of *hunk-magic*.

In this time line, she had no scholarship to attend a prestigious art program at a UC school. In this time line, she had no awards. No commissions from rich and famous Santa Barbarians. No job, even, unless she counted the restaurant job. (She didn't.)

But presumably, she still had her skills.

So could she live without the prestige and recognition?

As long as she could still paint like she used to, she could live without a lot of things. She gazed at her hands. Flexed them. Bad idea. That middle finger, broken courtesy of *Doucheous Bagus*, a Roman youth who'd been dead for two thousand years, was throbbing again.

"You okay?" Jillian must have heard her wincing.

Was she okay? Her brow furrowed.

"DaVinci?"

"Yeah. Actually, I think I might be."

That night, DaVinci waited until everyone was asleep in Father Joe's capacious vestry, which had a door connecting it to the Sunday school wing.

She'd been listening to the sounds of her companions sleeping for half an hour according to her fully charged phone. Jillian was on an air mattress beside her, with Quintus on the far side of the vestry, sleeping in the room's only actual *bed*, and Everett and Littlewood bunched on the other side of a bench Father Joe had set up for everyone on the floor to use as a nightstand.

DaVinci thought it was more likely Father Joe wanted a physical barrier between her and Quintus. They hadn't exactly been subtle, staring at each other all through their late-night dinner and that round of Polish liqueur. (DaVinci, who'd made plans for the night, had only pretended to sip the stuff.)

DaVinci's plans, strangely enough, did not involve Quintus. Or, not directly.

This was about her muscles, and the memories they had either retained or lost.

As quietly as she could, she scooted off the mattress she was sharing with Jillian. And from there to the door leading to the Sunday school classrooms. The door opened silently—Father Joe *did* seem like the kind of guy who would keep his hedges trimmed and his hinges oiled—and she slipped into the corridor.

Neither the kindergarten/first grade classroom

nor the second/third grade room had what she wanted. She struck out with middle school, too, and there was no high school. That left the classroom for the combined fourth, fifth, and sixth grades. She entered the room, closed the door behind her, and flicked on the lights. After searching the closet that had held art supplies in the other rooms, DaVinci found something that would work, in a pinch.

"Watercolors," she said, without enthusiasm. "It had to be watercolors."

She sighed. Well, watercolors were still technically *paint*. It was better than tearing construction paper into teeny, tiny pieces for a paper mosaic. Although, after those mosaics in Rome, she was going to have to explore that art form . . .

It took another few minutes to find paper and set herself up, and a long time to scroll through her pictures from Rome to find one she wanted to try, but eventually she found a photo that was perfect. Several, actually. And so, from the hours of midnight to four in the morning, DaVinci painted and painted and painted.

It was hard. A real challenge, but that was because watercolor was such an unforgiving medium.

"One mistake and you start over," she muttered to herself, laying down a Roman sky, complete with not-painted-over white sections that would become wispy clouds. Soon, though, she forgot all about how hard watercolor was and simply . . . *painted*. She captured angles, planes, highlights, shadows, Quintus's frowns, his eyebrows raised, his eyebrows pulling together, biceps, *latissimus dorsi*, the swell of fabric and leather draped over glutes (*wow* on the *gluteus maximus*, even under a skirt), the clenched jaw, the jaw when it relaxed, and those lips . . . Yeah. She could totally get lost trying to capture those lips.

When she was too tired to hold a brush any longer—it had actually fallen out of her hands twice—she took a long look at the three paintings drying on the counter, yawned hugely, and mumbled, without irony, "Thank God. I've still got it." And then she stumbled back into bed, sleeping soundly until ten the next morning.

It was the sound of Littlewood's laughter from somewhere down the hall that woke her up. She rubbed her eyes, sat up, and noticed that Jillian and Everett, too, had already gotten up. Quintus was still sleeping. He'd thrown off his blankets, revealing a body covered in bandages. DaVinci winced. Tempting as it was, she couldn't justify waking him up.

Instead, she pulled on the sweatshirt and sweatpants someone (Father Joe?) had set at the foot of her bed and traipsed out of the vestry toward the sound of Littlewood's voice.

"Ah," said Littlewood, upon seeing DaVinci. "Good morning. Did you sleep well?" Without waiting for an answer, he said, "I'm going for doughnuts. Do you have a favorite?"

"Old-fashioned," replied DaVinci. Her voice sounded raspy.

"There's coffee," said Father Joe.

At the sight of Father Joe, DaVinci's stomach knotted, remembering her nocturnal, non-permission-based activities in the Sunday school hall.

"Coffee would be great," she said, with a tug of guilt.

Well, she *should* feel guilty. She'd used up the entire supply of watercolors for grades four through six. She should have freaking asked before *stealing things from the Catholic Church!*

As soon as Littlewood left, DaVinci turned to Father Joe. "So, *um* . . ." She exhaled.

Yeah.

"Forgive me, Father, for I have sinned."

Father Joe quirked his head to one side. "Do I sense . . . irony?"

DaVinci felt her cheeks warming. "Only kind of. Come with me." As the two of them walked to the fourth through sixth grade classroom, she explained that she'd broken into the art supplies. That she'd really needed to know if she could still paint. She left out the part about time travel having created doubts for her on that score.

"In here," she said, guilt gnawing her insides. "So about my penance?"

Father Joe crossed to the paintings and examined them. "These are lovely," he said.

"I'm so sorry," said DaVinci. "I'll buy more watercolors for the kids. And paper."

"That seems fair," said Father Joe.

DaVinci's phone chirped with a text from Littlewood. She read it.

By the way, I told Father Joe everything. Felt I had to, and of course he's bound to secrecy since I told him in confession. Wasn't that clever? Anyway, I thought you should know.

DaVinci raised her brows and then her gaze. "That was Dr. Littlewood. So I guess my half-assed attempt—oh, *um*, sorry—I guess my, *uh*, attempted confession wasn't the first confession you heard today?"

Father Joe smiled.

"Right. You can't comment on that," said DaVinci. "But I can. So, yeah. These are all Quintus. Well, obviously." She flushed. "They're of Quintus in his hometown. Home city. Home capital of the empire. Whatever."

"Republic," said Father Joe. "Rome was a republic at this time." He gathered the watercolor paintings. "I wonder if you would allow me to give one of these to a parishioner? She's bedridden, and her favorite Bible story is of the centurion whose faith our Lord commended."

"Sure. Of course. Give them all to her with my blessing! *Um*, I mean, my blessing isn't, well, *um* . . ." She flushed.

"I should be delighted to give them to her with your blessing," said Father Joe.

DaVinci half groaned, half sighed and shook her head at herself. "You know, it *has* been a while since my last confession."

"Perhaps some coffee first?" asked Father Joe.

"Yes. Coffee. Absolutely. Absolution can wait."

Great. Now she was making bad religious puns. In front of a priest. She flushed a deeper red, if that was possible.

"Good one," said Father Joe as he led her to the coffee.

She frowned. "Yeah?"

"Oh yes."

DaVinci smiled.

She downed two cups of, honestly, pretty bad coffee, helped by an ungodly number of sugar cubes.

"Perhaps you'd like to take a cup to Quintus?" asked Father Joe.

"Oh, sure," said DaVinci. "I guess he's on bed rest?"

"Doctor's orders," replied Father Joe.

Unlike DaVinci, Quintus hadn't gone to the ER. Father Joe had called in a favor with a retired surgeon who had stitched Quintus up in the vestry, no questions asked.

She poured a cup of coffee and then frowned at it.

"What is it?" asked Father Joe.

"I don't know how Quintus takes his coffee. Sugar and cream?"

Father Joe smiled. "Milk and honey, actually. I used to wonder why, but now it makes sense—"

DaVinci finished his sentence: "Because, no sugar in the Roman Republic."

"No coffee, either," they both said at the same time.

DaVinci laughed. Father Joe was growing on her.

And then, with Quintus's mostly milk-and-honey coffee in hand, she walked back to the vestry. It was time she and Quintus had an "us" talk.

57
·QUINTUS·
Florida, July

Quintus had awoken several times in the night, although he'd fallen back asleep each time, thanks to the relievers of pain he'd been given. But every twist, every turn, made something ache. There had been no need for the physician tending him to advise bed rest; Quintus wasn't sure he would ever get up again.

He was awake when DaVinci entered the silent vestry, and he made an effort to sit up.

"Careful, careful," said DaVinci, setting down a coffee cup and rushing to his side. "Let me help you."

"I am ashamed, but I do not think I can rise without assistance," said Quintus.

"Okay, one, that is the stupidest thing *ever* to be ashamed of," said DaVinci, "and, two—" She broke off when their eyes met. "*Um*, I brought you coffee. With honey and milk."

Quintus smiled. "Much thanks."

Between them, they managed to get him propped up against a wall using every pillow in the room. It hurt, greatly, which Quintus did his best to conceal.

"Here's your coffee," said DaVinci. "*Hmm*. It might be a little cold now."

He took the cup and swallowed. Even swallowing hurt.

"Is it too cold?" asked DaVinci.

It was too cold. "It is perfect," he replied. He would drink cold coffee rather than have her depart. He didn't want her to leave. Not even for two minutes.

"When do you return to Sancta Barbaria?" he asked.

DaVinci's eyes twinkled. "Santa Barbara," she said. The twinkle disappeared as quickly as it had come. "And, well, I don't know," she said softly, her eyes down.

It was a terrible answer. It was the least satisfactory answer ever given.

"I was thinking," she began, "that it might be nice to stick around awhile."

This was a wonderful answer. The most satisfactory imaginable! He should say something. He should say, *I would like that*, or maybe, *Florida is a lovely place*, or . . . or . . .

How was one to know the right thing to say?

"The sunsets the last two evenings," DaVinci was saying, "oh my gosh. Unbelievable colors in the sky. It's the clouds, I think. Or the moisture in the air? I have no idea what makes the sky go all crazy with color like that."

"The skies here are the fairest I have seen," agreed Quintus. Yet she, the girl beside him, was fairer still. But no doubt she had been told this many times.

Why could he think of nothing to say to her, nothing that would convey the extent to which Amor's arrows had pierced his heart?

"And that doctor who sewed you up last night? He said there's a huge, *wealthy* population of retired people, and in my experience, *wealthy people* means *clients*. *Hmm*. Do you know the word *client?*"

"Rome invented it," said Quintus. How marvelous. He had managed to bring the conversation to Rome, a topic he had sworn to forego, in consideration of all the girl had suffered there.

"So speaking of Rome," said the girl, "I might have . . . well, listen, I took some pictures of you when you were at the second-hand jewelry place. The light was amazing. And I didn't have anything else to do. And, well, I'm sorry I didn't ask your permission first."

She had taken his picture? What did that mean?

"There was no need to obtain my permission," he said softly.

"Okay. That's good. Because I also made some paintings from the pictures, and Father Joe asked if he could give one to a parishioner. That's a person who—"

"I understand *parishioner*," said Quintus. He was on the verge of explaining that that word had Roman roots as well, but decided to hold his tongue. He didn't want to speak of words and roots.

"I know I acted like a total spoiled brat yesterday," said the girl. "I want to apologize."

"There is no need," said Quintus. "My behavior was also . . . regrettable."

"Well, when in Rome . . ." The girl trailed off, smiling.

"When in Rome?" asked Quintus.

"It's a saying. *When in Rome* . . . *um*, actually, that *is* the whole saying, but the implication is that if you are in an unfamiliar place, like, say, Rome, then you should behave the way the locals behave."

"I see. That is commendable advice."

The girl laughed again. The skin to the sides of her eyes folded in soft crinkles when she laughed. And on her round cheeks there appeared . . .

"What is the word for the . . . indentations, just here," he asked, touching her face.

At his touch, she took a hurried breath. "Oh. *Um* . . . dimples? Maybe? I have the worst dimples in the world."

Quintus smiled softly. "I do not think you are employing the word *worst* in its intended sense."

"Oh . . ." The girl smiled again.

There had to be a way to speak his feelings. To say something that would, at least, keep her here.

"Your injured finger," he asked, "does it pain you?"

"It's nothing. Seriously nothing." She examined her injured hand. "I don't even want to ask how you're feeling."

"My injuries are as nothing," said Quintus. It was both a lie and the truth. Compared to the ache with which he yearned for the girl, his injuries were nothing. Why could he not speak these feelings to her?

"Quintus?"

"Yes?"

"I want to ask you something. You don't have to answer, but . . . well . . . Look, I'm just going to ask it." She closed her eyes as if in resolve. "Do you still have feelings for . . . for your wife? Because . . . well, I might have feelings for you—"

"Beloved," whispered Quintus. Her eyes flew open.

"Okay, that is, like, the third time I've heard you use that word. To me. At me. Whatever. Do you actually know what that word means?" Her voice had grown soft as she asked the question.

"That which is treasured or cherished," replied Quintus. His heart began to beat faster.

She smiled. The . . . *dimples* returned. He raised his hand to her cheek.

"Dimples," he said softly. "Yours are the most lovely."

This time, when she inhaled at his touch, she seemed also to shiver. She moved closer. Quintus's pulse roared in his ears.

"Okay," said the girl, "I really, *really* need you to answer my question."

Quintus stared into her eyes, pools of luminous green. Question? What question?

"Your wife," she said, as if reading his mind. "Mucia. Sixteen- or seventeen-year-old with long straight black hair."

"Mucia?"

"Do you still have feelings for her?"

Oh. *That* question.

"It matters to me," DaVinci said softly. "I need you to be honest."

"I have . . . feelings," said Quintus. "Of disgust. Of disappointment. Of . . . regret. Yes, I have many feelings, but none are pleasing."

"Oh," whispered the girl. "That's good. Not

pleasing is very, *very* good."

Her head was now quite near his. He wanted to kiss her. Would she be offended? She had suffered so many affronts yesterday . . .

She was speaking again. "So, my feelings, the ones I, *um*, just mentioned a minute ago, they are very pleasing. I like you Quintus."

A smile broke across his face. The smile hurt like, what was the expression? Like Hades? His smile grew. "Never has a man been more favored by Fortuna," said Quintus. "I, also, like you."

The girl's cheeks grew pink. She looked down at Quintus's hands. "I might even . . ." She looked up, meeting his eyes. "You know what? After everything we've been through together, I'm just going to say it. I might be in love with you, Quintus. So as long as you don't have a problem with that, I'd like to stay in Florida awhile. Like, indefinitely, because, yeah. Totally falling in love here. And lust, too, which I might as well admit, right? Because, just, *wow*. Quintus, you are the most gorgeous specimen of man I have ever set eyes on, and let me tell you, I. Have. *Set. Eyes.* Lots of eyes. Lots of setting—"

Quintus touched her face, her beautiful pink and dimpled face.

"I'll, *um*, stop talking now," she said in a whisper. "Your turn?"

58

· *DAVINCI* ·

Florida, July

He wasn't saying anything. Well, he was touching her cheek like she was some freaking . . . *treasure* or something. Why wasn't he saying anything? Someone should be saying something.

"Listen, you've been through so much," she whispered. "I'm sorry. I'm so sorry for everything you've lost. I know what it's like waking up to find out you're not even sure who you are anymore."

Quintus's brow furrowed at this, but he didn't say anything. He just took her face in his large, strong hands. He touched his forehead to hers.

Oh God. She wasn't sure she remembered how to breathe. From somewhere outside the vestry, she was aware of the sound of voices. Laughter rising and falling in the distance. But that was *out there*, and Quintus was *in here*, his hands weaving in her hair— she probably had the worst case of bed head, like, *ever*—

And then she wasn't thinking about her hair or

Quintus's losses or her losses, because Quintus's mouth was on hers, hungry and wanting, and his hands were describing the curve of her neck, shoulders, and waist, and all she could think about was wanting, wanting, *wanting*, and she was reaching under his shirt, feeling the heat of his skin where her hand touched his chest—

Which was the moment the vestry door swung open.

Oh, dear holy saints and apostles! DaVinci pulled away from Quintus, gasping for breath and attempting to smooth her wild curls. She was making out in a *church* and she'd just been caught by . . . whom? A priest? She turned to look.

"Jillian," said DaVinci, breathless.

Not a priest. Thank God. Literally. She was literally thanking God for that one. She turned to Quintus, who was staring at her, eyes dark with longing, breathing hard. *Wow.*

She turned back to Jillian.

"So we were just, *um* . . . Yeah. I guess you saw—"

"I came to let you know there are doughnuts and coffee."

"Doughnuts," said DaVinci. "And coffee."

"Yes," said Jillian. "And Father Joe is wheeling them this way on a tea trolley, so you might want to—"

"Yes!" said DaVinci, leaping off Quintus's bed. "Yes, I might. Absolutely. Thank you." She hugged her friend.

Boy, when she finally got around to it, she was going to have to make one heck of a confession.

59

·DAVINCI·

Florida, One Month Later

DaVinci was painting again. Dr. Littlewood had offered her the entire upstairs space of the industrial unit above his basement laboratory. "I've never had a use for the space above ground," he had explained. "I needed a basement, to dampen the sound."

She was painting eight, ten, twelve hours a day—well, night. She'd adjusted her schedule to match Quintus's, sleeping from four or five in the morning until ten or eleven at Jillian's apartment. She knew she should pay rent, but every time she offered, Jillian shrugged her off. "Maybe when you get a commission."

She needed work. She knew this. She needed an actual job. But it felt great to be painting again, and she didn't want to give up the few hours a day she got to spend alone with Quintus. So she kept painting and not getting a job until one day when Halley and Edmund showed up with a package for her.

DaVinci was sitting at dinner with Quintus, Jillian

and Everett, and Halley and Edmund.

"Oh my goodness," said Halley. "I almost forgot. I visited your parents, and they wanted me to give this to you."

It was a package sent to DaVinci's Montecito address, coming from a *different* Montecito address that DaVinci didn't recognize.

"Go on," said Jillian, grinning. "Open it!"

"Is this from you?"

Jillian shook her head.

DaVinci looked at Quintus.

"Don't look at me," he said.

"Very nice use of idiom," said Halley to Quintus.

"Awesome, dude," agreed Edmund.

DaVinci opened the package. Inside she found a handful of photographs, a journal, a letter, and a packet of gummy bears.

"Okay, seriously, what is with all the gummy bears?" asked DaVinci.

"You tell *us*," said Jillian and Halley at the same time.

DaVinci shook her head. "I have no idea. Must be some alternate time line thing."

"Read the letter," suggested Everett.

"Aloud," requested Quintus.

So she did.

> *Dear DaVinci,*
>
> *It's taken us over eighteen months, but my sister and I finally finished going through Geraldine's things, and we thought you'd like to have these pictures. We read the journal, and we both agreed you should have it, too. (You might want some tissue, though.)*
>
> *Again, we want to thank you for making our*

mother's final months such good ones. You were all she could talk about on the phone—well, you'll see when you read her journal.
With warmest regards,
Ernesto and Amelia

DaVinci looked up. "Who are Ernesto, Amelia, and Geraldine?"

No one had an answer.

"Read the journal, maybe?" suggested Jillian.

So she did, curling up with it on Jillian's bed while the others ate dessert in the main room.

An hour later, with mascara streaks on both cheeks, she told Quintus, Everett and Jillian, and Halley and Edmund what she'd learned.

"According to this journal, I gave private painting lessons to a woman—to Geraldine—who was dying of lung cancer. She'd painted in college, in Italy, but then she quit when she became a mother, and, anyway, the point is, her kids Ernesto and Amelia, who are like, my parents' ages, hired me to give her twice-a-week painting classes for four months, which apparently, she didn't want at first, so that must have been fun, but eventually she and I really hit it off, it sounds like. Oh, and I guess I made her keep an art journal," she said, raising the journal.

"You never said anything about this," said Halley.

"You told me once you had an octogenarian friend," said Jillian.

"I don't know what to say," said DaVinci. "Maybe it was hard for me to talk about her, with her dying. Oh, and she had a dying wish I'm guessing I never talked about with you guys, either."

Jillian and Halley shook their heads.

"Of what nature was her wish?" asked Quintus.

DaVinci turned to Quintus. She suspected he took this sort of thing pretty seriously. "Well," she said, "it sounds like she was obsessed with taking me to Rome, staying at the St. Regis, and visiting the Vatican Museum to see the Sistine Chapel."

"Wait—you went to the Vatican Museum and didn't tell us?" asked Halley.

"And stayed at the St. Regis?" asked Jillian.

"No," said DaVinci. "We never got to do that. She was too sick. She just *wanted* us to, and she made me promise I would go on my own someday."

"Well," said Everett, "you made it to Rome at least."

DaVinci frowned as a sudden idea occurred to her. Had she been saving money to travel to Italy and stay at the St. Regis? Was that why she'd worked so hard at the fish restaurant?

"These photos," said Jillian. "You're in some of them. This must be Geraldine. I don't suppose she looks familiar?"

DaVinci shook her head. She wished she could say yes, after having read the journal. "Geraldine sounds like an amazing woman. I wish I *could* remember her." Then she turned to her friends.

"I have a question. Did, *um*, alternate-me ever explain my obsession with working forty hours a week at the Enterprise Fish Company?"

"You just said you were saving," said Jillian.

"For what?"

Jillian shook her head.

"Travel," said Halley.

"You should have told me," Jillian said to DaVinci. "I would have helped you get to Italy."

Halley gave Jillian a sad half smile. "That's why she didn't tell you. DaVinci told me her travel was something she had to do on her own."

"That sounds like me," said DaVinci. And then she smiled. Because, for once, this crazy, alternate-time line DaVinci *did* sound like her. She felt a sudden swell of gratitude inside, for this other DaVinci who hadn't given up entirely on art. Who had taken a job with an (apparently) irascible old woman and taught her to fall in love with painting again. Who had quit school to work forty hours a week, even though it made her smell like clam chowder, so that she could study art in Italy because of a promise she'd made to a dying woman.

"Wow," said Halley, who had flipped to a random page in the journal and started reading. "One thing comes across loud and clear—you made this woman so happy. She *loved* her lessons with you."

"I'm so sorry for . . . for what her loss must have meant to you," said Jillian.

Everett murmured in agreement.

"The journal entries ended on Valentine's Day 2017," said DaVinci. "I guess that's when she died."

Jillian's hand flew to her mouth.

"What?"

"DaVinci, that's the day you quit school."

"I quit school on Valentine's Day?"

Jillian nodded. "In 2017. Midterm. You didn't even try to get your tuition back or anything."

"I guess she meant a lot to me."

"Wow," said Halley.

"Oh," said DaVinci. "And there's something else. I think I understand now about the gummy bears. Why I liked them and . . ." She paused. "And why it was too hard for me to talk about them."

"Really?" asked Halley.

"Can you tell us now?" asked Jillian.

DaVinci picked up the packet of gummy bears from the box and looked at it wistfully, wishing she had the memories that went with it.

"I guess Geraldine didn't have much appetite on her chemo days. Her kids worried about that, and I, *um*, got her to eat. Sort of. She liked sour candy. Which isn't known for its health benefits, unless you're talking gummy bears, which are gelatin-based. And come in sour flavors, like lemon and lime. And I guess I was the one who picked the lemon and lime ones out for her, and I ate the rest, to keep her company and, like, make sure she got some calories down."

"Oh wow," said Jillian, covering her mouth with her hand. "That is so sweet."

"You know what?" said DaVinci. "I just figured out what I'm going to do."

"About traveling to Italy?" asked Halley.

"Oh. No, actually. Although I guess I'll have to work on that, too," she said. "Here's my idea. Florida is full of retired people, right? What if I advertised painting classes for the retired?"

"Like a geriatrics class?" asked Halley doubtfully.

"Yes," replied DaVinci. "Apparently I am skilled in working with the more challenging elements of that population. It says so right here." She lifted the journal.

"I think it's a great idea," said Jillian, clapping her

hands together. "So who wants to make a business plan?"

Much later that night, DaVinci sat with Quintus, putting the finishing touches on a proposal she planned to take to all the senior centers within a forty-mile radius of Wellesley, Florida.

"It is a most noble idea," said Quintus, speaking softly, his chin resting on her shoulder.

"Thank you," said DaVinci.

"In general, your culture holds not the elderly with the respect that is their due. I am pleased to know it is not so with you, personally."

DaVinci blushed. "Okay. You give the weirdest, best compliments."

"I have several more. I would speak in praise of the freckles upon your bosom."

"Wait. What? Oh my gosh. Is that why you're resting your chin on my shoulder?"

"The view is most praiseworthy."

DaVinci, laughing, shoved his head off her shoulder.

"I would speak in praise of your eyes," said Quintus.

"I've been told they're luminous," she said softly.

"Indeed? Whose report is this?"

She smiled. "Just some guy I met up with, who wouldn't mind his own business."

Quintus frowned. "I shall have words with him."

DaVinci laughed. "Yeah, good luck with that."

"This is an idiom?"

DaVinci nodded. "Generally used for sarcasm."

"Nevertheless, I shall have words with the man."

She leaned in until her head was resting against his. "Not advisable."

"I *shall—*"

"It was you, you over-testosteroned dweeb."

"I do not know . . . *dweeb.*"

"It means . . . dork. Sort of. Or idiot, but in a nice way."

Quintus frowned. "You give the strangest praise."

"Oh, quit with the praise and just kiss me, already."

And so he did. For a long time. And for a couple who had already traveled over two thousand years together, that was saying something.

THE END

For information on all releases by Cidney Swanson:
cidneyswanson.com

Acknowledgments

I owe a lot of people a lot of thank yous, so here goes. Huge thanks to Dr. Science for the formulae (a good Latin word) and answers to "What does that mean?" I also owe you for tromping around the Forum Romanum and its environs with me, even though I was running a fever and doubtless very grumpy at the time. Special thanks to Elizabeth and Jacob, who drove me all over rural central Florida in search of a perfectly dilapidated dock, and also general thanks for educating me about the area. Big thanks to Kimberley of www.kimrlustudios.com for answering my art-related questions. Thank you Nathalia Suellen for giving Quintus the hunktastic cover he deserves. Thanks to Mariette and the whole team at Kindle Press for all your hard work! And finally, for those readers who have been waiting for this book for rather a long while, thanks for your patience. There is so much to research! All errors regarding life in ancient Rome are my own, but now at least now you know, should you ever rent an apartment there (and then), not to expect a room with a view.

SNEAK PEAK INSIDE THE NEXT THIEF IN TIME BOOK

ONE
·NEVIS·

Florida, The Present

Nevis, driving north out of Florida on the I75, wasn't thinking about terrorists taking down the power grid. He was having trouble with coherent thought. What on God's green earth had he just witnessed? Three hours ago, he had watched as two people appeared between equipment that had been spitting blue fire in Arthur Littlewood's clandestine laboratory. Two people who had not been there a moment earlier. He saw them appear out of nowhere and slump to the ground. What had he seen? One thing was for sure, he was glad no one in that room knew he'd seen it.

Gripping the wheel of his rental car, Nevis made a mental shortlist of possibilities.

Secret deep-cover government agency technology.
Terrorist activity.
Alien technology.

Honestly? He had no idea what he'd just stumbled across. But he was pretty sure that whatever it was,

Jules Khan's death was mixed up in it. A shiver ran down Nevis's spine. Littlewood hadn't seemed like a killer. Neither had the young woman from Santa Barbara. Everett, the young man who'd opened the door—was he some high-level assassin sent to eliminate Khan when Khan had demanded hush money? But Everett could hardly even defend himself in a fist fight.

Unless . . .

What if his assailant had *pretended* to be unable to defend himself? They had all been intent on keeping Nevis from seeing anything, that was for sure. He shuddered, remembering the flashes of light. The two people who had appeared out of nowhere.

Nevis had FBI clearance for another two days. Less, maybe. He'd blocked calls from his SAC after passing the county sheriff back at the complex where Littlewood's secret lab had been located. He tapped his fingers against the steering wheel. He wanted answers. What had he witnessed? Something big, that much was clear. Littlewood had said his work was government funded. Okay. That was a place to start. Find out more about Littlewood's government funding. What branch was it from? How long had he been getting it? These were things that would be a lot trickier to research two days from now. That decided it.

Exiting the freeway, Nevis pulled into the parking lot of the Valdosta Walmart Supercenter. He needed to figure out his next move. If Littlewood's funding was governmental, then maybe the reason Nevis had been ordered to back off was because the FBI had been told to back off. The forces behind a secret of this magnitude must be powerful. And deadly.

Nevis swallowed and then reached up to loosen his tie. He shifted his seat, tipping it back to a more comfortable angle. As he did so, his keys shifted in his pants pocket, jabbing his thigh. Except . . . his keys were in the ignition. He reached into his pocket.

Huh.

It was the thumb drive he'd picked up in front of Littlewood's clandestine operation.

Nevis's heart began to beat double-time. Handing the thumb drive over to his SAC wasn't even a remote temptation. He fired up his laptop, inserted the drive, and examined the contents.

Five hours later, Nevis had a name and an address. He'd located the possible whereabouts of someone calling himself Ken Julius, a name he'd found on the thumb drive in a list of aliases once under consideration by none other than *Jules Khan.* Whoever this Ken Julius living above a bakery in Kansas City was, he knew something. Nevis swallowed. He should maybe consider adopting an alias himself.

Nevis would never know the complicated path by which the thumb drive had slipped from Khan's pants pocket to land between the Honda seat cushions. How it had been discovered, pocketed, and forgotten by Arthur Littlewood. How an unrepaired hole in Littlewood's jacket allowed the drive to slip out of his pocket and onto the gravel, unnoticed, where it lay until Nevis retrieved it. No, Nevis knew none of these things.

But he did know one thing: he'd seen two people appear out of thin air and this thumb drive contained scientific papers and schematics and blueprints that referenced *time travel* as though it was an actual *thing*. Benjamin Nevis had questions. Lots of questions. And he knew someone who might, with the right persuasion, be willing to answer his questions.

And so, thirty-one hours later, on a hot, sticky morning outside a hot, sticky bakery in Kansas City, Nevis waited until a compact man in need of a haircut stepped out with a cup of coffee and a day-old doughnut.

"Hello, Jules Khan," said Nevis.

The man dropped his doughnut, but not, fortunately, his coffee, and glared at Nevis.

"Who the hell are you?"

Nevis flashed his badge without a verbal response, allowing the question to hang unanswered for a moment before offering his most genial smile. "I'm the man you're going to have an extended conversation with regarding the contents of this thumb drive."

Khan's face, already pale, turned a shade paler. "That's mine."

"It *was* yours. It's mine now. But if you tell me everything about the time machine you invented, it could be yours again."

Khan swallowed, his Adam's apple bobbing up and down. "What do you want to know?"

TO BE CONTINUED IN BOOK FOUR

Visit cidneyswanson.com for the latest news on books coming out soon!

Printed in Poland
by Amazon Fulfillment
Poland Sp. z o.o., Wrocław